From the Author of
When Gucci Came First
And to you, homeboy I say thanks
&
Man Unnecessary

WildChild Press presents…
Kj Three Six Five
"The Diary" Vol. I

(Where every day is a roll of the dice)
Another Kalico Jones Joint

Kj Three Six Five

(The Diary Vol. 1)

Written by: Mia Williamson

Known by these works as

"Kalico Jones"

WildChild Press • Montclair, NJ 07042

©Copyright 2007 Mia Williamson

All rights reserved.

ISBN: 0-9753082-2-X

This is not intended for minors.

RAYOR – Read at your own risk

Printed in U.S.A.

April 25, 2007

Dear Reader:

I would like to first begin with a "thank you." I've received so much love and support from you with my first novel, **When Gucci Came First**, and it's follow up And **to you Homeboy I say Thanks** that it wouldn't be right if I didn't take the time to thank you FIRST.

KJ Three Six Five began as an online daily journal of the goings on in my life. The reason why I did the journal online through my website is because so many people were sending me emails and letters asking me what the hold up was for Man Unnecessary and my other unfinished, but registered works, Diggaz Incorporated. I am ashamed to say I was "caught up" in the world, helping everyone who knocked on my door (via email, letter, phone call) and so all my shit was subsequently put on freeze. Now its not like I WANTED to put myself on knock off, its just that being that I was grateful to be free of so many things, I felt it was my "duty" as a survivor to help EVERYONE I could and I did just that. My magazine, on HOLD, my newspaper, ON HOLD, my cosmetics line…on hold, the jeans…on FREEZE…Its just been me fucking up my dreams because I don't have enough sense to realize when ENOUGH is enough! And so as others succeed because of me, meanwhile my street dates are being pushed back further and further and you know what? I can't blame the people I've helped because hey….if you can get help and FREE help no less, what would YOU do? EXACTLY….milk it for all its worth. So now, as I type this letter to you its with a promise that I have rededicated myself to ME. And so you can bet, you will see nothing but the best of everything from Kalico Jones real soon. And as far as helping people, I'm not going to say I will NOT help anyone anymore, but I am going to say, "I'm all helped out until somewhere around mid 2008!" Sorry but I have to handle my business FIRST and since I am behind…I've got a lot of things to accomplish quick! Who have I helped? Well I'm not going to list the names of all the people I have helped get into the publishing game, or the music industry, (lucky for them) but I will say this, "There are a LOT of self published and traditionally published authors and a few up and coming rappers / singers who should begin their books and CDs with '…If it weren't for Kalico Jones…' and that's me keeping it real. So between trying to find my OWN way as a single parent, a single woman, an author, and a friend to the friendless, I have been busy. My life has been filled with nothing but drama (family, friends, associates, lovers, etc.) and it has gotten to the point where I had to recently MOVE and cut my phone off just to get a LITTLE peace and quiet so I can concentrate on YOU, my readers and of course, myself and my little one.

Its hurtful to live in EXHILE when it comes to former associations but its for the best, because I can honestly say that 85 percent of the people I have met over the span of my days as the infamous "Kalico Jones" have been PREMEDITATED INTERACTIONS on behalf of the person who made it almost impossible for me NOT to notice them. It's such a shame to be 35 with NO friends. I can't even tell you. So…with this book KJ Three Six Five, I try to discover myself on a day-to-day basis, while trying to understand why I continue to go down the same sad ass roads. And before you ask…. No I haven't relapsed; I'm still DRUG FREE!

So…in this book I give you ME, in the "raw" living life as I know it, sometimes making terrible decisions, but that's a part of life…you live to make mistakes, and hopefully you learn from them, and move on.

Please keep in mind these are dated entries – a true diary, taken straight from my website, at the urging of my readers. Enjoy!

May God grant you everything you ask for during your quiet time with Him.

Take care of YOU!

Respectfully,

KJ

This book is dedicated to everyone who
WILL NOT GIVE UP

In loving Memory of:

Two-5 "Mr. Mt. Vernon" (Mt. Vernon, NY)
And all those who life gave up too soon
"Rest easy my friends, until we meet again."
xoxoxo

To my daughter, Ivana

You were truly meant to be

So here it goes, my life as I know it for the past year and some change. I am publishing this in hopes you will grow from my mistakes, my successes, my obstacles, transgressions AND lessons learned…oh and some times…lessons RE-learned.

This is a REAL diary with REAL dated entries.

Fasten your seatbelts, its gonna be a bumpy ride.

08/19 - Hello all...today's reflections are a product of family circumstances. On my website I mention how the truth will set you free...so I will say this: What good is keeping "the peace" when the peace is fake? It's our place to demand respect from others and family is no exception. When difficulties arise, get your point across and don't waver your feelings for the sake of keeping peace. You'll only harbor resentment.   -   kJ

08/31- Or what I like to call, "The Final Day of Summer" School shopping, looking for a new place to live - possibly a relocation, and completing my second book. I'm tired, I've got some things going on and I just deleted myself from the long list of Authors groups I belonged to. No reason to explain, just I feel at this time I do not need to be part of a clique to advance in publishing. I feel as though the streets are my reviewers, so no thanks on that. I'm not trying to be funny, I don't think I'm better than others...but lets face it. I'm FROM the streets and so that's who I let judge me. Kalico send us 9 copies of your book for review? NO. Kalico we would like to add you to our web page, just let us review your book, and by the way...we need 4 copies. NO thanks. I will continue to let the streets handle my book sales, and reviews, your help is not necessary at this time. Publishing to me is a business! I'm not here to make friends with everyone who comes across my path. I'm just here to make a difference. I'm sure you can understand that. **So today I say, Blaze your OWN trail. Be your OWN judge and don't let anyone   dictate   your   life   to   you!   peace!   KJ.**

09/01 - Today's topic. When enough is ENOUGH! You have friends, you have family, you have associates, all out for one thing, Your time. But when do you begin to put a dollar amount = value on YOUR time? When does your time become valuable to you? I have come to the conclusion - just for today, of course - that my time is VALUABLE and therefore should not be wasted. Don't waste my time. You need something, ask, get it and move on. Don't expect me to baby-sit you. don't expect me to allow you to reach your goals via my time. I've got my own goals. So any time I take out for you is time taken away from me. So please if someone is nice enough to help you, learn whatever it is they are doing for you, so you can do it for yourself. Don't be a time waster. - **KJ.**

09/03 - Well today I will be traveling, actually for the next week I am traveling. Going South. Maybe find a home for my family and me. Check out the book stores in the area, been getting a lot of country love re: When Gucci Came First, so you know a sista gots to go around and check in on those who have supported me. Introduce them to the new books - that's right, BOOKS, plural and just relax. Tried to have a conversation with baby daddy this morning, too bad it didn't go as planned. Ok see this is why ladies WE have got to do "it" for ourselves. WE have to be independent of the b.s. Life is better for you when you treat baby daddy like a business transaction. Damn shame I have to say this, but you know your girl Kal, she's gonna be real...If he ain't going to give your child the love and respect and most Important, TIME...then make sure your child gets the money. **Don't try to force him to do what he should feel in his heart. Always keeping it real, KJ - over and OUT!**

9/13 - The day after the weekend it stormed... I can't even tell you guys how this weekend has made me stop and think, "When did Kalico become a punk?" First, my car was Impounded, yes, Impounded and I was given five tickets two of them court appearances, then I had drama with baby daddy You see, unfortunate for him, he didn't enlist what I like to call, **CONSEQUENTIAL THINKING.** It's when you think about the consequences of your actions frame by frame prior to acting on dumb ass Impulses. You have to evaluate how your irrational behavior is going to affect the overall relationships (you and your children, you and the mother of your child, you and the relatives of the mother of your child, your children's relationships with your family, etc). All these things should be taken into consideration, because when they are, you usually don't show your ass. Today is eviction day for those people who have taken up too much of my mental and emotional time. Eviction day for those individuals who feel as though they are going to affect my life in ways that force me to act out of character...to you, the space holders..."YOUR LEASE IS UP!" The flip side to this is they're all going to make me rich in the long run. **So on this day, Monday September 13th, I say to my former tenants "Thank you...now pack your shit and go!" Keeping it real as always, your girl Kal**

09/14 - The day after the day after the weekend it stormed... and I think I'm going to move. Relocation may just help me sort the givers from the takers and provide the space between us I need to be able to get things in order. Just because you're an author, of which I do not consider myself to be because my books are truth based and not "made up" (to those who read the original When Gucci Came First: true tales of a tramp). So as I was saying, just because you're an author does mean you're Immune to daily drama and believe me ... I've got my share. Although it has been quiet today. Thank Goodness...**Love you all - KJ over and OUT!**

09/16 - Haters. Today I want to talk about haters in the "writing community" why? Authors don't hate on me because I'm trying to do my thing. Don't hate on me because I deleted myself from all of your groups, don't be mad because it APPEARS that I may be selling a book or two...I say this after seeing a post re: my book. Now for all y'all who know me you know I'm going to keep it real...this post was classless. called my book **INANE PRATTLE**, etc. Now that would have offended me **HAD I NOT** been selling books, that may have offended me **HAD I NOT** been doing my thing on so many OTHER levels, but fortunate for ME, I AM NOT a hater. I don't have to diss any of you authors, and why should I? and why would I? I've got all y'all books! I have support many of my peers, many authors' books are in my home and **I DIDNT GET THEM FOR FREE!** The ONLY book I have that I didn't pay for is by someone named Natalie, all the others...RIGHT OUT OF MY POCKET. I was the ONLY author out at the Harlem Book Fair giving out my books for FREE! I was the only author who can honestly say they went around and showed loved to EVERYONE! And in the midst of me being KJ...Not one of them said, "Oh let me buy a book from you kj." But did that stop my flow? Hell no. Did that make me not want to support you? Hell no! So why diss me? If I don't want to send books to be reviewed, don't take it personal, I TOLD Y'ALL I WAS WRITING, LIVING AND DREAMING FOR THE STREETS, its NOT personal. **Kalico Jones is a MOVEMENT**, WHERE STREET CREDIBILITY MEETS CORPORATE THINKING. I **AM THE BRICK LAYER FOR ALL THOSE LITTLE KIDS COMING UP WHO ARE IN SITUATIONS WHERE THEY FEEL AS THOUGH THEY CANNOT TURN TO ANYONE.** I do many charitable events, **I give my time, my money and my spirit for the kids, and don't you even THINK FOR ONE MINUTE YOU CAN JUDGE ME! Please. Now I have better things to do for others, and I cant get them done by allowing the B.S. to get in the way of my goals. Y'all be cool out there. KJ over and OUT! peace**

09/27 - The REAL meaning of keeping it real...and today I'm forced to axe yet another person out of my life. But don't cry for me though, its all good. Now let's get to what I've been up to, my daughter being in a fashion show, dance class, karate, a festival, shopping, dinner, etc. and its been non-stop since Friday afternoon. I've been all over with an authors meeting, a book club meeting and just being a mommy. So between my little princess and my own stuff, it's been one heck of a couple of days. Her fashion debut...well you know how that went down...SHE DID HER THING! she was cute and professional, let me tell you, I may be grooming the next T. Banks. And the dance class, she was terrific! Did you expect anything less than perfection? Of course not! lol. I'm a proud mom. And I should be., it's really all good and I can look and say, **"this is because of me" and God has my back and YOURS too! See ya when I see ya...Kali**

09/30 - It's almost my birthday and I'm excited. It's the first time I am actually excited about having a birthday in years. I'm healthy, I'm happy, I'm doing my thing... Kalico Jones is now a name brand and things are on fast forward. My clothing line is going to drop the same time as the new book and cosmetics. I am in negotiations with a realtor in relations to the flagship store in, NJ. It's going down folks. I've decided I am not going to self publish any authors right now because I'm too busy. But I have a host of friends who own publishing companies that are willing to take the load off me. What else is going on with me? Oh I will be in Harlem on Saturday doing a signing and attending a family event. I'm meeting up with Myron, a friend from D.C. he's relocating to NY and looking for work. We're putting together a game plan for him. He's got a great look and personality, he's definitely a fashion forward individual. So we're going to get together. I'm anxious about meeting him. Oh that reminds me, our mutual friend is expecting, I have to call her to see if she had the baby. What else is going on? Well I'm single again and loving it. I've decided that celibacy and getting to "know thyself" is more Important to me than having a "boyfriend" so its back to the drawing board for me and its about time. It wasn't working out and he and I just aren't compatible in the "more Important" ways. **He was nice and all, don't get me wrong but there were "issues" and so it's best to say bye bye. and no...you wont find him in the next book. ha ha. I'm out...PEACE! kj**

10/04 - Well, well, well...Today I have decided to go with a publishing company. When Gucci Came First is going to be signed over to a major company in the next few days (hopefully, cross your fingers). Its just I am tired of doing the bookkeeping, dealing with printers, stores, etc. The only thing I want to do is tour and cash checks. I just don't want the headache drama of the paperwork. I have to say I have a new respect for those in the publishing game. Keeping track of all this stuff is a LOT, trust me. My cosmetics line is on the horizon and I took the weave out...I'm on a diet and have joined a gym in my area - even though I have exercise equipment in my house - the exercise equipment has become abstract art and a hanger (for my clothes), its a shame, but true. I have to get back to my "fighting" weight so I have to let go of the champagne, brie, pesto and pathmark fried chicken (don't you just LOVE pathmark fried chicken?). My family event on Saturday was what it was. No comment. We love each other and that's what counts. ha ha ha. My birthday is QUICKLY approaching and I have no plans. I think I'm just going to take out my favorite person = my daughter. I don't expect family or the few friends I have to do anything for me because they know I would not like that. I just want to be low key. I am however, going to slip into Mt. Vernon = my hometown for a night of dancing with some of my people at the AAC on third street, that will be on Saturday. But afterward, it's back to NJ to resume my life. I've been contemplating a move as you know (north carolina) and now I have three choices re: relocation (1. North Carolina 2. Atlanta 3. California). I am asking (praying) for clarity so I can just be out when I get the "sign" to roll. Its nice not having to consider others in my decisions. It's the kind of freedom money cant buy. Let me see, what else is going on? Book two is going to be held up a month. Sorry, but I cant make the deadline, so you guys are going to have to wait until November for the follow up to Gucci. A Man Unnecessary will hit the stores sometime around Thanksgiving. And my third and fourth books will be in January and then in April. after that, I am just going to relax and do things I really want to do: work with teens, push the make up and live somewhere where shoes are not required. I will keep you posted. **Have a great day, don't forget to pray and give second chances, KJ over and OUT!**

10/05 - Today I am free!!!!!!!! Well as most of you know, I've been working part time for a religious organization and was very unhappy during my time there = 4 months. The person who hired me doesn't enjoy her position and has on several occasions complained to me about the workload she is expected to keep up and she doesn't like the overall behavior of the lead minister...that's right I said minister. I can tell you in my years of being able to determine what is real and what is fake, I cannot for the life of me understand what kind of religion allows its ministers to drink = liquor, wine, etc, and curse. his behavior (lead minister) was typical of a person with control "issues" and his need to be in control requires and demands complete attention from everyone who comes in contact with him. His meaningless banter during staff meetings was laughable = reading what I like to call h.w.m.i.c. "scriptures" and forces the staff to listen. My dear friends, today is the day I break the yoke. you know in the bible it clearly states, "two cannot walk together unless in agreement." I was not in agreement with them at all. and to top that off, isn't there a such thing as the separation of church and state? He takes positions with his congregation that are clearly unethical and uses subliminal content in his monthly newsletter to send "messages" to his people without being outright noticeable to others. When you have staff meetings where the renters are being discussed in derogatory capacities, you have to say to yourself, "what in the hell am I doing here?" I leave knowing I don't have to use them on my resume because I just don't have that kind of need. Oh and you know I absolutely had to tell them I am an author. How I write entertainment news columns for magazines and freelance for ad agencies. Ha ha ha. you should have seen the look on the face of the lead minister and my supervisor...they never knew who I was at all. I've decided to write an article and submit it to several local papers on my experience at the church. I figure he (h.w.m.i.c.) would love the attention . Other than that, I am just perfect. Have a bunch of things on the horizon and life is wonderful. I'm dancing with life right now and it feels GREAT! to all those who are in jobs that are beneath their talents and skill sets, I say to you...Keep your focus on your dream while dealing with your reality. You have to position yourself during your off time to discover what opportunities are waiting for you. Its ok to reinvent you, that's what keeps things interesting. If there are things you want to try, then try them...don't allow a job to trap you. Be loyal to yourself because in the end, the only reason you are there is because THEY NEED YOU. and don't you know the supervisor had the nerve to walk me to the door, like I wanted something out of there. She and the rest wouldn't even be able to drink from the water fountain in the lobbies of the places I have worked! Ha ha ha, but true! I'm shaking this off because I have business to handle. **I will keep you guys posted as always, your girl,**   **K.J.**

10/08 - and my birthday is Sunday the 10th. I cannot wait. I'm not approaching mid thirties and loving it! It's a blessing for me to get this far in life with regards to everything I have been through. My computer systems are now up and running and it is my goal to complete A Man Unnecessary. Which still does not have a cover and to be honest with you...I may just drop it without one. Let me see how this develops. Or maybe I can drop a photo of myself on the cover. Hmmmm that's something to think about. I may do something at my house for my birthday, a small party. Some of my friends want me to do it tonight, but I haven't really touched base with anyone about it. aside from that, I'm thinking I may just spend the bday with my daughter and my man. Let's see. So I told you guys I took the weave out and I look cute with the short cut - I had it before, the spiked look. jet black, etc. and once I lose some of these 160 pounds, I will be back to myself again. Now don't get it twisted, I got it going on, but I would like to see myself back to my "fighting" weight. Now if only I could give up the champagne. lol. I have dance school tomorrow with my daughter, then arts and crafts, then ...nails, then food shopping, then hair, then relax....and try to figure out what I am going to do re: my birthday. I will keep you posted....Say a birthday prayer for me, I think I'm going to visit my old church Steele Memorial on Sunday. Hey, that sounds like a great plan. **I will chat back on another day. Your girl...Kalico J! to my friend Leticia in Cali, CONGRATULATIONS ON YOUR NEW BUNDLE OF JOY...I'M PROUD OF YOU. AND LAURYN IS A CUTIE PIE!**

10/14 - The Big Decision!!! OOHHHH, life is funny. You go through peaks and plummets to make you the person you need to be at the time when you big break comes. There have been so many things done to me directly, indirectly, etc. and all I can say is, "I'm still here." I have to quote a fellow author, "No weapon formed against me shall prosper." This author quoted the Bible after going through what I hope to be a controllable "rumor" - Why can't blacks get along with each other? Now don't be going around saying Kalico is putting down her own race, 'cause that is NOT what I am doing. I am making a general observation based on my exposure to several situations, including ones that have involved ME! We'll be nice to Mr. & Mrs. Indian, Mr. and Mrs. white folk, Mr. and Mrs. oriental, but I'll be damn if we are nice to each other. **Lets try this challenge: Be cordial to each person you see of African American descent** (whatever color, shade, or origin of birth, if they cant get a cab in midtown = be nice) lets try that for one week. **If you are in a position where you can help another person of African American descent help them out** (whatever color, shade, or origin of birth, if they cant get a cab in midtown = be helpful), try that for one week. Lets see what happens. I think we need a "blacks be nice to each other month" Where we have to hold hands and sing or something, 'cause we are off the hook with each other...No other race should be able to tell US we treat each other poorly = that's exactly what happened during a conversation I had this morning with a Jewish man. He said, "you people always complain about us, but what about you? You treat each other poorly and have no value for the lives of people within your own race..." and you know what? **BIG MOUTH KALICO, WHO FIGHTS THE GOOD FIGHT FOR EVERYONE, COULDNT SAY A WORD.** What's most disturbing about his comments besides the year (2004 and NOT the fifties and sixties), he was so right, he didn't even care about how his "observation" would make me feel and he and I are friends. I know some of you are reading and saying, my Jewish associate and me are NOT friends, but we sure are. Its his right to make an assumption as such based on his perceptions = his experiences and beliefs. I've learned peoples perceptions are their beliefs and so they are correct in how they feel...its up to ALL of us to change the perception of the world...**Vote, USE CONDOMS, STOP HAVING BABIES, get off the crack, weed, whatever drug you are on if you are on anything, AND GET SOME EDUCATION UNDER YOUR BELT. .. Let's be responsible for ourselves. Keeping it REAL as always, your girl Kalicooooooooooo ! peace**

10/15 - Meeting New Friends All The Time Now...Today I took my daughter to family buffet in South Orange and met a few young women who are employed at Seton Hall... Now how did I NOT know Seton Hall was in New Jersey? Dag on shame. I thought it was in Brooklyn = St. Johns Kalico, NOT Seton...DUH. I guess the S threw me off. Well anyway, they were nice young ladies and then...I got on the 92 Bus, that's right, KJ took the BUS...and met the bus driver and a lady bus driver. She is 26 with an 18 month old. We discussed potty training, etc. and the bus driver lent me 25 cents. KJ was short for the bus...well not short, but I didn't have the change...dollars but no change. Sorry Mr. bus driver...Ok so I'm chilling, meeting people in my new area and I gotta tell you...They are nice over here. Well, I have many things to do this weekend, beginning with dance lessons at Sharon Miller in Montclair for my daughter tomorrow morning. If you have a little one...try the school, you wont be sorry. **Well I have to go now, Kj over and OOOOOOOOOOOUUUUUUUUUUUUUUUTTTT!**

10/22 - Friday and I'm feeling good. I've decided it is time to throw the weave back in...sorry I know I told y'all Kalico was going "all natural" but I miss my big hair, nails and full face make-up. And please, the entire time I was going natural, I rocked a Christian Dior baseball cap. So it's off to my girl, Tye at I'm ages of Tye Salons on Bloomfield Avenue in Montclair to get a FULL head weave. After I'm done there, I will go next door and get my FULL set of acrylic tips and you know the eyebrows must be arched outward. I think I'm going to do a "Italian Girl" look = big hair, nails, jewels, etc. I want to be all I can be for my evening out tomorrow. Going to Papillion 25 = South Orange Avenue, South Orange (by the railroad) heard Thursday, fri, sat are nice nights for US to go. So what else it up with me? Man Unnecessary is giving me a hard time re: page count and I have to do "other" things with it to get it to completion. I have the cover concept banged out, courtesy of my best Author Friend, Moody Holiday, I know you've heard of her, right? If not, you better ask somebody. Anyhow, I'm just happy to be here people. Now Election day is QUICKLY approaching and we've got to not only encourage each other to get registered (unless you are in the state of nj, 'cause the deadline has passed) but we've got to get the polls. WE stand to lose a lot of liberties we have taken for granted. The only way you can complain is if you vote because THEY won't take us serious if we do not. Case in point: Last week I encountered a problem with a government funded organization, I called into Trenton and began my complaint's with, " I am a registered voter and..." and guess what? they actually listened! I know, it sounds like b.s., but it happened. And I got the end result I was seeking. So PLEASE GET YOUR BEHIND OUT THERE ON NOVEMBER 2nd and VOTE. **Its our time to show the world that WE can come together when OUR back is against the wall...and its sooooo true, OUR backs are against the wall people. Ok. well that's my time for today, It's your girl Kalicooooooooooo, over and OUT!!!! Y'all be good out there! (wink...wink...)**

11/10 - It's been a long time...Sorry I haven't written in so long, but you know its hard being me. It seems as though everyone in the free world who has written a book in the past month has my private email address. I have no idea how it got "out" but ...whatever. So as I was saying, everyone seems to have my email address on their "list" to solicit business for their book. HA! you've gotta be kidding me! So I sent out "one liners" i.e. "Good luck!" and "Keep it going!" in an attempt to be "nice" but let's be REAL, KJ is not your publicist. I am NOT going to forward your information to my friends or my "list" and its not because I'm hating...Its because how DARE you invade my privacy by using my personal email address to not contact me re: anything I'M doing, but to promote YOUR book or party. Come on, if you want press, I own a magazine set to launch in January = The Kalico Jones Report, return $300 with a signed insertion order and a pdf of whatever you want the "people" to know and I'll put you in. Distribution is the entire East Coast and parts of Cali. But don't insult me with your back door antics by sending me your stuff like I'm your personal ad agent or whatever....See people. I told y'all I had a normal life. I know you have friends and family who try to pull the wool over your eyes once or twice and lets face it, when enough is enough...we BLACK OUT! LOL. Now onto ME. Well, I told you me and my boyfriend have taken some time off. He's in the music industry and I...Well y'all know I'm all over the place, just trying to make a dollar out of fifteen cents. The separation is not one I am enjoying, but I understand when a person has to be alone to focus. We spoke last night. He's a nice guy...but again you know the music industry, so I don't have to say no more! I have realized over the past few weeks my circle of friends is getting shorter. and I don't mean one or two, I mean like seven...seven chicks ousted! that's right. I have No time for fake ones. and since I'm not going to put them on blast...just know this for your files my friends, **When you are married or in a committed relationship, please find married or committed women to hang with. Leave your single friends to things that are holiday oriented, i.e. Christmas Dinners, Thanksgiving, etc. things that do not require you leaving the house and hopping around with chicks that don't have a care in the world.** I'm not going to elaborate because I don't think I need to. What that situation makes for is DRAMA **'cause as soon as your man finds out she's a ho...whenever you go out with her and the rest, you will find yourself answering a shit load of questions at 3am.** And there is no reason why a married, single parent, or person in a committed relationship should be out at 3am. See that's the Fast and Free chicks getting you in a "mess." (sigh) what else is going on with me? I found someone for the cover of my magazine. I cannot share that with you, all I can say is I'M GOING to ask the questions YOU would want me to ask of this person. My other issue of the day is this: Why are so many women SINGLE PARENTS? Men what in the hell are you thinking? All these women raising these kids alone, it's disgusting. This world is going to be a mess in about ten years when all these little kids are big enough to confront these so-called men. but have no FEAR 'cause **Ladies, I GOT YOUR BACK IN BOOK TWO: MAN UNNECESSARY.** and **don't you even THINK about calling KJ bitter! Where would I find time to be bitter, I'm too busy trying to make a living and raising a kid all by myself. Your girl KJ, over and out!!!!!!!!!!!!!!!!!!!!!**

11/11 - People I tell ya... just when you think its safe to go back in the water.... I get this email from someone who shall remain nameless...but she's making comments on When Gucci Came First...ok so what in the hell do you expect me to do? NOTHING. People I tell you this because this book...Oh MY GOODNESS...you would think I have stolen the keys to the gate...Everyone's a fuc@#@ critic! For the LAST time, When Gucci Came First is written in conversational format from the mindset of Kalico Jones...who is not only on drugs AS SHE IS WRITING THE BOOK, BUT She is working through many issues (sexual abuse, abandonment, physical abuse, etc.). Now I'm going to say this again because this is how I would like it to be: NO I don't want your "organized" review. The streets have my back and I'm doing just fine. Why are so many authors uptight? Get a grip. Stop focusing on me. I'm out here just like you, trying to sell books. Why hate on me? I NEVER said I was a writer...**I never proclaimed to be an author, that's for YOU to take ownership of (a title)...**I will tell anyone, **ANYTHING I DO IS FOR THE PEOPLE WHO HOLD ME DOWN. MY LOYALTY IS NOT WITH YOU AUTHORS, EDITORS, ETC.** I pay for your books, I pay for your services and I correspond with you when my email box is cluttered and I have no choice but to respond to your countless emails. So why bother me? Why make back door comments about what I am doing? People if you don't believe what I'm saying is true, just join three online groups and **I bet you one dollar to your dime, the SAME PEOPLE belong to the SAME GROUPS.** Its just a clique thing...but 4REAL...**You better HOPE you sell as many books as me!** and I'm keeping it real. My books are in constant need of replenishing at every store I'm in...online and otherwise. **and when the book thing wears off...I DUST OFF MY DEGREE IN BUSINESS ADMINISTRATION AND GET A JOB.** It's a small thing to me. **and MY LIFESTYLE WON'T SUFFER.** You bad mouthing me and my thing to other authors, editors, etc, in your crews and cliques **won't help you get your numbers up (books sold).** Use the energy you put in your attempts to bother me...into getting your businesses and your lives up and running...**REAL FOLKS SEE THROUGH ALL**

THAT CRAP! Well off of them and onto me...My girls at sista connection are onboard with the magazine and I've got big names coming through for me for the launch. It's coming along people. Tonight I get this 260 dollar hair shipped from Cali sewn in. I have to see how this comes out. then it's off to the nail salon where the little one and me will have full services executed. I'm thinking of having her hair braided since we may be traveling for the holidays. I have to think on that a little bit. Other than that, things are what they are. **I'm working hard putting together literature for my Crossed Legs campaign**. I have to talk to a group of teens in Harlem next week. and its just full speed ahead. Oh...LA weight loss ...I forgot to tell you guys I am going on the LA weight loss plan. Yes, Kalico is trying to lose a few pounds = 30. putting me back in a six. I'm 11 now. which is mostly a nice bottom, thighs and hips. I just don't want it anymore. So I'm checking for LA weight loss, I will tell you guys how it goes. they are in Caldwell, nj. Ok. well that's about it for today. **I had a lot to say, I know...but hey, that's just a day in the life of...Your girl KJ signing off. Have a great day and be happy for someone other than yourself. Peace**!

11/18 - Preparing for Thanksgiving...Well I am now responsible for the dinner...and I have one question for you...Is Demetris open next Thursday (restaurant). How do I get myself into these messes? I volunteer that's how. Your girl KJ, done (Ebonics) volunteered to cook the family dinner and I've got the be honest...I don't have a clue! I'm going to fix a turkey, wild rice, mashed potatoes, yams, collard greens, mac & cheese, apple pie, sweet potato pie, white rice, gravy, stuffing, and some other stuff. (now y'all see where the LA weight loss would come in) ha ha ha. So far that's what I have. should any of you know things I should add or subtract for that matter, please be kind, look out for you girl...and EMAIL ME suggestions. and is Egg Nog not the thing to serve on Thanksgiving? Well, I don't have much time today, so that's it for me. I hope you are doing fine and if you are a single parent, **"Keep your head up!" Your girl...KJ over and outtttttttttttt!!!!!!!1**

11/29 - Happy Monday Everybody! Well Thanksgiving is over....AND THAT IS WHAT I AM THANKFUL FOR. HA HAHA. I have cooked, cleaned and hosted my first Thanksgiving dinner for the family and I must say, it was a success. We had lots of food, great conversation and lots of fun! and for the record...If I see a turkey never, it would be too soon. I have been eating the same foods since Thursday. Today my mom is fixing an Asian themed dinner...I can't wait. This week is my first Internet Broadcast show and did I mention it's going to be LIVE? That's right, you can catch your girl Kal on www.artistfirst.com this Wednesday from 9-10pm EST. Real Talk with KJ is going be advice, book stuff, party stuff, entertainment news and gossip. I am waiting for Jo Jo Brim's people to contact me with a time slot. It's hard trying to catch up with these celeb types, but he's cool people and I would like to have him for the first show. I also have Tina McKinney "All That Drama" Strebor (Zane's publishing co.) on the show. Tina has already been picked up by Black Expressions and she is QUICKLY making a name for herself and check this out...THE BOOK HASNT EVEN DROPPED YET! So I can't wait to hear what's on the horizon for this Diva enroute. I am also going to be interviewing someone from Spot TV Network. www.spottvnetwork.com. see what's popping for entertainments best kept secret. That's going to be a blast. and then we'll talk about me. And then there's a little thing called "ambush" is when I devote ten minutes to celebrity gossip. It's going to be rough, rugged and RAW, just the way I like to give the business when I have to give the business, if you know what I mean. What else is going on? Well nothing. Just trying to figure out which way to turn. Have so many people counting on me, sometimes it gets to me, but NOT today. I'm a warrior...and everyone that knows me will say that. I'm too busy being busy to let things bother me today. **Have to finish up some work for the show. I don't have an intro, have to get one of those. will do for the NEXT show. I'll holla later....Your girl Kal, over and out!**

01/15...Well Merry Christmas, Happy Chanukah, Kwanzaa and Happy New Year to you...I know, I've been slipping with

Kj's diary but its not because I don't want to write, I literally do not have time to get on the computer and do this web maintenance every day, but I will go back to the regular schedule of at least once or twice per week. Well, so many things have been going on with me lately, I don't know where to begin. My show on artistfirst.com is moved to Sundays and that's because I requested to be moved away from others. Want to establish my own fan base and really go off on my own. I didn't want to follow authors, etc. so it's better for me. and since its late night, I get to do and say a lot of things on during my show (wink. wink.). So I'm getting a lot of hits and I enjoy doing to radio thing, who knows, there might be a future in that for me. Man Unnecessary is giving me a little bit of a problem, but I worked it out and although advanced copies won't be available, the release date is going to be the same, so you have about one month until the BIG day. So have you guys heard Fantasia's cd? I heard the song, Baby Momma last night, my friend Karen played it for me and I was like, that's it...that's going to be my show opener. I just have to get the vocals laid for it. I will work on that this week. What else is going on? I'm just all over the place. Mending fences, burying hatchets, etc. but only with those who I feel enough time has passed, mostly family...I really don't have too many friends. Tomorrow I have the Whitney Houston EXCLUSIVE...you have to listen to my show. Oh..also, I may take a quick trip to North Carolina this week to hang out and check some things out ...I will keep you posted. **Life...It IS what it IS...Your girl KJ wishing you the very best in coming year...over and OUT!!!!!!!!!!!!!!!!!!!!!!!kj**

03/11 - Is it almost two month to the day? Damn my life is hectic. Ok. so I have many many things to tell you guys. First on the horizon we have my two books. **when Gucci came first** the remix and **Man Unnecessary.** I BET YOU BY THE END OF MAY...y'all are going to be like: I knew her when. I have a bunch of stuff set to jump off after tax day and all up through the summer. I'm working at a newspaper and I'm going back and forth to North Carolina - Garner / Raleigh - Holla at your girl....I'm loving the south and they are loving me when I come through. next week I am in Virginia for a minute and then once my daughter and me get back, we are going to the circus - and hopefully next week we can catch the knicks , I will keep you posted. My peeps is on the knicks so we're going to hit him up for tixxx...what else. . . **listenership for the kalico jones show on www.artistfirst.com Sundays 10pm - 11pm has gone up 50% over the past five weeks. I LOVE IT. PEOPLE ARE FEELING ME.** I'm getting ready to take that to another level, but not until I finish up with these books. RE: the trilogy...I'm not feeling a third book on me...I have two other treatments waiting in the winds and so I think I'm going to move on one of those. and after 2005 no more books. **All I'm going to do is chill and put my feet up somewhere in North Carolina with my husband and daughter**. Ok. so if you haven't caught the show, shame on you. I'm going to have several book launches so check back for dates at a city near you. for now: ny, nj, nc and maybe somewhere in VA. but again...I have to get my schedule situated. what else,. I took the weave out but I called Lavar hair design (72nd - nyc) for a consultation on a weave. I think I'm going to try them. took the nails off and got a short hair cut at Images of tye salons and then took myself shopping. you know I needed new clothes for the new haircut. there are so many places to shop in jersey. Oh. you have to check out my other site www.thekalicojonesreport.com its about my show and topics I discuss on my show. Its snowing out and I'm getting ready to leave work, then go home and work some more and maybe have a nice glass of wine and get on my Ab lounger - yes I purchased that thing off TV. and since I've gotten it, it's been a hanger. lol. But I ordered a treadmill with all the extra space in the apt. since I threw out the pool table. getting ready for what life has to offer. **Well. that's it for me folks. I love you guys. I'm glad you have my back and you know I got yours as well. Stay safe, focused and REAL...your girl, kalico jones.**

03/14 - Happy Monday People....Well my show on artistfirst.com is moved up to 10pm on Sunday nights, so check me out at my NEW time. I had to check one of the females I work with. its a small thing to a giant = ME, and so

I'm not going to even get into the particulars, just know the next time she even thinks about saying anything to me, she will think twice and then re-think her position prior to approaching me. I am getting ready to do some things with my daughter. next week we are at Madison square garden to see the circus. we missed the continental arena thing, well not really because we can still attend, but at this point, I would rather see it at the Garden. Ok. so what else is going on? I have lots to do right now and I'm just enjoying life. Making sure I move mountains and not let little distractions take me off course. I am getting ready to do some work, so I will have to holla at you later...OH before I forget, why are authors bored? Ok. this is in response to the hate mail I have been getting online from them. Grow up already. they are so into When Gucci Came First...they are in a shit load of trouble in a minute, because my books are going to dominate the game. and you can say what you like and post what you want online about me under all the alias of your choice, but **PLEASE BELIEVE**...you better hope you can sell as many books as kalico jones...you better hope your fan base is as loyal to you as mine is to me... and you better hope you've got something to fall back on when the game spits you out...if not, rethink YOUR position and stop trying to come for a GIANT, **'cause KJ is NOT the one. Well that's all folks. Y'all be easy out there and have a wonderful day! Your girl...KJ>**

03/16 - HAVE YOU EVER MET SOMEONE WHO TOUCHED YOUR LIFE IN WAYS YOU CAN'T EVER REPAY? Well that's what happened to me last night. I can't say much about this person...I would have to get her permission first, but I can tell you this; She was a member of the Panther Party, her son is famous and is deceased or as she so eloquently put it, "Transitioned" and his father is what we would refer to as a "Political Prisoner" - I learned a little something...no a LOT last night. I had the kind of History lesson most of us will never get the opportunity to even be EXPOSED to. All last night I kept saying to myself, "Why isn't she on Oprah?" How I wish I could facilitate that ...but don't count me out, because I sure as hell am going to try. So we talked and she autographed her sons CD for me. It was truly a pleasure. I made a promise to myself last night about teaching my daughter REAL history. I mean its all good going to the top schools in the country, **but what good is it if you DON'T HAVE KNOWLEDGE OF SELF? exactly...means nothing. Ok. well that's it for me today...KJ and I'm OUT!**

03/22 - WHAT'S UP? It's your girl KJ coming to ya on this fine Tuesday with a question: "How far would you go for your best friend?" I ask this question because although I DO NOT have a "best friend" I have a few and I mean very few friends of whom I would go the distance for. But have you ever had someone who you DON'T consider to be a friend ask you to do something or ask you FOR something ...like a HUGE favor that only a FRIEND aka BEST friend could ask for and it makes you stop and think, "Hold up Dog...I don't know you man..." Like how would you handle that? Well I'm asking this question because I have people sending me emails and letters from past travels asking me for money, items, shout outs, etc and its like...Dunn, I just ain't up for that. I do what needs to be done or as Mike put it to me just yesterday, **"Women do what they want, girls do what they can."** I don't know if or how that statement applies to what I just said, but I would like US ladies to learn how to handle our **first business...FIRST**. Meaning our career paths. Our educational goals. Teach our children respect for self and others. In order for us to take care of our children, we have to first take care of ourselves: drinking, smoking, getting high and bringing different men around our children should be a NO NO. When we handle our first business first, everything else will fall into place and we wont have to go around expecting someone to help us out. NOW I am NOT saying its bad to ask for help...and its not uncommon for people to lean on those they feel close to but don't waste anyone's time. get yourself together while you're getting the help you need so that you don't have to go back to them. that's all I'm saying and when you ask don't act as if the person who you are asking for help OWES you something. Just ask, take the help and get yourself in a position where you don't have to ask again. What else is going on? **Well people continue to be fake as ever sending me emails asking me, Remember me? and then try to engage me conversation and then REPEAT the contents of my email...**well trust and believe contents...I'm careful with those because now that I'm making my way, I have to be. so treasure the correspondence because it WON'T happen again. going around telling people I holla'd at you. You'd think that one email is your life. this is why people you have to be careful of being overly nice. If you leave a place, LEAVE those people BEHIND YOU. You can't help everyone and you damn sure cant be nice because people will take that and RUN with it. ha ha ha. How boring ... What else is going on? **Well I'm back from Vacation on Sunday (vacation from the show) and so It's going down on Sunday, so be ready. 10 - 11pm on <u>www.artistfirst.com</u> THIS SUNDAY FOR THE THUNDER...THAT RIGHT AND YOU HEARD IT STRAIGHT FROM ME...Your girl Kal...Be happy, Live happy, LOVE hard. K.J. Moore (now figure that OUT...if you don't know...now you know).**

03/23 - Its Wednesday.....Wuzzup? I'm chilling. No complaint's today. Just happy to be here. I'm working out the "kinks" in a project that's been on hold. I know y'all are tired of me pushing back the street date for Man Unnecessary, but I've decided not to push a trilogy and so I have increased the page count to finish up the story in two books instead of the three as originally planned. I'm sorry folks, but I want to do some other things. You know I have the radio show and I've got the magazine, which is now a NEWSPAPER...and I've got a bunch of other things that I have to complete out. When Gucci Came first is being re-dropped with a NEW cover and "remixed" with added bonuses. I have to finish up that project this week with AC and Ndigo Designs. I have put them on back burners because I'm burning myself out with all the stuff. So I have made the decisions to get the Remix of When Gucci Came First out with Man Unnecessary and that's not going to happen until the end of the month. The END of the month meaning April. Which is fine with me. the newspaper, well I am in the process of soliciting writers, reporters, and editor, etc. for that project and since I am doing it this way...I can make it free to the public, as initially planned AND EXPANDED distribution. so I wont be in just New York and New Jersey. and so I can cover other states. The first one is going to drop in May and it's going to be monthly. So I have about Five things that are going to be completed out over the next two to three weeks and THEN....I can sit back and promote, market, and sell. What else is going on? I sent my big brother an email asking him to pick up the new play station gadget dropping at midnight...My brother will wait on line in the cold for a pair of Air Jordan's - he has done it several times - and he will wait on line in the cold for anything that has to do with the Play Station and so since I know he's going to be out there getting one for his son, I said for him to pick up one for his niece, ha ha ha. These kids are spoiled rotten, I tell ya. But it's a good feeling when you can do something special for them. **Savings Bonds, that's what I wanted to tell you....If you have 25 extra bucks, get a 50-dollar savings bond for your child. Put it in a safe deposit box and wait and see how much money you will have ready for them in a few years.** Try to do that at least once per month. If you can do it twice per month, then do it. We've got to have something to give our children to help them along. Ok. so I've been keeping up with this as much as I can, just because I have to go in hiding for a few days to get things together and books / projects completed. I wish you all the best life has to offer and **PLEASE PROTECT YOUR CHILDREN**...Oh no, wait...I'm watching CNN a lot lately. You know I have to stay up on what's going on in our world. so I'm watching this Terri Shiavo thing and I'm pissed! It's a damn food tube, not a respirator? What is going on people? Uhhh. I'm just disgusted by the actions of everyone involved including her parents who waiting until 2005 to handle their FIRST BUSINESS, FIRST. and now the husband is winning and everyone is up and armed including the president = who really tried to help this woman and her family, but as always, it was a day late and a dollar short. and **did you know that foreign countries own stock in our country?** Yes they do. in TREASURY BONDS. . . Our concern should be what happens in the event these countries want to cash in those bonds? we will be in trouble. The global economy would be in a horrible condition and really we are so dependent upon foreign goods, from oil, to food, to electronics, cars, etc. you name it...its IMPORTED. Do you know that if we were cut off by china and the Middle East, we wouldn't be able to rebound. **People we have got to wake up and smell the coffee. Ok. that's my time...I'm outta here...Your girl...Kali J. - aka Mrs. M. Moore**

03/25...It's GOOD Friday everyone, so be GOOD and remember: Jesus is the reason for the SEASON. Go to Church and PRAY FOR SOMEONE YOU DON'T LIKE!. You know people, I am very excited about life and love and family....Its been a nice ride for me thus far. My daughter and me are going to Brunch on the World Yacht (cant publicize the date - sorry). But it's a nice little thing for you to do with your little girl - or family for that matter. there is a full brunch buffet, a live orchestra and....**CAVIAR SERVICE!!!!** You know that's my thing. but it's a great way to spend 2hours. You get to dress up .
I told you guys I work for a newspaper and I am branching out on my own. I have teamed up with someone in Louisiana...She is a great writer and we will all learn from her Together!!!! What else is going on? Hmmm. Nothing much, just trying to plan my daughters Moving Up Ceremony and Its going to be a FORMAL AFFAIR. ...Gotta buy an Easter Dress and shoes for us between today and tomorrow and get us to the salon. Just a lot of running around and cooking...A LOT OF COOKING...Having friends over tonight, tomorrow and Sunday...My girl Yolanda is flying in with her daughter next week so that should be a nice treat. she's a shopaholic and so I have to prepare myself for the experience. I can't mess with her, cause when the cash stops, she pulls out a wallet FILLED WITH PLASTIC! lol, Yolanda is funny and her daughter is SPOILED OUT OF THIS WORLD. she's coming in from Marietta. I can't wait. My circle of friends ...those chicks hold me down and I love them. So I look forward to that. Well, I have to go now, have a deadline for one of my projects for my DAY job. **I wish you nothing but Inner peace and Sunshine...Your girl, Kal J Moore!**

03/28 - The day after Easter! WOW...I gotta tell ya, I'm sleep walking. I've been to the laundry, Pathmark, Shoe stores, Dress shops, beauty shops, etc. I'm whipped! and all day Saturday my little one showed her behind! I was truly at my wits end. But as the trooper I am...I got through Saturday and Sunday and when we returned home from Church...**WE SLEPT THE ENTIRE EVENING TO THIS MORNING! THAT'S RIGHT FOLKS ROUGHLY TEN - 12HRS OF SLEEP.** I didn't even do my radio show last night and they didn't even bother to put on a rerun. So I have to say, I may be going over to voice America soon. I have to see how our (me and the stations) business interaction goes today because I expect more from them than that. And to be quite honest...I am TIRED. I am running in circles and I just have so much to do and I can't do it all like this. So maybe I will put the radio show on hold for a minute. I will keep you posted on that. What else? Nothing. Just doing what I have to do. The message in Church was "who will move the stone?" It was great. It was something I really needed to hear. You know some stones (obstacles) we can really move (get over) ourselves. If we make serious attempts to get through things on our own, then God will gladly step in if we need him to. but we should really make the ATTEMPT. I have to say again, the message was one I really needed to hear. At any rate...the Church my daughter and me attend (not going to mention the name because someone will mess around and come there to bother me during my time with God) is very close knit. the people are wonderful and have embraced us...My daughter is in the choir and we have a nice time. Ok so this week I have what seems like a million bills to pay. Ugh, how I hate the end of the quarters. So much paperwork with having the businesses. and as Oprah would say, "I'm rich because I still sign my OWN checks." (I'm NOT rich yet, so don't even THINK about robbing my black ass – for my "thug" readers – lol) ...So I only let the accountant step in to file stuff, but as far as paying bills, etc associated with the household and businesses, I do that stuff myself. Royalty checks and charge backs, consignment forms, outstanding accounts receivables, this is a LOT OF WORK. BUT I can't say I would trade it, because I probably wouldn't.

Ok. well have a nice day and be happy for someone other than yourself....your girl kj. over and OUT!!!

03/29 - NO MORE RADIO SHOW...I am tired! I just got off the phone with my girl who gave me some advice, "Kj, you are spread too thin..." and she went on and on after I complained to her about "things" in general and artistfirst.com not respecting me enough to put the rerun on after listenership has increased over 50 percent since I came aboard. OH no...I've got others trying to get me to radio stations in NY and Philly and although I haven't seriously entertained that yet, I'm just too drained to deal with the show during that time slot on Sunday and besides that...I have to get ready for a book tour and I'm going to be on the road beginning May. **So to all my listeners, "I'm sorry to do this to you, but I have said farewell to the show...and I hope you understand." I don't want to say its temporary, but I will...**ONLY because I am going to be on somewhere else in the near future, but I have to stand my ground and I have to make sure that at the end of the day, I am happy...and being spread too thin is not my definition of being happy. Once I have completed out my stuff, then I will holla...but I have to get the businesses where they need to be first and then I can do some other stuff. Being a full time mom (primary and ONLY caregiver to the child), is my first business, but we EAT via books, events, etc. so although those things are not FIRST in my life, they do require a HUGE amount of attention, I'm sure you understand. **Well that's it for me today. I hope you are well and I really mean it....your girl KJ Moore, Over and OUT!!!!!! "KJ.com where street credibility meets corporate thinking"**

04/01 - APRIL FOOLS DAY!!! AND My secret crush played a joke on me...and my girl Laverne played a joke on me...and I'm just all joked out...I worked so hard today I absolute didn't even relate the 4/01 to April Fools at all. Anyway...Happy Friday Y'all, I hope your week was great and I hope the weekend is good for you and TO you as well. As for me, I've got things to finish up and since it's going to be raining...I get to stay in and complete this dag on book. It's taking me through the fire, but It's all good. So I spoke with Hubby this morning about some things that has been bothering me...not about him or US, but about just "being" its rough out here sometimes and between friends, family, work, work, books, helping others, etc...I just need time to Vent...and sometimes...EXPLODE! so that's exactly what I did...And now its 5:30pm and I'm on my way to see my girl Laverne and chat about things...and maybe check in on a few of the businesses and relax...Me and my little one are going to see that new princess movie I think tomorrow with my friend and her children, so that should be nice. It's been one hell of a week (had a few parties at my house this week Tuesday, Wed, Thurs) and I'm tired. Oh...Have to get a bday gift for Mike. Ok. well that's about it for me. Gotta go. My daughter wants to get a plant and so I have to take her to the florist and see what kind of plant we can get out of there. she wants to grow one, so hopefully we can get seeds or something...I'm thinking CHIA pet right now (ha ha ha)...but I know that WON'T fly with my little girl...Well maybe it will. I'm going to ask her....**Take care, be safe and this weekend, be selfish....put yourself FIRST! Over & out, your girl, KJ Moore**

04/05 - Happy Tuesday...and my daughter is ill = stomach virus and now I'm coughing, it's a mess. Well my girl Yolanda from Atl touched down this morning about 6 and we are going to do some things today. I will keep you posted as to what exactly, but you can REST assure there will be some serious shopping involved. I'm almost done with one of my projects and so I'm excited about that. I have so many things to do, I can't really chat with ya today, but as soon as I have something to tell...I will. **I love you all, be safe and stay real...Your girl KJ over and OUT!!!! 1**

04/06 - Just when you think it is safe to go back in the water...I get alerts about authors hating on me once again. and y'all know I'm accustomed to this kind of "acting out"

s@#@ these authors do. going and posting negative reviews about MY book, like I really give a damn. Ha! you can't be serious. those online reviews don't get my numbers up like that = books sold. I do that all by my lonely. **It's called Networking, it's called STREET team, it's called, IN STORE accounts and Credibility BEEYACHES...**Ha! the hate consumes you authors and you come for me like that? Don't waste your time. I told you **KJ is a Brick layer**. Those types of behaviors DON'T effect me at all. **My street credibility is LEGENDARY and my corporate status is PHENOMENAL...**I won't be BEAT and **the GAME chose me 'cause all of Y'all were at a standstill**...so please, by ALL means, continue to post the b/s, cause I'm covered and PROTECTED and it really is a small thing. Extremely small, like tiny, like molecular small, just like that. All these little people with big mouths...and what's makes it comical Fam...is this..."two of these haters are veterans in the publishing world..." have MORE BOOKS than whatever I could come up with...have sold more books than most and have literally paved the WAY for people like me and to hate like this...where they are trying to play with my money...HA! that's what let's me know...I am doing my thing. **When the VETS are SHOOK...then you know I'm doing something RIGHT.** so I thank the haters today...fore they have allowed me to know my book business is headed in the right direction and that When Gucci Came First is a true literary PHENOM and so to thank them, I am going online to purchase the books of the people who can't make it unless they diss others. . . Now off of them and onto me...What's up Everybody? I know you are doing well. So...How is your day thus far? I hope great. Listen. You cant let negativity stop you in your tracks because during your "stuck" time, the haters will progress...So do you and Love God and the rest will fall into place. Ok so enough of the preaching. My child is still a bit under the weather and this cough I now have it "bothering" me. My secret crush...ha ha...don't tell hubby = Mike, but my secret crush just left my presence...Oh boy, this is going to be DRAMA. but the man of the house doesn't care. Not about stuff like that because we have a different kind of bond. the kind where you can say "I knew her / him...when...." and no one can tell him anything about me and visa versa because we have been down from day one. It's nice. Toys r us in times square...PLEASE go there. I took my daughter and it was nice. We went on a shopping spree at the Hello Kitty store and we went to Barami where I purchased a pair of shades...OH and they are ALL that. We went to tad's steak house because I haven't been there in YEARS. What else? We went by the Wax Museum and I'm sure a bunch of other places ...**OH. found a shoe store for kids...its called...(looking for the card, damn, I can't find the card),** I will give it to you guys tomorrow, but the shoe selection was incredible. got her a pair of Ralph Lauren track sneakers and Kenneth Cole maryjanes for 67.00 (total)...I will find the card and post it for you guys tomorrow. Ok so I'm done today, getting ready to figure out what Kind of hairstyle I am going to get today...thinking of another weave to go with those Barami shades...lol. But my cousin - who is a manager at **Victoria Secrets** on 34th street, told me to leave it alone. Oh that's the other place we went and I purchased **"love spell"** that smells good and we went around trying to buy up all the Rocco Baracco perfume I could find. Its discontinued and since I wear the silver version...I have to go around and purchase all the bottles I can find...it was funny. I was haggling...its going to be a collectors item I'm sure. but the smell is my SIGNATURE SMELL and My hubby likes it. and so does everyone else I go around for that matter. So that's what I am doing in my spare time. I know its stupid, but I love it and I have to make sure I have enough to last me until I find something else that makes me crazy like that. **Well people I'm outta here. I love you and please take care of yourself. use condoms, drink in moderation and TAKE CARE OF YOUR CHILDREN...1 Love KJ Moore**

04/08 - Happy Friday "peep"le - Ha ha. Well today I'm here just being me and although I cannot elucidate the particulars, just know I'm good. Spoke with A.B last night...he's got a bunch of shows lined up - he's rapping. I think I'm going to North Carolina - Fayetteville on Friday to catch one of his road shows, maybe Bless him with a backstage, "special." Nah, I'm only kidding. He's with some cats out of Alabama and

I'm proud of him. So I think the little one and me are going on a road trip with a stop over in V.A to see hubby and then off to NC to catch AB on the road and let the little one go chill with my father, step mom and brother Josh. That would be a nice pop up present for hubby, me and his stepdaughter in V.A. His Bday is Sunday and so I've got to figure out what I can get him. I was thinking about shoes, I know a place where you can get a pair of banging Ostrich loafers...I have to think about it. I know the maurys aren't what they used to be and I think he's got enough pairs to be quite honest. Well I'm getting ready to move - I think. I have to look at a place in the same town, but I'm upgrading the neighborhood and the flat (apartment). Today would be a nice motorcycle day. I have to call cyn and see if she feels like dusting off the unit for a ride. what else? well my girl is still here from ATL, she is having a blast. Tomorrow we are going to get the hair done. I just got a hair cut. It's like the girl from soul food but the way she wore it in "shorty wanna ride with me" video...just like that...spikes and all. I LOVE it and everyone is loving it as well. Huh, well my little one is still a bit under the weather. I hope she feels better to go to brunch tomorrow. We ate from Tierney's today (me and the "girls") Chili & cheese fries...and a sprite. Oh that combo is going to have all of us SICK...not because the food wasn't good, it actually was GREAT, but because that kind of stuff fucks with my stomach. But it was good going down. LOL. Ok well I have to go now...I'm listening to my girl Shannon complain about me getting some "work" done to myself. she's bugging. I have two grapefruits and one hell of a plastic surgeon and so I'm going for it. but that's NOT all...I got lips on hold and some other stuff. I'm trying to get myself ready for the tour and just meeting people. and although I'm GOOD now...I just want to do some stuff for me. For my OWN selfish, self centered reasons. **y'all know I'm narcissistic (spell check on that) but I am and I'll be the first to admit it. I'm going to go now...I have something to finish out. Have a great weekend and please Be easy ...KJ - Moore. aka "Mrs. Gadget" ;)**

04/11 - What's up everyone, its Monday! and I am alone....awww, yeah feel my pain. My friend Yolanda went back to ATL yesterday with her daughter...her daughter is the most beautiful and INNOCENT 17 1/2 year old you'd ever want to see. she left Jersey yesterday a little after 11am and reached home about Midnight. **translation: SHE DROVE TOO FAST.** LOL. Ok. so Yolanda is home and I think I'm going that way some time soon. I'm just tired of my telephone ringing...you know it rings CONSTANTLY and I mean from 6am to 4am BOTH numbers are off the hook. I may change one of them, have to check in with Mike. Oh today is Hubby's Bday and so I have to do some things for him today. My little one is feeling better, thank goodness. but she didn't want to ride the bus to school today so I took her in a car service. SPOILED. During the time Yolanda was here, we shopped and ate and shopped and ate...Oh. We went to **Amy Ruth's = 116th Street (Harlem).** We were there on Saturday and it was a nice experience, but next time I'm going to have my help call ahead so we can be seated promptly. Today I am also forced to cut two people out of my life. OH well and screw them because I am NOT going to be fake. One has a "problem" keeping her nose clean and the other, well she has a problem with being herself and the both of them together makes for a mess whenever the THREE of us are out. And although I don't knock anyone because Lord KNOWS I've just about done it all...I believe there are things that should not be added to your list of habits at 50, period, point black. and OHHHH. I met these guys on 34th street, they were selling their cd's **you can find them at <u>www.RU1records.com</u>** and I cant think of the other guy, but I will post his information tomorrow along with the name of the children's shoe store on 7th avenue. Well what else is going on? Well my secret crush is female. Yes, I put it out there...and there's nothing wrong with that. There are many ways to admire someone you know. What else is going on in my world? Just living. and doing what I feel I have to do to keep myself happy and a smile on my daughters face. People I have to tell you...I'm getting closer to just jumping up and moving. It's really coming to pass. I will keep you posted. **make today the BEST day of your life...Love yourself, handle your**

FIRST business, First and please give someone deserving a second chance. I love you all....your girl KJ

04/12 - and boy am I tired. Well let me start by reminding you guys of my statement yesterday regarding cutting two people out of my life, well...it actually was three. One I have to work closely with sometimes (unfortunately) and the other two...are just plain ass freeloaders. and I would be lying if I told you that any of them meant anything to me. its not that I never liked them, but I'm just so fed up...that I could care less and therefore do not wish to go forth with the current association in place. I'm sure you understand. At any rate, I was up late last night talking to my secret crush. She is breaking me down people...LOL. Ok. so what else? One of the girls in the "crew" asked me about Lot 42 = that's a new club in Mt. Vernon, NY. and since I'm from there BORN & RAISED, I guess she felt I would be the better source in respects to the goings on out there...NOT!!!! I have no idea what's going on there. I don't know, I don't care to know...s@#@ people don't even have my number out there. but have no fear, KJ was polite and quite the lady when I answered stating, *"Girl, I wish I could tell you, but I cannot. I would assume that since Wendy (radio personality) is hosting the parties there, it is safe to go."* she fell for it and so that's good. LOL. what else is going on? My brother is going to Tokyo this week and so we are having a party for him. He is doing very well...We all are, I know my mother is proud. I'm happy that she can say, "all my kids are doing well." and it be true. Oh...I have to find something to wear for my girl Puddas bday party and a hat for Church (haven't been in two weeks = 2 Sundays) miss the congregation and I miss the "connection" so me and the little one will be there with bells on this Sunday getting our message. What else? Oh...Hubbys bday was yesterday and we had a nice chat about life and the businesses...I'm like...why do you want to talk about business on your birthday? he said because next year we're going to be too busy to discuss anything. I'm thinking of having another baby for my daughter...I figure I may as well...but really...I remember promising her father that I would never marry or have children by anyone since he and I didn't work out the way I'm sure BOTH of us wished we had. Awwww....makes me sad to think back, but hey...it is what it is. and so ....OK. well I'm over that. (taking a deep breath) but I love him still and so that's that and everyone knows it. Ok. what else? nothing really, just trying to make a dollar out of fifteen cents, loving life, myself and all those who love and respect me. hey I forgot to tell you guys I am going to another radio station. **I will keep you posted. Your girl KJ. "Lets be good out there, ya hear?"**

04/13 - Do the humpty hump...Its Wednesday, shake your booty...Its Wednesday, shake your booty...Hey Everybody!!! What's good? Holla at your girl...its Wednesday, the middle of the week, two days before the IRS comes and kicks the doors in on us all and I am feeling kind of good. My girl Fredell has Tupac on her voicemail...so I'm forcing her to put the same on the KJ Fam Hotline because it captures the zone I'm in right now. So I'm doing things, making things happen and you know...YOU cant sit around and Wait for someone to give you YOUR fifteen minutes...so if that means you have to take your 15 by force, then do it. OK. that's what I am going to call a book. 15 by Force. Y'all look out for that and DON'T EVEN THINK ABOUT JACKING MY S@#@#! LOL. BUT 4REAL..don't even think about it. Ok. so I'm doing some things...trying to complete out projects - which will happen by the end of the month so I'm not worried. I have a ton of things on the horizon and they are ALL set to jump off in May...(taking a deep breath), it's a lot. Oh and why did I have a dream about my kid's father last night? I don't know, but we had a "closure" conversation. That's strange,...especially since I assumed, "Bitch Be gone" was the closure...ha ha ha. Nope let me stop before people be running up on him talking about KJ said this and that...Really I did have a dream about him I think because I spoke about him to someone yesterday. At any rate...the dream was very "real" in that it was detailed...I don't know people...I gotta be honest...it was one of "those" types of dreams kind of sort of...(taking a deep breath), but enough about HIM. I have to go shopping for myself and the little one for nine pieces each and maybe two shoes. We have to make sure we are put together for our weekend back home aka Mt. Vernon. Maybe and THIS IS A JUST MAYBE...YOU WILL SEE YOUR GIRL A LOT 42 ON BROAD ST. lets just see how I am feeling. Life is good. Tomorrow I have a 3hr meeting and I'm sure they are not going to serve breakfast...Ugh...how I hate going to places in the morning and they don't even have the courtesy bagel and coffee (I don't drink coffee) but damn, offer me SOMETHING....I think breakfast meetings at 8oclock in the morning should have a mandatory breakfast clause. What else is going on? Oh...NC may be calling me a little earlier than I had planned. The house I saw back in Sept. is back on the market. I had my step mom go over there today to speak with the people because the only reason why I didn't get it was because the person before me left a check. So hopefully they will give the house to me and if this should go down...I will be packed and outta here before the 10th of May and I mean it. Gone, by mothers day. the good thing is that my daughter will have her yard and pony...and I will get the peace I would like to have. Just a little "slower paced" living. Not that I am not going to work the way I work now, but I think I would like the change in scenery...**No sidewalks where I'm going. Only trees and an acre and a quarter of land. Lets see. Say a prayer for me, please. well that does it for me today...your girl kj over and OUT....1**

04/14 - Magic Wand....To play or not to play that is the question. LOL. What's up everybody????????? I'm back from my three hour meeting and I have to tell you, it was INFORMATIVE in the respects that it expanded my knowledge base and y'all know how I feel about being SMARTER THAN THE AVERAGE. So today is bill day and I've got to get things sent off by tomorrow and that's going to be a chore within itself. I don't have much to say today. I am busy as a bee and I have to get from under this report by 4:30pm. going to the Eye Dr. to get my glasses and next week I begin my dental work = BRACES... Life is GREAT. Now today's assignment is simple: If you can help someone...help them...If you can't ...don't say you can / are and if you give someone something...DON'T BE AN INDIAN

GIVER (meaning take it back - no disrespect to my native American sisters and brothers). **Have a great day! Your girl Kal J Moore**.

04/15 - I GOT THREE LETTERS FOR YOU...THE "I" THE "R" AND THE MUTHATRUCKING "S" AS IN DA INFAMOUS UNCLE SAM...I just finished speaking with my accountant and my directive was as follows: "I don't want to go to jail, but I'm not afraid of a little probation." aka "do what YOU have to do to keep them off my ass!" lol. Can I tell you that if the numbers don't add up...I'm going to hold off and take the penalty for filing late. I put some stuff away in things that are exempt translation: I can put them under 2004 and be SAFE...y'all better ask somebody. and it's ALL legal, which is what we want right right? (wink...wink...). Ok so today I have to help a friend and tomorrow I will be at **Downtown Music** hanging out with some of today's HOTTEST underground HOUSE / Club music Dj's...its going to be a GREAT event. I won't be there for long, but I will go to support Soul Groove records and Downtown Music - Orange Road in Montclair NJ. What else? Well I just got the application faxed to me for the house in NC. I will be writing this weekend AND PRAYING! I will be praying because I need the Lord to come down and personally handle this for me. because I am going to have to move a mountain to pull this off before Mother's day. So let's see what happens. What else is going on...Well I have helped so many others and now I find myself in the SAME situation with regards to me not wanting to help people for a little while. Like I don't want to be super save-a-ho. LOL. I have puddas b-day, her moms b-day, my brothers going away party and I've got two events and 100 pages worth of work to complete out by end of Sunday and I'm talking about THIS Sunday. So NO champagne, I have to be focused and so there you have it. OH...973-342-1039 is the KJ Fam hotline number, you DO know this, right? Ok. well if you didn't, there you have it. Its Friday everyone...go out and enjoy yourself and for those Johnny come lately with respects to taxes, handle your business...get your asses out there and get the stamp on the envelope. or for those of you who work in offices with the stamper...you know how to get it done, put a few sheets of paper in an envelope and weigh it for the postage amount, and stamp your envelope for TODAY...shit...do the damn thing and send it out later...its NOT YOUR fault if it got held up in the mail...Who says I don't have your back? **I told y'all, I don't want to go to jail, but I AM down for a little probation...ha ha ha. Your girl Kali...over and out...PEACE.**

04/18 - Happy Monday. I'm getting ready to go to the doctor and pick up the little one from her Au Par - if that's how you say it. I'm behind schedule in my writing and just for the record...I didn't complete the 100 pages, but I did something BETTER...I CLEANED the flat. That's right...I figured I would do a thorough cleaning, change over the little ones clothes (from winter to spring / summer) and mine as well. I gave clothing to the local kids and adults through the school and so its all good. My little one is on spring recess and loving it. I just got a call from her on her CELL phone stating that she would like to visit her pop pop...Uhhh, I don't think that's going to happen, but hey...you never know. At any rate, I am going to make sure her vacation is GREAT. She has the au par (spell check), my family says to stop calling her a nanny or a sitter. lol, that's funny. I'm from the projects, where a TOE is a toe, period. Ok. so this chick I work with looks like she's been rode hard and hung up wet. LOL. That makes no sense to me. It makes not sense to have a wet ass and broke pockets. Lesson for today: If you're going to play in the big girls park...Please Act like a BIG girl. - **I'm outta here for today. Have to handle my FIRST business first aka My daughter. Have a great day, Your girl KJ over and out.**

04/19 - Hey Family...How are you doing today? Ok. so if you recall, yesterday I told y'all about chicks running around with wet asses and broke pockets...well I got a call last night from the QUEEN DON MOMMA MEDINA straight outta Florida...shit, I haven't seen Medina since Dwight Gooden days..been a long time. Anyway, she's returning to NYC in a few weeks, so you know I've got to catch up with her ass as soon as she touches down. I'm going to talk that one into writing her story. If you chicks reading this ever want to know how to handle **B.I. = Business Interactions** on a **NATIONAL** scale, this is the chick to learn from. So she signed my guest book and we chatted for a few...I'm hopeful we'll catch up on things this evening after me and the little one come in from dinning out with my secret crush (a girl) and a friend. aka **"The Broad and HER associate"** - Ok so have you people gotten your taxes out? I hope so...you know Big Brother IS watching, but you also know that if you work in an office or know someone who does, get them to turn the postage machine backward...you need a pin to do this...get a safety pin and stick it down in between the numbers and turn those suckers BACK and get your stamp on. **LOL "do at your OWN risk" aka MY disclaimer.** I don't want y'all to be running around talking about KJ done told us to do some illegal shit. so there goes the disclaimer, I threw it in for protection. OK> so lets get to the little one...she's doing absolutely marvelous. Those Ralph Lauren sneakers of two weeks ago....FILTHY!!! It's like she is purposely running them ragged. I have to now go out and purchase another pair. I think I'm OVER doing white with this girl. Maybe I should call her dad and ask him to do a few pairs of sneakers. But he's so damn preoccupied with living life without her...You know what? I'm NOT even going to get into that. **Just handle your FIRST business FIRST if you are a parent**. There should never be NO ONE or NOTHING that prevents your from being active in the lives of your children, period, point blank and there IS NO excuse. and my days of holding out for hope ended when my brother told me **the story of the tortoise and the scorpion** for those of you who don't know the story: *A scorpion wanted to cross a pond and so he asked the tortoise to allow him to ride on his back across. the tortoise said, I cannot, you'll sting me and I will die. The scorpion then says to the tortoise, I wont sting you, for if I do that you'll drown and WE will surely die. so the tortoise thought about it and agreed to allow the scorpion to ride on his back. Midway across the pond, the tortoise feels a sting...the tortoise turns to the scorpion and says, why did you sting me, now we're both going to die ...the scorpion responds, "I couldn't help myself, its in my* *nature"* Now take that and do what you will with it family. We have to stop being the damn tortoise. and really, you know I hold it down...we don't need him to kick out for a pair of kicks. Nah, Oh No...we don't get down like that. but I have decided that instead of purchasing 9 pairs at a time = 5 pairs of shoes and 4 pairs of sneakers - **ALL THE SAME SIZE, MIGHT I ADD.**(I KNOW THAT IS STUPID TO DO, BUT I LIKE HER TO HAVE AN ASSORTMENT) I think I'm going to do two shoes, two sneakers and two sandals through the summer months and then back to school, I can get my man at the Heat Sportswear in Montclair, new jersey to run me the timberlands for 30 a pop and go from there. Maybe just try not to spend so much on stuff she ain't even getting a chance to wear basically. we're giving away shit with tags on it. but it's all good. Oh...that reminds me...furs have to go in storage. Ok. so I have to put together some kind of reunion for me and the old crew. We are so busy being moms, we haven't had time to mingle with each other. Since motherhood I have been busy 24/7 but I'm sure I don't have to tell you that. and to be honest...NONE of US would have thought we would be mothers...**let alone MARRIED AND SETTLED DOWN...THAT'S CRAZY WHEN I THINK BACK TO JUST EIGHT YEARS AGO. Damn, I was a mess.** and all over the place. But that's in my mid twenties and now I'm mid thirties and so its different and shit...**WHO IN THEIR RIGHT MIND WOULD WANT TO BE OUT THERE WITH ALL THAT'S GOING ON: AIDS, DRUGS, CHEATERS, ETC.** I tell you, that's why I'm the way I am. NO one is going to look out for yours the way YOU do, so keep yourself in good health so that you can live to see your children mature. **Use condoms, Don't get high and drink in moderation if you chose to drink...give second chances, but don't be nobody's TORTOISE! I love u, u love me...give me a call if you like: 973-342-1039 you know the kj fam hotline is up and running. tell me your thoughts. you know I'm interested. and if the recording comes on...LISTEN to it. Its Tupac in the movie JUICE...my girl Fredell put it on there for me. It's really inspirational for the STREETS. Also, I'm looking for authors...if you wanna write a book, hit me up ...lets talk. and to all the bitches (yeah I said bitches** because **REAL women don't deal with a man who doesn't take care of his children)**...So to all you bitches who deal with DEADBEAT DADS aka the "Sperm Donor" **Shame on you.** you NEED TO BE encouraging the DEADBEAT to be active. OH I forgot why would you ever when the father of your kids ain't helping you....Ugh, you chicks disgust me because when I was "out there" I NEVER dated anyone who didn't take care of their children - Mr. NBA, Mr. Old School Rapper, Mr. NFL, Mr. Boxer and all the others with real jobs (construction, police, etc.)...every last one of them TOOK CARE OF THEIR CHILDREN AND I'M NOT TALKING ABOUT SENDING A CHECK THAT DOESNT EVEN COVER THE SHOE / SNEAKER/CLOTHING BILL. **and that's why I decided to drop man unnecessary on FATHER DAY. SO YEAH, THE STREET DATE IS PUSHED BACK AGAIN. FATHERS DAY SO BE PREPARED.** ok. so **I'm outta here for today...I'm whipped and its sunny outside...your girl kj moore OVER AND OUT...1 oH HI RASUL AND I GOT YOUR MSG.**

04/20 - It's Hump Day!!!! Whoooo HOOOOO...now this doesn't mean to go out there and literally HUMP people (to all the freaks reading) Ha ha ha. Its means its WEDNESDAY and we're at the half way point of the week. THAT'S ALL. Ok so My girl **Big Medina Da Don Momma** called me this morning and its settled. I put in a call to Dr. Bellin and we're going under the knife. I was on the phone with her complaining about trying to take off 20 pounds and after five minutes of me telling her about the Ab Lounge 2 and all the other shit I purchased, she yelled, "I don't have time for this, just go under the knife!" Well you know what fam...she's right. I mean it won't be the first time I've had some alterations done and so what's the big deal? I've decided to RE-alter some things and move forward and you can say what you wish...cause if you ask me, I'm going to say, "yeah I had them done and what's your point" - Ok. so Medina better hurry up and get her ass back into the tri-state. I know her kids are going to have culture shock coming back here when they are accustomed to the "ocean view" lol. that's funny because back in the day...WE were a mess. The only ocean view any of us wanted to see was the one from the balcony of the hotel rooms we laid up in with the sports and entertainment dudes. Damn, have we come a LONG way and I wouldn't trade it for the WORLD. Being able to get out of that game FREE and CLEAR - drug free and clear of disease...I'm telling you family I don't know WHY a person would purposely be "out there" - especially now..when you can't get rid of this shit with ampicillin and amoxicillin and tetracycline, etc. y'all better be CAREFUL out there. Oh. so let me tell you about my night out with **the broad and her friend**. lol. It was very nice. good food, great conversation and FUN! **The secret crush** took my daughter shopping...I was there TOO, so don't even go there. I don't let my little one go ANYWHERE with ANYONE and I don't give a damn who it is, so you know I was there. Ok. so enough of me explaining that. So...we went shopping and then we went to dinner...WE had a blast! then my daughter came home and opened ALL that stuff - **over twenty things OPENED AND ALL OVER THE FLOOR!** what else is going on? Well just another day for me trying to survive Oh, I've gotten several emails in regards to me pushing the street date back for Man Unnecessary so I will repeat myself: **"IT DROPS ON FATHERS DAY" THAT'S ALL FOLKS. I AM NOT GOING TO PUSH IT BACK AGAIN. FATHERS DAY**. Or as me and ALL my friends call it, **"Single Mothers Day!"** Because if you are doing it all by yourself, you **DESERVE TWO days** to celebrate so this year I will be taking my two days, single parent's...take yours too. so **if you are a single parent and you are MALE, take mothers day AND then take your Fathers day.** I say this because I have gotten emails from men saying they read my diary and feel I am not being fair to the men...I got one thing to say, **"WAIT UNTIL BOOK TWO DROPS...Y'ALL ARE GOING TO ME MAD." Shit...my kid is still holding onto the Christmas gift she brought her father four months ago. that's a damn shame, but I guess it's only right being as she didn't even get a call or card and NO one can justify his behavior NOR the behavior of his family. DISGUSTING, I tell ya...just horrible.** I'm happy to know my mother and the rest of my family don't cosign bullshit by backing it. Ok. so that's all I want to say about that. No more calls, no more msgs from my little one, that's OVER. We're chilling and moving on...Ok. so hubby is chilling and I have to get Yolanda and her daughter back here for memorial day. I think we are going to have a BIG bbq in New Jersey. I will keep you posted. but its only going to be for KJ Family Members so you better join in....send an email to wildchildpress.com or click on guest book and write...I wanna join the family and put your email addy in there and I will have shayna - my hired help (office girl) get you going and on the list because the bbq is going to be guest list ONLY. It's going down folks. (taking a deep breath). Well I have to call Pudda back, I will chat with you tomorrow. OH. I got this guy I am working with on the cover...he's an artist....**www.artwanted.com/k.e.** and check him out. Y'all better BE ready. **Ok. so today please mend fences. You got someone who you haven't spoken with in a while? call them up and ask to move forward. Get your mental back on track... FORGIVE, YES...BUT DON'T BE ANYONES TORTIOSE. Love you...Your girl Kali Moore...**

04/21 - Thursday and I missed a meeting this morning - ooops. but the car service fu@# up and I got the short end of the stick. Ok. so hopefully I can reschedule, but to be honest...**I absolutely can't stand it** when people reschedule with me after taking time from my schedule even if it's just me penciling them in...(taking a deep breath). so **Mr. black man tell me where YOURE headed?** My brothers in this journey called life...I know y'all think kj is a bitter beeyach, but I'm not. I know you have hard times and I know between your bosses riding you on the job and the kids and the bills and US women sometimes not understanding that the only control you really have is in your own house and so you need and WANT peace aka a safe haven. I know this...But its like I say in my book, **Man Unnecessary**, *"by the time we find Mr. right, or Mr. right finds US...we've been slapped, shaken, burnt and broken down and so when something good comes along...either we cant recognize it or we're just to emotionally bankrupt to give it a chance."* I know you can understand that. and so to all the REAL men who I have walked past and when they said hello I responded with, "hey" with my head down and kept on walking take...this as a formal apology...Now with hubby...those head down days are over (or maybe NOT ...find the joke in that sentence)...But really...we - REAL women - understand your pain, but sometimes it's just not worth the loss potential...so we don't stop to respond. Well, I'm a little tired right now. It's about noon and your girl is feeling the medicine I just took. what else is going on? NOTHING...absolutely nothing. Life is great and I'm dancing on a cloud right now. I hope you can say the same, if not...**then do something for YOURSELF. Today...ask yourself, "What can I do right now to make myself happy?" and wait a few minutes...take FIVE minutes to really think about it...and then DO IT!!! I LOVE YOU ALL. YOUR GIRL, KJ MOORE.**

04/22 - If you're happy and you know it clap your hands "clap, clap" What's up everybody...its Friday y'all and your girl is going OUT! That's right you can catch me, your girl Kali J Moore at Richie Ceceri's and don't get it twisted...its an UPSCALE venue. So that's where I'll be. What else is going on? Well I was supposed to go out with my secret crush (female) yesterday, but I had family business to deal with and so I had to decline in the eleventh hour. Dr. Bellin called me regarding my consultation for my "alterations" and so I will be in midtown sometime in the next few days. My little one asked me a question yesterday, ***"mommy what's a liar?"*** I almost said something derogatory about the **"other people"** but I refrained. that's right...your girl has **self control** ha ha ! I sure do. Not about to go there, it's Friday and we're happy. Ok. so last night I FINALLY get some sleep and my doorbell rings for fifteen minutes. I was pissed. It was my office girl coming to use the phone...OH no...girl you better use this phone and get the hell out. I'm tired and I better be able to go back to sleep. You know when you get into that GOOD sleep? and someone comes and disturbs you. it pisses you OFF. and I went off on her. she came upstairs, used the phone and LEFT. I told her not to EVER do that shit again. Messing up my sleep like that. and I had the little one sleep at 8pm...and you know she's a night owl...You better NOT ring my bell. and what's up with people calling me like they are on fire? **Ugh, don't you just hate that. I have a kid, don't call me on my warm line late at night and there NOT be sirens and screaming in the background because I will flip.** LOL. KJ is no joke when it comes to disrupting the home front...WE (me and Mike) don't play that. Home is where your peace lies and you cant have people thinking they can just call at midnight to say goodnight or ask a BUSINESS question...I'm not open 24/7 for that kind of stuff and I am NOT a non profit organization so people STOP calling me at home to get FREE consultation for your book or business...I'm ON to you and it ain't happening no more. Ok. **today's assignment: JUST SAY NO. LETS SAY NO TO THE PEOPLE WHO ARE THINKING WE ARE NON PROFIT ORGANIZATIONS AND PEOPLE WHO TRY TO USE US UP FOR OUR KNOWLEDGE AND PEOPLE WHO DRAIN US EMOTIONALLY BY PUTTING ALL THE PROBLEMS IN THEIR LIVES THAT THEY ARE NOT DOING ANYTHING ABOUT ON US.** "SORRY THE COUCH IS CLOSED" TRANSLATION: I AM NOT YOUR PSYCHIATRIST AND DON'T TELL ME...TELL JESUS" YOU KNOW IN CHURCH WHEN THEY SAY, **"BRING YOUR PROBLEMS TO THE LORD?"** WELL THAT'S EXACTLY WHAT I'M TELLING FOLKS FROM NOW ON, "DON'T BRING YOUR TROUBLES TO ME...BRING THEM TO THE LORD." AND I'M NOT TRYING TO BE FUNNY, BUT LETS BE REAL **people tell you all their shit, drain you for advice and comfort and then don't do any of the shit they tell you they are going to do to get out of those same sad ass situations they are complaining to you about. so WHY bother? Bring it to Jesus. I'm out...Your girl KJ Moore ...going global. See ya!**

A BONUS ENTRY FRIDAY - APRIL 22, 3PM BONUS ENTRY BONUS ENTRY...LETS TALK ABOUT MISREPRESENTATION SHALL WE? ok. so I just got a call about this girl who claim's to be a "bad ass chick"

MEANING SHE HAS IT GOING ON...always bragging about her furs and the men taking care of her and her looks and blah blah blah...why is her telephone disconnected? figure that out. I'm told the police are looking for her as we speak for Impersonating a Rich Bitch. I mean why lie? Why front? It's always been like that with me and females. they approach me and automatically want to tell me about how Niggas is looking out. PULEEZE (intentionally spelled incorrectly). Step off with that crap. If your phone is disconnected and it's not due to relocation or a number change...YOU AIN'T a "bad bitch" as you call yourself. Ha. I have to tell you this because the misrepresentation that goes on among women is ridiculous. I'm putting you fakers on blast THIS time as a courtesy...**next time you get caught fronting, I'm calling the POLICE! Stay in your lane and don't pop shit if your business AIN'T in order - kj. and NOW what?**

04/25 – What's up and Happy Monday everyone! Well today started out like this: Aggravated! First off I couldn't sleep last night – anxiety attack a.k.a. "panic" got about three hours and that was riddled with nightmares = have to stop taking things I can't control to bed with me (lol) that sounds a bit suspect...ha...let me break it down for ya...I have to stop allowing things to upset me to the point where they fuck up my sleep. Ok. So you think life is all gravy and biscuits and it is for the most part...BUT I have my fair share of shit...'cause "More money...more problems" So now I'm taking things I can't solve to bed with me and That's NOT good. So today when I get some time...I am going to cook, clean and exercise and then take a nice hot bath in the soaker and RELAX...and who knows...I might pull out my "Magic Wand" if I find the soak and exercise doesn't take the "edge" off. Ha ha. Yes, it's by Hitachi and works wonders. Its a massager...THAT'S ALL, you can't do NOTHING ELSE with it, so don't get no funny ideas...and matter fact...GET your dirty minds out of the gutter. But I gotta tell you on the **Q.T.** = **quiet tip**...If you strategically place it "south" ... you might be able to **BREATH, STRETCH, SHAKE AND LET IT GO!!!! WHOOOOO HOOOOO....**Ok.

so I know you've read my **five star seller, When Gucci Came First**, right? If not, you better go get that, cause you're going to need it to follow **Man Unnecessary...**Go online to **Barnesandnoble.com** if you can't find it in a store near you or **amazon.com** or **borders.com**, etc. **If it's not at a store near you...then order it!** Ok. So like I was about to say...**EVERYONE** in **When Gucci Came First** has re-entered my life over the past few months...and I mean almost everyone last one of them: **Diamond Bracelet, Mr. Realtor, Russ, Heavy from Brooklyn, you name it...they ALL have reached out to me** and just recently as in the other day, I get a call from Heavy with another **blast** from my past. He's a nice guy and very focused. I can't say his name because you know all my past people have to go under an alias...so lets call him ...hmmm, let's see...**Mr. Cinema Production AKA "C.P." (you know how I adore initials)** and we had a nice conversation about "back in the day" etc. 'cause you know your girl Kali was a MESS. But he says he's proud of my growth and excited for me with regards to the businesses. Yes, I'm a busy woman...I tell you all the time, **"ain't nobody gonna give you YOUR fifteen minutes, so you might as well buckle down and get them minutes for yourself!"** You know if you are organized in your personal life, you will see your dreams more clearly and then you will be able to focus more on attaining those goals you've set for yourself. Ok. so Today is the day we get organized... **Today we are going to organize our lives... and what's the FIRST thing we do in our house when we want to get organized and back on track...we wash our mother <u>fu@#@</u> dishes – KJ's TRANSLATION: forgive all the people who you feel have wronged you and MOVE ON! Today We're going to cut off all the scorpions in our lives. We're going to let go of all those who drain us for emotionally support and comfort, we're saying BYE BYE to people who have borrowed money and not paid back, people who ask us to watch their kids and they don't come back when they say** (oh yeah, I've got those too)...**people who have ulterior motives in their dealings with us...Today we are going to clean our house ONCE AND FOR ALL.** Let's not continue to allow undeserving people to have our mental , EMOTIONAL AND PHYSICAL time. **SO HOW DO**

WE DO THAT?????????? We GET IT DONE by just cutting them off and moving beyond giving a RAT'S ASS AND A SMALL BOWL OF COCOA PUFFS what they do after we cut them off. As long as they are not somewhere bleeding...we DON'T care. Shit... WE have to SAVE OURSELVES. You know...motherfuckers can be detrimental to your health...you do know that don't you? Yeah, They can...Stressing your ass meanwhile they aren't doing a damn thing for themselves. **(Taking a deep breath). What else is going on...hmmm let me see. Well I'm working hard and loving EVERY BIT OF MY FIFTEEN MINUTES... my daughter wants hello kitty sneakers...ugh...say it ain't so...I don't want her rocking hello kitty footwear**, but she's is INSISTING ON HELLO KITTY KICKS. SO I MAY HAVE TO 'GO THERE' WITH HELLO KITTY. UGH. **WELL that's my time for today...I'm good and GONE...your girl kJ over and OUT! Be Easy out there.**

Tuesday, April 26 - I miss my days at "Tiny's lounge" in Mt. Vernon, NY, we had so much fun. What am I doing on this lovely day? I'm listening to 107.5 fm WBLS...you know you can stream them online at <u>www.wbls.com</u>. *Over like a fat rat...(I'm singing)* in my heart...we will never part.(still singing) Hold...as we take this love to the stars........Over like a fat rat...Ahhh yeah...I'm Jamming this afternoon fam...Ok. so today I had to pull a "jack" move on someone. I don't like to go there but sometimes people let my high heels and suits fool 'em into thinking that 'cause the bag, shoes and belts match...I'm NOT KJ...So I had to just plain ol tell this former business associate that I would forget about my suit and shoes for five minutes. **Ha...you should have heard the voice...got real low after that.** And rightfully so because your girl was about to set it. **Now don't be talking about KJ ain't grown...I have grown, by leaps and BOUNDS might I add, but I ain't "fin na let" (ebonics) ANYONE FORCE ME TO do something I don't want.** I maintained my sexy and calmed myself down because I ain't trying make the news like that. Now don't get me wrong...ALL news is great news when you have a business, but I didn't need that "kind" of drama especially since AND after my "don't be nobodies tortoise" speech of the other day...**Hell, my ass should not have been helping her in the first place! See that's what I've been trying to say...about cutting people lose, etc**. You have to family or else they will have you just like my EX business associate had me, outside in the street about to act like an idiot. Now when I say outside, I don't mean in the street, I mean in public...I was outside in public with someone who was asking ME for a favor. And a MEGA favor at that!...don't you know she had the nerve to get upset when I was like...**OH NO, I ain't gonna do that dog...You gotta meet me half way if you want me to pitch in, but I am not by any means doing your business FOR you,** you've gotta be kidding me. Well...don't you know. Old girl began to yell about **BEING DOWN FROM DAY ONE! Now family...**don't get what I am about to say twisted...but **you know I've got to keep it REAL...your girl KJ...had NO ONE down from day one.** That's why when the money gets to where it's going...I OWE no one. The only person who had my back and encouraged me was my daughters father...HE kept pushing me to complete the book. HE did that...NO ONE else was there. **So I OWE no one with respects to loyalty. EVERYONE after him, was just that...THEY CAME AFTER IT WAS ALL DONE.** I got Moody Holiday who holds me down and Andrea Blackstone, both authors. Other than that...NO ONE can step to me like that and so I had to let her know...**Dunn, its not that serious and I ain't saying I'm NOT going to help you, but listen...**Its not my place to do this kind of a favor for you, this is MEGA and the money on the return is going to fuck up our association so let me do this little bit for you free and clear and you get one of your peoples to handle the rest for you. **But she didn't respect that.** She got loud and really her vocabulary became egregious and I was livid and I ALMOST had to step back to the KJ from about 9 years ago... **I guess that's what happens when you sleep with people you do business with.** Oops did I say that? At any rate...She and I are cool, but as far as me helping...WE collectively decided that would not be a good idea. **So good for me!** What else is going on? Nothing. Just trying to make a dollar out of fifteen cents, that's it. Jamming to the radio. WBLS is playing Jeff Red "You called and told me" I love that song. And I have an "issue" with the broad **(female crush)...** Call me up, can I see you, no you cant, then I'm going out...then she does and now she's sick. **I have to say this: Whether you date men / women or BOTH...whether you are female or male, TAKE CARE OF YOURSELF. And don't be a cheap date. Ok. So that's my time...what's up for today? Today lets finish yesterday assignment of "cleaning our friendship closets" Lets wash our dirty dishes and Please...you guys have got to love the new wbls format. The music is GREAT. Makes me wanna dance. Go KJ., Go KJ, shake your booty...shake your booty....Whooooooo hooooooooooo.... Have a great day fam. I'm in here dancing and singing...Holla at me on the hotline if you wish 973-342-1039 Kali J Moore, over and OUT**

04/27 - Happy Hump Day Folks! It's the middle of the week and your girl is just happy to be here! What's up with me today? Nothing really. The little one is excited about visiting her relatives over the weekend. My home-girl landed a nice gig with nice pay. My other peoples is on her way out here for a visit, and I'm planning to go to the **Tribeca Film Festival** this year, again. Last year I gave out free books but this year, I am going to pass out my promo items and stuff like that. So you know where to find your girl on Saturday - Greenwich Street in Manhattan by BMCC. **So Saturday its Tribeca for family day...If you have children...this is a great place to be. There are so many activities out there and did I mention all the FREE stuff? Yes, there are a lot of giveaways (face painting, kite making, etc.) ALL FOR FREE...scholastic has a tent there every year...they have Clifford out there – the big red dog, Dora the explorer, etc. YOUR children will have a great time.** So come out! **Ok so now I wan to talk about US women putting ourselves in useless situations**...THIS part of my entry was "requested" by a fan... **QUESTION:** "Dear Kalico...I am trying to move and I have no money to relocate. I have been dating someone for a few years, and he can't help me. He has no money due to loss of job. I did have money, but I didn't save it." Help! **ANSWER: "Dear Help..."** (you guys do remember my advice hour during my show on artistfirst.com, don't you?)...Again...Dear "Help" Your failure to save money during good times has afforded you this situation. My advice is to not become involved with someone for YEARS who can't help you. Now I'm NOT saying to sell your ass, but what I WILL say is when you are out there picking a "partner" you have to consider finances ALSO. You want to move, but the truth is...YOU WOULD LIKE to move and you have to now rethink how you are going to get that done. Relocation is costly and deserves not only a plan A, but a contingency plan AKA plan B. Take some time and THINK of ways you can make additional money to move, please keep it legal and please consider WAITING until YOU have saved enough to relocate AND relax while you put your ducks in a row in your NEW environment. And the next time you get your hands on some BIG paper or short paper for THAT matter, SAVE FOR A RAINY DAY even if its 20 bucks a week. Because had you done that, you would have MORE than enough money to bounce." With love & respect – kJ. Now for those of you reading and listening...let that be a lesson to you. There has to be a rainy day savings and you can take this from someone who has been out in the rain (me) more times than I would like to admit. So...If you can save a little per week...even if its five bucks...hell don't Newport longs (cigarettes) cost more that that? If you buy a pack of smokes, save the equivalent to that for the week. If you buy a bottle of champagne (ME), then I should be saving the equivalent to that. All the things you spend money on that you should not be doing (harmful to your body), you should put aside THAT amount of money aside for a rainy day. **Today's assignment: SAVE MONEY! And if you have a child(ren), empty the change from your pockets every day and put it in a bank or jar...My daughters father taught me that and it WORKS...I don't know how much money I've saved for her (in addition to other things) by taking the change from my purse each evening...Well that's my time for today...I love you and I am YOUR girl...Kali Jones. "I'll hollaaaaaaaaaaaaaaa!"**

It's Thursday!!!!!!!!! April 28th, I'm a FAN of WBLS, I gotta tell you. I'm here relaxing, doing some work and guess what song comes on? The song I used to sing to my daughter while she was in my stomach... "Overjoyed" by Stevie Wonder - I want to say that's the title of the song, but it may not be.... ".(singing) *I've come much to far, for you now to say that I have to throw my castle away...and though they don't believe that they do....dreams do come true...fore did my dreams came true when I looked at you..."* **My song for my little one. My song to her father? Its by Maxwell** "(singing) I can let my life pass me by or I can get down and try...work it on out this lifetime...lifetime" **that's the song I played on the "departure" the songs that remind me of our time in space are " Beauty" by Dru Hill, and the one by Jon B** *"(singing) Don't listen to what people say, they don't know about...about you and me...put it out your mind, cause its jealousy, they don't know about this here."* **One song I absolutely cry to right now is by Glen Lewis** *"Don't you forget, don't you forget your way home...hold on to your world...."* It's funny how certain songs can spark emotion. Today I want to talk about YOUR favorite song. What makes you smile, what makes you happy and what makes you REALLY FEEL. **One of my favorite songs, I play this every time I have a BIG decision to make or a move... "And the Beat goes On..."** *I love that one! , but* **MY ALL TIME FAVORITE SONG...PASSED DOWN TO ME FROM MY MOTHER AND YES...I HAVE PASSED THIS ONE DOWN TO MY LITTLE ONE...SO THIS IS A 3RD GENERATION ALL TI'ME FAVORITE SONG: "NATIVE NEW YORKER"** *(SINGING LOUD THIS TI'ME) "You grew up riding the subways, running with people, up in Harlem, down on Broadway, you're no tramp, but your no lady, talking that street talk. You're the heart and soul of new York city...love, love is just a passing word...its the fallout you had, in a taxi cab that got left at curb...when he dropped you off on east 83rd ...oh ooh ooh, you're a native new Yorker..."* **that my DEAR friends is my ALL TIME favorite SONG.** Today I want to take it light...Its going to be a nice day...I'm putting this in early (a.m.) so I can go out to support one of my friends...he's opening a business today...**Smokey's American BBQ - In Montclair, NJ...**you name it...he's got in on the menu and I cant wait. **Oh...I got the WEAVE put in last night and I look GREAT! So I went into the shoe closet and the new clothes closet and pulled out the cream and orange (courtesy of my secret crush - female) . and I look cute in it, which makes it bad for HER 'cause we're not speaking. I'm done. It wasn't a physical thing and so NO BIG deal. Hubby, is cool with that and so it's NONE of ya business Fam...ha ha**. So I'm feeling great and just happy to be here. Let me know what YOUR favorite song is. **Today's assignment is? PLAY YOUR FAVORITE SONG AND DANCE TO THE MUSIC. ACTUALLY GET UP AND DANCE. AND SING TOO. LETS BE HAPPY TODAY. OPEN YOUR BLINDS / CURTAINS, WHATEVER YOUR WINDOW TREATMENT IS...OPEN IT UP AND LET THE SUN COME into YOUR HOUSE AND TURN ON THE RADIO AND SING AND DANCE...I LOVE YOU ALL..YOUR GIRL 4REAL...KJ MOORE.**

Friday and I'm feeling kind of lucky...April 29, So what's up family??? Did you dance? Did you sing? If you did...didn't it feel GOOD? I know it did. If you didn't...then shame on you. And ...you missed a chance to make yourself feel good. That sounds a little suspect, I know. But YOU know what I mean so don't EVEN go there! So today I would like to talk about being FREE and I am also going to get into the secret crush (female) and why you SHOULD NOT deal with people you work with. We're going to get into life after a bad break up and the don'ts. So fasten your seatbelts and get ready to ride the wave fantastic with your girl....Now. **To be free, or not to be...THAT my friends is the question. The answer, lies within YOU.** This week we discussed leaving people alone, and moving on, and being happy by way of SELF...**ALL are pathways to being FREE.** FREE of a situation that makes you uncomfortable and FREE from bills (remember we talked about saving money) and FREE of just being used a.k.a. Being someone's tortoise. So for the weekend, I would like you to take time out of your schedule, just five minutes and jot down (make a list) of the things that prevent you from being FREE. Once you've made your list, read it, rip it up and throw it in the trash and not the trash in your home, take it outside and either put it in the sewer or a trash can on the street, but do not keep it in your house. **Once you have discarded the list from your home, discard those things from your LIFE. Let "it" go and MOVE on...Let's be FREE family.** (taking a deep breath). **So lets talk about the secret crush (female) and why you should not form relationships with people you work with, shall we?** First DON'T ever deal with someone you work with...be it emotionally, physically, whatever...don't do it because it's only going to serve as a MESS in your life some where down the road. **My advice:** Before you get involved with someone you work with, take time to THINK about it first, because when you THINK about things prior to doing them...more likely than NOT...YOU WON'T go forward. **Ok. Family...KJ is being FAKE right now... Lets keep it REAL...its like this: Before you fuck with someone on your job, please enlist what I like to call, CONSEQUENTIAL THINKING ... its when you THINK prior to acting on DUMB ASS Impulses and to even THINK about fucking with one of your co-workers is DUMB.** Now for those of you who don't understand it in THOSE terms...I have another: **Don't SHIT and EAT in the same spot.** Now...I'm NOT saying you can't take a piss every once in a while (flirt)...but by NO means should you SHIT. Got it? Good. The secret crush is an ass. Coming around me acting "a fool" I can't believe in even Entertained the thought (taking a deep breath). Ok. so enough of that...She's an idiot and I'm through. the bad thing about this is that we WORK together and so I don't know how this is going to play out. (taking a deep breath). Oh well, thank goodness for my ability to keep good notes and records of things aka interactions or else I would be worried. Ha. Ok **so how do you move on after a bad break up? Well first: you DO NOT** step out of character by dealing with someone right away and **number two...you don't** deal with someone who is NOT your style **and third: do not** sleep with someone until you can be OBJECTIVE about what it is YOU want out of the relationship (which should be more than dick / puss) OK? So you already have the assignment for today...**NOW go forth and behave yourselves out there...'cause the streets**

have a habit of remembering all the bad shit you do. Your girl, Kali J Moore over and FREE!

May 4, (did you miss me?) Do the Humpty Hump...do the Humpty Hump ... what's up y'all...It's Wednesday and You KNOW how I feel about Wednesdays. The week is almost over. Mother's Day is Sunday and you know what? Your girl has changed her home number! That's right. The number was changed this morning. .. I'm saying "Peace out!" to all those I cut off over the past few weeks....but the hotline number will remain the same so if you want to holla at the girl...do so...973-342-1039. And I DO answer the phone. Ok...so **Mr. Diamond Bracelet** came to see me around 4am and so I'm a bit tired, but its nothing I cant handle. He comes under the cover of darkness for "federal" reasons. But I can be sure to see him once per year and around a Major holiday. So Mother's day is coming and there he was, all up on my doorstep and I have to say, **Hubby really didn't give a damn. He knows I come with "extras" and so it doesn't bother him and why would it?** I'm married to HIM and I DO act like it. But my old friends...especially Diamond Bracelet, well he and I are going to always be cool. And so we stayed up and talked about the late eighties, and the nineties and I said, "Damn I'm getting old" when I met him **I was a baby from Mt. Vernon, NY** and **he was Harlem's baby boy.** (thinking back)...we were great back then and to be honest, he's 100% responsible for my shoe habit. HE made me love the shops. HE did that. It sure was different back then. But I'm married with children (some step, one is mine) and he...well he's got a fiancé and she's pregnant...I'm happy for him and so is my family ...NINE and a half with him **during the Kali Jones Street dreams days** and so we've got a lot of history. So there it goes my once per year visit from Mr. Diamond Bracelet and yes, your girl got the Jimmy C. shoe budget for Mothers day and money for this piece of jewelry I saw...yes, **all my peeps look out for their girl and if you think Mother's day is big for me...CHECK ME OUT ON FATHER'S DAY...ALL of my family...EVERYONE goes ALL OUT for me on Father's day...**its a damn shame though 'cause I would rather them go out for the kid's pops, but hey...it is WHAT it is. (taking a deep breath)...Y'all know that really bothers me. It really does. But I gave that situation enough time to fix itself and homeboy has YET to do the right thing by his daughter other than the child support so...(exhaling), I'm sure he'll holla one day (sucking my teeth) What else is going on? **Well today I want to examine the terminology: JUMP OFF.** now for all those who don't know what a Jump Off is I would say this: **a jump off if a person who you get with for sex only.** Today I want to clarify its meaning because a dear friend of mine who is married has the meaning confused and **so I believe many of you may be going around misrepresenting Jump Offs across the country**. ha ha. **A jump off is a person who** you call for SEX ONLY. Preferably in the middle of the night or wee hours of the morning, but nothing is out in the open for others to see. **A Jump off does not** go to the movies. **A jump off does not** go out to dinner. **A jump off is not someone who gets pregnant and wants to flip the script by keeping a kid. A jump off is not** going to say hello to you in front of your man / woman. **A jump off is NOT** thinking long term because a Jump off cannot BE long term **BECAUSE ANYTHING LONG TERM INVOLVES FEELINGS. A jump off is not** going to ask questions **or** expect you to explain anything about your life outside of f'ing around with them. **And a jump off shouldn't be based on ANY emotion other than a "NUT"** *(sorry but you know I have to keep it gangster).* Now based on those characteristics, ask yourself? AM I A "JUMP OFF" **Oh and before I forget...THE JUMP OFF ASSOCIATION IS THE ONLY ASSOCIATION WHERE BOTH PARTIES INVOLVED ARE CONSIDERED EQUAL. MEANING: BOTH PARTICIPANTS ARE THE SAME THING = JUMP OFFS. I'm getting out of here. have to get the little one to the dentist. You guys be easy out there. Your girl, KJ over and JUMP FREE! ha ha ha.**

05-06 - IT'S FRIDAY AND ACT LIKE YOU KNOW! What's up fam? It's your girl kj on the check in...this week has been very busy for me and I know I've neglected you

guys a bit with the entries but hey a sista is trying to make a **dollar out of fifteen cents (still coming up short)** ha ha, ok so this week we discussed the TRUE meaning of a Jump Off and I hate to admit this but a LOT of you are running around thinking you are in committed relationships when you are really a Jump Off and then...there are some of you...and JUST a FEW , who think you are being jumped off when in fact you are in committed relationships. Its funny because until I addressed this on Wednesday I kind of thought I was being jumped off by way of hubby...ha ha ha, but much to my surprise, I am actually a WIFE...lol. but to all those married and committed folks who are reading, ..hmmm in the middle of the night....don't you just love to be "jumped off" every once in a while? Y'all better act like its Friday....so, kj is feeling great. I got the new hair shipped in from cali from my girl.I'm getting the hair done like free from 106 and park done tomorrow and I think it would be good with the summer months and all....you know with the whole wet and waved thing going on. what else? Well I want to say happy mothers day to all the parents out there and fathers you're included in this. **if you are a single parent doing your thing, then happy mothers day to you as well. if you are taking care of others people's kids, then I want to give a special mothers day shout out to you .** Have a great day on Sunday and what else is going on? well I have a million things to do over the next few days and I just don't know how I am going to get all these thing accomplished. I have cut out one more person in my life. well really two. just don't have time to deal with the crapola that derives from being friends. **lets me make myself clear. I don't have time to confide in people who BIG MOUTH me afterward.** so since the beeyah did...I had to past tense her ass and since Nik was the one who introduced me to this hussy...I had to past tense her by default. **you know how it goes...your association...YOUR ass.** period and point blank. so this ho betrayed me. and that's not what's up. now I have to think "where am I going to hear my business in the future" I can't believe I fell for that shit. **thinking I'm having a personal conversation with a WOMAN and all the while I'm talking to a tape recorder.** If I wanted everyone to know how I felt, I would have put it in a book and you know I'm not shy. **My** personal life is my personal life and don't even think about fucking with the little one. I am too protective for that. so today's assignment is: make a card for your mom or the mothers in your life. lets get back to the basics where love meant everything; I love you. Y'all be safe out there KJ. moore. I hope hubby gets me a car for mother's day. kj. over and out. peace.

05/09 - HAPPY MONDAY FAMILY!!! HAPPY MOTHERS DAY TO ALL THE MOTHERS AND THOSE WOMEN TAKING CARE OF OTHER PEOPLES KIDS... I want to amend something I said to you on Friday about celebrating Fathers day if you are a single parent – mother. WE cannot be MEN. **Its NOT our duty to be a FATHER to our children...the ONLY thing we can be are GOOD MOTHERS.** So WE are NOT going to celebrate Fathers day...WE are going to have our OWN single MOMS day. I am working on that. and its NOT going to be on FATHERS day...**this is because despite MY situation and some of your situations...THERE ARE MEN OUT HERE WHO ARE PARTICIPATING IN THE LIVES OF THEIR CHILDREN AND ARE GREAT DADS AND US WOMEN SHOULD NOT WANT TO SHARE A DAY WITH THEM...** So...I'm thinking that since Mothers day is May...Fathers day is June...**Single Parent's day should be in JULY.** This day is going to be fore ALL OF US...**Single Parent MOMS & DADS. We should celebrate TOGETHER because WE deserve a day of our OWN. So On THE FOURTH SUNDAY IN JULY – WE ARE GOING TO DO A SINGLE PARENTS DAY.** If you are reading this : **SPREAD THE WORD.** From now on...**the 4TH SUNDAY in JULY is for SINGLE PARENTS -** what else is going on? Hmmm, well I DID NOT get a car for Mothers Day so now I'm just going to come out and say, **"Babe...ani up...your girl needs a new set of wheels."** That's it. Ha ha ha. I'm sure he's got something planned because that's all I talk about lately. Bills and Wheels, that's ALL I talk about. Ha ha. What else? Well Mothers day my "friend" took my daughter out and they came back with a beautiful bracelet for me. And I got a lot of cards and stuff like that, flowers, etc. It was a very sentimental Mothers Day and I really enjoyed that. My daughter also made me about five cards and she gave me two plants. It was very cute. I'm glad she found me, 'because I swear I was a mess before her father...they really "grew me up." Having him and then becoming a mother. (thinking back). (taking a deep breath). So this Mothers day was very nice. Now today I have to finish up my book business with a distributor...they were suppose to send my check for two weeks now...this is crazy. I can't stand when people do this, but I need them and so I can't complain. **I'm short of going there and taking it back to "the day"** ha ha. But ok so I called the rep this morning and was told that I would get this check tomorrow. Lets see because I NEED it. And I'm not about to allow these book checks to come like the child support checks – all willy nilly and just whenever 'cause you THINK KJ got it going on... Hell no. **CTC = cut the check! Mariah Carey's CD...I am LOVING it: Favorite songs – track 1,2,3,5,12, and 14 ...I know there is one or two more in there...BUT I am in-love with NUMBER 5 (it reminds me of a jump off) ha ha ha. And Number 14 – MARIAH GOES TO CHURCH ON THAT ONE...I LOVE IT. Played it all day yesterday and its in my office on the CD player. Today's Assignment is for ALL the SINGLE PARENTS: "LETS MAKE A COLLECTIVE PROMISE TO NOT SPEAK ABOUT THE DEADBEAT PARENT AGAIN." LET'S NOT ALLOW DEADBEAT PARENTS TO RENT SPACE IN OUR HEADS...OH I FORGOT...TO RENT MEANS YOU ARE PAYING FOR SOMETHING...OK. SO LETS NOT ALLOW DEADBEATS TO SQUAT IN OUR SPOTS. LOL. Let's move AWAY from the past if not for ourselves, then for OUR CHILDREN. I'm proud of you all, but ONLY if you're proud of yourself. Your girl KJ Moore, over and SQUATTER FREE.**

05/11 - Its hump day everyone...and I'm just happy to be here. It's Wednesday the middle of the week and y'all know how I feel about the middle of the week. What's up with me? Hmmm, about FIVE bags of laundry. Damn! How did I let it

get like this right? Where do I begin…Well I'm very busy first off and as long as me and the little one have clothing, it's not a big deal. I shop too much not to have this under control. Maybe just maybe if I didn't shop so much… Each month I make a promise to myself that the next visit to the laundry won't be far in between. The place I go is not too far from my house, but its like everyone knows Kalico…and so I don't have a minute to be just "me" and so I get a lot of "where's book two" and ""I figured out the identity of Mr. Nba" so its a lot of that going on. I will get there though...possibly tomorrow because I do not like my weekends to be filled doing housework. and Since I have to leave the premises to do laundry, I have to **plan** the experience in advance…Two to three hours UGH!. What else is going on? Well I am getting ready to go car hunting. That's right and I think since I need to do book stuff and the kid needs space, I am going to get a wagon or a minivan and trick it out...**Route 22 here I come!** (taking a deep breath). **So the little one is doing great and we are just having fun right now** planning her graduation party - which may go down in Westchester - and her birthday parties - which will go down in jersey - I'm going to do the cheerleader themed one. **So I finally got my royalty check today and THANK goodness because a chick needs the dough.** What else is going on? Well I am just happy to be here. **Today's assignment is: DEAL WITH THE REAL YOU. whatever short comings you have, FACE THEM. GET IN THE MIRROR AND DEAL WITH YOU. APOLOGIZE TO YOURSELF FOR WHATEVER YOU HAVE DONE IN THE PAST AND MOVE ON. DON'T CARRY WEIGHT FROM WAY BACK WHEN. EVERYONE FUCKS UP. JUST MAKE A PROMISE TO YOURSELF THAT YOU ARE GOING TO BE AWARE OF THE MISTAKE PRIOR TO ENGAGING. LETS LEARN FROM OUR MISTAKES. LETS NOT CARRY THE WEIGHT OF LIFE ON OUR SHOULDER ANY LONGER. FORGIVE YOURSELF AND MOVE ON. I love you all and I'VE got your back! Your girl, Kali J Moore...I'll Hollaaaaaaaaa :)**

05/14 - Its Saturday . Sorry I've been slacking off on this diary thing, but the past few days have been filled with turmoil. Ok so where do I begin? First of all, the secret crush - aka "female" turns out to be a REAL ass. Now I know I told y'all she was bugged out before, but this girl has LOST her mind. Let me tell you what she did. ..you know what? I'M NOT even going to go there...in a nutshell, its like this: She is a head case and she really needs to be in therapy. I sincerely hope she gets the help she so desperately needs. so "Andy Griffin" needs help...that's ALL I'm going to say. Ok so the good thing about this is: the association will be professional from here on out because I have made it that way. I can't really get into the particulars because there are some who read this from the job...but trust and believe...this weekend I will be thinking of how I am going to fix this the K Jones way. What else is going on? Nothing... I told y'all I was a regular ol gal with the same shit going on in her life as many of you. This weekend I am going to finish cleaning and think about how I am going to move beyond this bitch attempting to ruin my day. one thing is for SURE...she better stand CLEAR of me. **Oh...I did the laundry y'all every bit of the 60 bucks worth. three hours** and I am just putting up the clothes this afternoon. Me and the little one went to the park and after carefully considering a request...I am going to decline on an offer to pass along information. the reason: I just don't know who to trust. this is why KJ don't do anymore interviews. This is why KJ stopped the book signings, but (taking a deep breath) **I know that living in a bubble is NOT living in REALITY** and so as I stated early on...I took the little one to the park. We had a great time. I met a woman "Faye" and her children. We had a nice chat and you know what? I NEVER MENTIONED SHIT ABOUT BEING AN AUTHOR, NOTHING. I never do because that time belongs to my daughter and NOT kalico jones. I know you feel me but we did exchange numbers. what else is going on? OH my radio show will be back on artistfirst.com beginning the first week in June. I am going to Sunday nights at 11pm. so be ready for that. Its going down ladies and gentlemen. Oh...(taking a deep breath). **KJ 365** is going to come out. Its going to be a compilation of all my diary entries. I'm sure you guys will find it amusing. Tonight I will be at Just Jakes in Montclair NJ checking out the flying Mueller brothers: a cover band and I can't wait. I haven't seen that band in years...Ok so **today's assignment is: Seize the Day! Go OUT, enjoy the fresh air. Even if you don't have money. I left my purse home. KJ went out today with a buck in her pocket just in case the ice cream truck came to the park...It didn't bother me one bit. So Seize the day and don't worry about having money to go out. Go out and take a walk and tomorrow...GO TO CHURCH. So we have two things to accomplish over today - Saturday and tomorrow - Sunday. Well that's my story and I'm sticking to it. Your girl KJ over and seizing the day dammit! I'll hollllllllaaaaaaaaaaaaaaaa peace!**

05/16 - Happy Monday "Peep"le. How in the hell are ya? I hope good. As for me, I'm taking it light. I have cleaned the flat, taken my daughter to the park and I have cooked: That's right KJ has got kitchen skills: Fried Chicken, REAL mashed potatoes and corn and PYT was happy. "PYT" don't even worry about who...just know that all YOU need to know. (taking a deep breath). So I spoke with hubby yesterday who has not seen or heard from me in a minute and I have to tell you...his last letter...was NOT good. So (taking a deep breath), I think I'm going to VA over the weekend. (another deep breath). I just don't know what I am going to do about all this "life" I'm having right now. I'm looking good, I'm feeling great, BIG things are happening for me right now. My radio show is back on **www.artistfirst.com** as of Sunday June I believe 13th or 5th so things are going well. My daughter is now a "daisy" that's the girl scouts. Back in the day the smallest you can be was a brownie, but no more...now you can be a "daisy" and so I already put everyone on notice about my baby and those dag on girl scout cookies "ANI UP!" when you see little KJ coming through. ha ha ha. What else is going on? Well my baby is getting ready to graduate out of pre-k to kindergarten and so I have to put together a party for that. its in THREE weeks, (taking a deep breath). Can you say "empty purse?" ha ha. my nephew's bday is coming in two weeks and so we're having a BIG thing for that, he's turning one. Then its my older brothers bday and then he had the nerve to have a son the following day...and then the little ones graduation is two days after that. Ugh, the money we are going to spend and then just when you think its safe...**FATHERS DAY COMES...THEN WE GET TWO WEEKS OF REST FOR THE WALLETS AND THEN MY SISTER IN LAW AND THEN THE LITTLE ONES BDAY THREE DAYS LATER...money, money, money...all of which I DON'T have. at least not like this. Damn, this is BIG money, not baby bucks. My child wants a dog and so we're getting that for graduation. and a party of course.** What else is going on? Well I spoke with my older sister...she will be coming out to jersey to live. it would be a great change for her. she has a few kids and so ...it will be nice. so lets see. What else is going on? Well today I'm going to just hang around the house. I'm thinking baked chicken and mac & cheese for dinner. No bbq chicken with mac, cheese and spinach. No STEAK onions left over mashed potatoes and spinach...no STEAK, onions, baked potato and salad...BINGO...THAT'S IT. AND I am no longer mad at the secret crush "female" I just hope she doesn't do that to me again. We have decided to be working buddies and that's it. See y'all KJ does have a very busy life. **So get ready for the tour. I've got bookstores coming** for me and so it's coming along. I will post the dates and places for you at the end of the week. **Anyways, today's assignment is simple: Don't be bitter or talk malice about others including those who have wronged you. That was the message in Church yesterday. The service was nice and did I mention my daughter had a solo? sure did. and she was GREAT! (but I'm sure you know that by now). Well take it light. I love you all. KJ over and NOT a bitter bitch!**

05/17 - Tuesday and I'm feeling good. Today I was in an ALL DAY meeting...and yes, BREAKFAST WAS SERVED (Y'all know how I feel about being up in the morning for meetings where food is NOT provided) and there was lunch as well, so that was great! The meeting expanded my knowledge with regards to publishing and so you can look

forward to me putting out stellar products soon. My show on www.artistfirst.com is coming. I have yet to figure out a day of the week, but I am thinking on it and so I will be able to pass that information along to you soon. **If you would like to be a guest on my show, send me an email: Kalicojones@yahoo.com and put SHOW GUEST in the subject** so I can make sure I get to it. (exhaling) what else is going on? Well I'm getting ready to cook dinner for the family and get a few hours of writing in. I do everything by hand and then transpose to computer so its time consuming, but things hit me in the middle of the night and so I sleep with a pen and pad on the floor next to my bed. Tomorrow is Hump day! THANK GOODNESS because I could really use a weekend. **Oh tomorrow evening I have an event, don't** ask me where because I really don't remember the name of the venue. I am going to have a **launch party next month and its going to be invite ONLY so if you want to go...you need to send me an email.** This is the benefits of being a kj fam member because fam members already have their e-vites and since its free for them...including food, but YOU will pay for drinks if you like. I think I'm giving a champagne toast, as a matter of fact, I KNOW I AM...but aside from that, **I am NOT getting y'all drunk.** At any rate, I hope you had a good evening yesterday and completed out the assignment. So today I have to call my girl Pudda and check in. She called the office today while I was out. and I'm trying to get back to people who have reached out to me over the past couple of days. So this evening I will be on the telephone. BEFORE you ask; The little one is fine. A bit under the weather, but only a bit. She is still running around and you know what? I have to purchase a smaller bike WITH training wheels because your girl kj don't really know how to ride a bike and so I cant teach her (pathetic I know). but hey...I have to get it done. So we've registered for tennis lessons and she's back in karate...no more dance...didn't like it anymore. Damn shame though because she's good at it, but you know how they (kids) are. She's coming into her OWN little personality and so therefore I don't fight with her on changing activities because once she find her niche, I'm sure she will stick with it. but the tennis, that is going to be MANDATORY and we're going to do bowling lessons. Once per week for an hour. **Listen: AND**

IDLE MIND IS THE DEVILS PLAYGROUND AND KIDS THAT PARTICIPATE IN ACTIVITIES ARE LESS LIKELY TO PARTICIPATE IN DRUGS AND ALL THE REST OF THE CRAP THAT'S OUT HERE. PARENTS WE ARE RESPONSIBLE FOR OUR CHILDRENS HABITS. **SO TEACH THEM TO BE RESPONSIBLE AND DON'T LET THEM SLEEP ALL DAY BECAUSE LIFE IS ONGOING. THERE HAS TO BE CONTINUOUS IMPROVEMENT BECAUSE TECHNOLGOY, PROCESSES AND LAWS CONTINUOUSLY CHANGE (EVOLVE OR IMPROVE) AND OUR CHILDREN HAVE TO BE READY TO COMPETE WITH NOT ONLY WHITE CHILDREN, BUT ASIANS, INDIANS, AND OTHER AFRICAN AMERICAN KIDS AS WELL.** SO **Today's assignment** is: **Call your parent(s) and tell them that you love them.** I know most of you read my book and so you know some of the turmoil I have had with family. I'm happy to report those situations have changed for the BETTER. It took some time, I ain't gonna front, but WE ARE family and we ACT LIKE IT. I'm speaking to my cousins on a regular basis, not all of them, but some of them and although my sisters are in a different world than me sometimes, we do take time out to call each other. **So today, call your parents and say hello. If you're parents are not living or if you do not know who your parents are then TELL GOD hello, you know HE loves you right? and HE IS YOUR FATHER.** I love you, that's my time...I gotta bounce, KJ

05/18 - Do the Humpty Hump, ah do it baby, ah do the humpty hump just doing the humpty hump....WHAT'S UP EVERYBODY? Its your girl KJ coming to you on the fine afternoon wanting to discuss getting your grove on with a kid in the house? or as I would like to call it "SEX and the Single Parent" Now for those of you who already know...yeah your girl kj is a single parent, but NOT single. But since y'all know I take questions from the kj fam members, its time for me to speak on this topic. The question of the day is: *"Dear KJ, I have been separated from my son's father since 2001 and I have been dating someone since - but no one knows so don't say my name -*

the person and my son have met on several occasions but the guy has to come to my house while he is sleeping to avoid me having to answer questions the next day. I am ready to go to the next level - move in, how should I tell my son and should I tell his father as well? his father is NOT active - he hasn't seen him in over 8 months). Troubled in Texas. **ANSWER: Dear Texas, spare me with the troubled portion of your alias because if you have been with someone since you left your son's father, YOU ARE NOT troubled...fast maybe, but NOT troubled. Ok. So** *the only thing I can say is you should begin slowly with introducing your friend to your son...because it's only going to confuse your child if you hurry. And by the way, what are you going to call him? your BOYFRIEND? this is terrible to me because as a person who has clearly been down this road before - noting unsuccessful relationship with someone you had a child with already, you should be more focused on having a HUSBAND to introduce to your son. We as women are too quick to put stand-ins in the lives our children. And what in the hell are your thinking with regards to telling his father. Someone who could give a damn LESS about his son (if he did, that much time would not past between visits). Its none of his business what you do with YOU and with YOUR son for that matter. Lets not be dumb. Or do you feel as though you have something to prove? Leave him alone and don't introduce your son to this person until you have a ring aka ARE ENGAGED. because as adults WE can move on, but it's harder for children once they become attached. He's already had one person walk out on him...lets not make it TWO. But I wish you well. KJ.* **Now let that be a lesson to all the single parents reading.** Don't be bringing people around your kid so quickly. Especially since they've dated FOUR years and have yet to make it to the alter. Don't you know MEN know after a 1 month if YOU are the one for them and they act accordingly? meaning:" THEY WILL MARRY YOUR ASS!" So ladies, stop selling yourself short...lets hold out for the RING. **Today's assignment: RE-EXAMINE your relationship. If you are in a relationship for over one year, and there is nothing but drama, you need to LEAVE. Lets stop wasting valuable years being MISERABLE and then you've lost your spunk and end up a bitter old person. Lets make sure we are** not wasting time on dead relationships. Lets let them "go" if its not working out, because eventually it will end anyway. I love you all, Lets stay the same 4Ever! Your girl Kalicooooooo PEACE

05/20 – Happy Friday Everyone! What's REALLY good, Family? Today let's talk about competition among children, shall we? Ok...now keep in mind what I am about to tell you took place among a small group of five year olds: (taking a deep breath, y'all know I'm dramatic like that) My daughter is friends with a couple of little girls. They have their "clique" they are the children of ...for lack of a better word the "elite" we've got a nice little clique going and they are all black and their parents have it going on. So they play together. They just went to the Circus, graduation is coming and you know about the activities, parties, etc my little one participates in., well my daughter was with the "clique" yesterday and a new little girl was at the facility and chimed in during a conversation about their upcoming birthday parties and the graduation party (June 14th), etc. Really my little one and the others were "bragging" to the new little girl. I don't know why, I don't know what was going on in their little minds, but they were bragging to the point of really TEASING the little girl. And you know me, I was NOT going to intervene...Kids have to learn how to stick up for themselves and they have to learn that teasing is not nice and so whatever the new little girl said to my little one was fine with me. I sat back with the other parents and watched the situation unfold. There were Five little girls standing in a semi-circle when the new girl (fed up with my daughters mouth and the others) says: **"My daddy plays for the NFL and he's getting me one thousand balloons and roses and we're going to have a barbecue for my birthday and you're not invited!"** and my little one turned to her and said, **"Well my mommy is Kalico Jones and Dora the explorer is going to be at my party with boots AND the power puff girls so I don't need to come to your party Treasure!" (The little girls name)** and then Treasure responds with, **"That's nothing I'm gonna have lots of candy and cookies AND a parade!"** and my dear sweet child says, **"Oh yeah...well that's why my mommy's gonna buy me a cake the size of a window!"** And the "exchange" went on and on...ha ha ha. People I have to tell you. That interchange was so funny. Children are funny little people. But it made me stop and think, "Why are our children so competitive?" you think that may have a little to do with US, the parents spoiling our children to the point where they STAND OUT among others and have a "I want it now Mommy" attitude. For instance: My little one the other day asked for cereal. PYT and her were having breakfast before work and school and so I assumed she – my little one – wanted Fruity Pebbles as well (pyt was eating that brand) ok so I poured the fruity pebbles and brought it into my little ones room ON A TRAY, might I add, and she glanced down and said, "I want the Kellogg cereal NOT this, take it away" and flicked her hand in a "please go from me now" motion. What did I do? Instead of saying, "you have to eat this cereal." I politely left her room and got the frosted flakes. I know...I'm a wimp! So SUE me! I'm just trying to keep her happy and yes...VERY spoiled. By spoiling her...I spoil myself. But what at what cost do we spoil our children? **Today's assignment...well the assignment for the weekend is this: Let's take back control over our children and discontinue being wimps. Lets stop spoiling our children to the point where they think they are privileged and allowed to speak to other children in a capacity that could be considered "down" lets not raise children who will be slapping our asses around in ten years. Let's NOT do that. So...Let's say NO to the ridiculous demands our children place on us. No to having TWO bikes. NO to having sleep overs every weekend. NO to ...(taking a deep breath) I'm sure you catch my drift. Ok so I love you, you love me and We're one big ol' worldwide family. Be Easy. KJ.**

05/24 - Tuesday and I'm feeling "hot ...hot...hot" and It ain't because I look good either...I'm talking about hot like on FIRE...Like how dare Homeboy not send a check for his kid? I have to tell you it makes no sense. With all the expenses that come with raising a kid, you would think (Ugh - taking a deep breath) ...I'm not even going to GO THERE! Just know...You pay your CAR NOTE...PAY YOUR FUCKING

CHILD SUPPORT! Its not rocket science, or is it? (sucking my teeth) Maybe it is and I just don't know it. I mean listen...and then I'm not going to address it any further...If all you have to do is SEND A CHECK (which doesn't really cover shit) then why should it ever be late or partial? EXACTLY family...it shouldn't be. I mean you ain't checking for her now going on month NINE and it was Six months the time prior. Your family ain't checking for her in what seems like maybe almost three years AND BEFORE THAT NEVER...On no holiday, that includes birthday and I'm sure I will be saying the same shit in three weeks on her Graduation day so give me a break Dog...and get your shit together. Terrible I tell ya, just terrible. I'm trying to bank heavy while things are what they are so that she can have something later on in life and not depend on anyone and this late and skipped payment / not in full shit is counter productive to the goals of my household. Ok well enough about his ass. I'm a little under the weather. Have a cold and swollen glands so I will be going to the doctor this afternoon to find out what is going on. I'm hard at work and so I cant really chat with you today. But life is good. the little one is great. She sung in the choir this Sunday for the Pastors anniversary. It was nice. She loves Church. Oh...and the secret crush "female" purchased her a bike. so that's two bikes in 8 days. She's giving the bigger one to charity, so at least it wont be taking up space in the house. **This weekend my girl is coming up from ATL and PYT is going to Miami and the following weekend, I will be at the Nick hotel with the little one. Sponge Bob, Dora the Explorer...you get a "themed" room and so we're going to do that. Hopefully I will be feeling better. I'll holla, KJ. NO assignment for today, just "live and LET live" and if you are a non-custodial parent...PAY YOUR DAMN CHILD SUPPORT, LEARN TO HANDLE YOUR FIRST BUSINESS, FIRST!**

05/25 - Its Hump Day folks and you know how much I love Hump Day!!!! So, I have a throat infection. YUCK - aka Strep Throat. So I'm on an antibiotic...the Z pack. I think that's what you call it. PYT took me to the E.R. yesterday evening and then the Secret Crush aka Female, went to the pharmacy to pick up my prescription...that was nice. So

what's up with me? Well I've been corresponding with my cousin "Trouble" - he's been married and has been out of Mt. Vernon for a lot of years now and is doing great for himself. Right now I'm trying to get some things in order. I have re-arranged the flat and so I will be getting rid of some stuff. I'm thinking of just putting it on the curb with a "FOR FREE" sign and let people just take whatever. The little one is still a little under the weather and so I'm not happy about that because between her and I...this week has been nuts. So tonight I think I'm going to fix beef ribs, corn on the cob and salad. I have to see how I feel. I'm expecting people over, and so I have to make sure there is plenty of food and Yolanda and Brit will be here on Friday so its off to shop til we drop once again. Oh...so will my Dad...he's coming up here from North Carolina with dreams of taking me back with him. Lets see. Hmmmm....Y'all know I want to be in N.C. so bad. I just love it there. **Today I will be replacing the hired help with regards to my daughter.** She stepped over the line yesterday and I just don't see how I can move forward with her at this point. Its a shame, **but you know what I realized fam? "People don't respect a buck anymore" translation: back in the day...you hire a cleaning lady or a cook...and they cleaned and cooked, said yes, finished their jobs and went about their business and during the time they are working for you...they would keep their mouth shut and their opinions to themselves**...BUT NOT NOW...You hire these people and they mistake "Hi how are you today" for a "friendship" and then you have what I had yesterday, SOMEONE OVER STEPPING THEIR BOUNDARIES.AND THAT'S NOT COOL. **ITS LIKE THIS: I PAY YOU, YOU DO YOUR JOB AND SHUT THE FUCK UP! SORRY BUT HEY...IT IS WHAT IT IS.** So since this is not the case in this situation...and I'm the type of person who has a hard time forgiving...and I will be the FIRST to admit it...I don't think I can go forward with the current situation in place. and truth be told...I don't know if I want to. Ok so what else is going on? I'm getting ready to take a nap. Didn't sleep much last night due to stuffy nose, sore throat, fever, etc. **Today's assignment: FIRE SOMEONE USELESS! If you are not in a position where you can fire someone...then cut someone off. and if you**

happen to be one of the BLESSED ones who are surrounded by nothing but love and competency...THEN THROW YOUR HANDS TOWARD THE SKY AND SAY "THANK YOU JESUS!" Have a great day! I love you all...Kali J Moore.

05/26 NO POST...JUST PURE PANIC AND CHAOS IN THE PUBLISHING INDUSTRY...Kj has done it again...Everyone wants to know why I'm not checking emails, why I am not getting back to them...why my phones go straight to voicemail...well this is why... MY masterpiece is almost complete....WORLD SAY HELLO TO "DIGGAZ INCORPORATED: *Closed Legs Don't Get Fed*" a story about four friends from Yonkers, NY ***********Hopefully I can have this out before Winter Have a great day! kj.

Its Friday, May 27, and I'm trying to book a spot for a gathering. This is crazy I tell ya...this town I live in...you cant just renegade yourself and party into a park and fire up a "q" – no....not here...you have to go to the "town" and get a permit. You have to PAY for it and you have to PAY for an attendant to assist you (on staff with the town) and you have to PAY by the hour (of which I believe is about 25 bucks) and you have to PAY for someone to clean up after you are done. DAMN...I thought "Milk was chillin'?" ha ha ha. 'Cause based on what the town charges, I'm being "Milked" – Y'all remember that song..."Milk is chillin'...gizmo's chillin' what more can I say, top billin'...I absolutely loved that song. I'm laughing at myself because my sense of humor is so "off key" but I think that "I thought Milk was chillin'" comment was just the funniest. So what's up family?...So its come to my attention that we may have members of our family walking around saying to themselves, "I thought I Had to die to go to Hell" their lives are so miserable because they have allowed a few fuck ups to throw and KEEP them from obtaining their goals. Family, this should not happen. If I allowed every fuck up to make me miserable, I would STILL be a mess. We have to learn how to **FORGIVE OURSELVES**. We are ALL works in progress. WE have to learn how to *dust ourselves off and try again.* (R.I.P. – Aaliyah). Now y'all know I always talk about PEACE and a time or two I may have mentioned "taking your problems to Jesus" etc. but I have to tell you…In all my millions and trillions of fuck ups, back slides and go arounds coming back around on my ass…I have always PRAYED. I remember in the height of my offenses I met an older woman who said, "Mia (that's my real name) do you pray?" and I looked at her and said yes. She said , "I mean REALLY pray…get on your hands and knees like you did when you were little and PRAY…you'll make it through…I know you will." And Family, let me tell you this…(taking a deep breath because I'm getting emotional and I'm about to testify) I prayed family and STILL to this very day, with all my potty mouth, baby daddy drama, family shit and books about my PAST life and all the OTHER bullshit y'all really don't want to know about (pyt, hubby, secret crush and the other one), …I get on my HANDS and KNEES and I PRAY…I humble myself to the Lord. Its not that God wants us to feel inferior or degraded in His presence, its about **showing God some respect. Get ON YOUR HANDS AND KNEES. I'm telling you, IT WORKS. IF THERE IS SOMETHING YOU ARE ASKING GOD FOR RIGHT NOW AND YOU ARE NOT GETTING ANSWERS…IF YOU ARE SEARCHING FOR CLOSURE, OR ASKING GOD TO OPEN DOORS FOR YOU AND YOU FEEL AS THOUGH HE IS NOT RESPONDING…get on your hands and knees and really give God time out of your schedule. And be specific.** Most of us, when we pray, we pray for others and our family and do this whole spin prayer…NOT me…NOT anymore…I am specific when I go to Jesus and so you better be too! When you go to the Lord…(clearing my throat) you better be careful as to what you pray for. Let me share something else with you: Y'all know I want to move down south (north carolina) and so me and my daughter have been going back and forth there looking for a house, right? Ok. So the last time we went to see the house I really wanted (that's the three bedroom on 1.25 acre of land with the pony stable and playground and lets not forget the biggest garage – two levels – I've ever seen)…well, me, my father, my step mom, my daughter and my little brother were standing on the porch and I asked my dad to pray. We stood on that porch all of us, holding hands and we ALL prayed and although I cant recall the EXACT prayer my father prayed I can tell you it ended with **"Lord if this is NOT the house for my daughter, don't give it to her"** and my daughter said, "God I want a backyard" We ended the prayer and we left. I called the seller ALL day for the next few days and nothing…it was all kinds of excuses…and eventually the house was given to someone else. SIX months later….the house was back on the market and I was back on the phone with the seller. My step mother was on the phone, my dad filled out the paperwork and NOTHING…they chose someone else again. House is off the market. **But am I upset? Not at all, why? Because Jesus has something else in mind for me and the little one and that house was NOT it**. So in the meantime, I keep what I have, save more money and be patient. To be honest with you family, when I go to God, he tells me the SAME thing over and over again, so I KNOW what I must do in order for me to have the things I go to Him for. WE all know the little things we do that we have NO business doing. Those things that we know we need to give up in order to get ahead. I have two things and NO I'm not telling you what they are, but just like I have my two things, YOU HAVE YOUR "things" as well. **So Today, Lets RENEW ourselves through Jesus. Lets pray today and lets get on our knees and pray…Take it back to the old days with the prayer. Lets be SPECIFIC when we go to Jesus…SAY WHAT WE WANT AND NEED. And lets GET RID OF those "things" we know we should have said goodbye to a LONG time ago. LETS stop blocking our blessings by holding onto those "things" that we have allowed to take residence in our lives. Because its these "things" that hold us back from reaching our FULL potential. Don't believe me? Give up one of your things and see how God moves in your life…Try it. I'm going to do it as well. And lets meet back here in a few weeks to discuss. So you have the knowledge, you have the assignment, now lets go forth! Have a wonderful weekend. Enjoy Memorial Day and lets be safe out there. Your girl 4Real, KJ**

Happy Tuesday May 31, the last day of the month... and I'm constipated. Ugh...its like it wont come out. I know...too much information, but its true. My girlfriend Yolanda is still up here from Atlanta. last night we had dinner on the world yacht it was very nice. my little one didn't want to get off the dance floor. well I have to go. I don't know if I will check in later. this post is short because as I said, I'm constipated and I have to fix myself. YUCK. (don't be frowning your faces...I know, I'm graphic).I may be getting closer to a relocation, especially since the building I live in has been sold and these new owners seem to be assholes. never introduced themselves, never responded to my calls and then they have the grounds keeper push a note under my door telling me to whom to address the rent check...YEAH RIGHT...ha ha ha. **Today's assignment: Give someone a compliment...it might just make their day. I love you, you love me...your girl 4real kj moore.**

Do the Humpty Hump, ah do the Humpty Hump...What's up family? Its your girl KJ checking in on this fine Wednesday the First of June and I'm feeling much better than yesterday, I gotta tell ya. Oh, I gotta get some fiber in my diet QUICK. (don't worry I'm not going to get graphic on you today). Well, my friend is still here from Atlanta and having a blast. Oh I forgot to tell you. Monday we hung at the lobby of the Marriott at World Financial Center...can I tell you it was very nice. and the MEN in there...Ladies if you are single and LOOKING...put that on your list and lets not forget the Grand Hyatt at Grand Central Station during baseball season...THAT is the place to be. There are also a few other favorites on my list of places to go to "meet" and "greet" but you hookers reading these posts...Y'all might run up in there and misrepresent the Legend that is I and We wouldn't want that, now would we? So I'm looking good. Got on the Chanel Shoes with jeans, white t-shirt and baby blue blazer and the NEW weave...I've got the Julia Roberts look. I love that look in pretty woman when she has the jeans, shoes and blazer (oh and you have to see the bag - its AWESOME) and the hair...well my new hair style is longer than usual (14inch), jet black with lose flowing curls, just a little glam in my life for this week family, just a little glam. Well (taking a deep breath)...my little one graduates from Pre-K on the 14th and I'm excited. She's growing up so fast, sometimes it makes me afraid you know, because this world is so crazy...eleven year olds stabbing nine year olds to death (did you see that on the news the other day?), its terrible. But one of the reasons why I think all these children are violent is because of the family structure. Meaning: there is almost always something missing within the family structure, whether its the father (due to abandonment or just working too much to keep the bills together) or the mother (doing the same, yes there are mothers who abandon their children) or maybe its just other things...but one of the most Important things is the fact that there are **NO MORE TRUE generations. Mothers are no longer 25 years older than their children...their children are 12 and the mothers are 26.** So the two of them are basically interested in the same music, clothing and boys, so when it comes to being a parent, **HOW CAN THEY when they are children just the same?** (taking a deep breath). Its just a shame you know. When I had my daughter (after so many abortions and yes I can keep it real, that's between me and my God, so get over it)...I was 28 going on 29 and her father was a year older than me. Both of us had no children and have since elected not to become parents to additional children. (At least I know I kept that end of our "agreement" up). But the reason for that is simple: **Children with a bunch of different daddies just don't feel "related" like they should.** I know because I have many sisters and brothers and we (most of us) have different mothers and so its hard having the "loyalty" you should to family. So me having other children just wouldn't be the same. I hope some of you reading this take the time out to USE condoms and just keep yourselves together because **this world is not designed for anything other than the PROPER family structure. In the Bible it clearly states the order of operations with regards to rearing / bearing children and we have to adhere to that.** Now this doesn't mean everything is going to be perfect, but when the two walk in AGREEMENT...the difficulties wont get the best of you. Ok. so that's my time for today...**The assignment: Spend time with your children. Read your child a bedtime story. If you are not a parent, then spend time with** someone special. and that doesn't mean have sex...(for those of you who don't know the meaning of spending quality time)...watch a movie or just talk. Do you know your special persons middle name? favorite color? second favorite color? mothers name? What do you know about the person you are with? So get to know the person you are with. What is your child's favorite color? or favorite friend? Have a great day and remember: I am happy for you, but only if you are happy for YOURSELF> I'll holla.....KJ Moore w/luv!

Have you ever woke up in a bad mood? Oh my goodness...I was a maniac this morning (car service late, problem with home phone line, cell phone wont work, dead zone where I live and my daughter missed the school bus). (taking a deep breath) Its Thursday, June 2nd and I am just worn out. I threatened to relocate this morning. Went into the office and just said, "You know what? I'm done...I have to see how I am feeling over the next few days and make an Executive Decision." You should have seen the look on the faces of the people who were in attendance...and you know what family? KJ don't give a shit. I'm just to the point where I feel as though I need to make a "run for it" Its just like damn, I can't get a break. So much shit gets side tracked off one thing. and it rolls downhill from there. So...after my daughter's graduation, I will make my decision. I think I should just "go for it" and keep it moving. Hubby is in Jail...never told y'all, but it is what it is. PYT is cut off. The secret crush aka female is a true ass...I mean she has reached "legendary" ASS status. Family shit is just that, family shit and the only constant thing is the relationship I have with my little one, God and my father. Now don't get me wrong, I have a relationship with my mom and brothers, but what I am talking about is the "peace" factor. I can't explain it, but I am just thinking aloud. **So KJ is saying, "is it time?" My father and I had a conversation about FAITH and stepping out on faith and how can I tell you guys to do this and that and just go for your dreams and whatever makes you happy if my black ass ain't taking my OWN advice? EXACTLY ...I cannot. So if its not something I am willing to do, then I am going to keep my**

mouth shut because the LAST think I am is a fucking hypocrite. So what else is going on? well I have decided to cut one more person out of my life. **Unfortunately I have come to the end of the road with her. Reason being: a Man, and being deceptive...what else would it be?** You know how us chicks are when it comes to a man...man first, all else...SECOND. its going to be something to see how her own personal situation develops, God bless her. So what else is going on? lets talk about Indian giving (no offense to my native American brothers and sisters) but let me tell you what happened: Friend comes over, stays a few days, gives me a shirt...I accept it (knowing I don't accept shit from anyone, but she's a buddy so its all good). The shirt is new retail 98.00 don't know what the SALE price was because that part was torn from the tag...ok. so friend gives shirt. I put it in my closet with all the other shit I don't wear, but I liked the shirt and decided that I would wear it to my launch party. Ok. so friend leaves while I am at work to go off and be a cash cow (no comment TRANSLATION: I wont elucidate the details) OK so later on that day, I have company...go to show the nice gift my visitor gave me and guess what? **GONE!!! SHIRT GONE Y'ALL...WHAT'S UP WITH THAT. hanger still there, but SHIRT mysteriously missing. Now don't get it twisted...the shirt...IS NOT THE ISSUE.** The issue is the fact that she went in my closet and took it and didn't say a word. I guess she figured I wouldn't notice it any time soon and you know what? to be honest...I would not have noticed it until a few days prior to the launch party. So what did I do? I called her and asked her where the shirt was...you know why? At first I was going to let it go because quite frankly...I HAVE MORE than enough stuff and the shirt is not something I can't get ...**but it was the VIOLATION** that had me by the balls. and before I called her ass, **you know I got on the phone with my girl Pudda and asked her for her opinion...she said the same thing: ITS THE VIOLATION that was crazy...and therefore it should be addressed.** So I addressed it (oh and by the way...she has no idea what happened to the shirt, but will "check her bags for it") why would you check your bags if you know you don't have it? and things got nuts between that and her lying to me about something else...so to make a long story short...I went to western union and wired her the money she paid for dinner the other night (small thing to a GIANT = me) and I left her a not so nice message with regards to her attempt to "play" me and I move on. **No blood...no foul. See the thing about me that bothers people who DON'T like me is my ability to not allow PEOPLE not liking me ...BOTHER ME...I could give a damn LESS.** I love those who love and respect me and I teach my daughter the same and that goes for FAMILY as well. I tell her, **"don't let the last name and blood type keep you from speaking your mind or detaching yourself should the need arise!"** because FAMILY are those who treat you according to your standards **PERIOD AND THERE IS NO ROOM FOR COMPROMISE and don't feel bad for not settling.** I'm sure you guys understand where I am coming from with that. **Well I'm outta here for today. Today's assignment: Don't worry ... BE happy. and if that means you have to not worry about others...THEN FUCK 'EM. Your girl KJ Moore over and out...**

Happy Monday "Peep"le!!! Its June 6, and today I resigned from my day job. It was a very liberating experience to say the least. I didn't give the particulars as to why, but I can tell you this...In life, you have to know when to hold 'em and know when to fold 'em. and it was time to fold family. So your girl KJ had to roll out. But have no fear...I was professional in that I gave them two weeks notice. So after that is up...I'm going to head south and house shop and vacation with the little one and then ...come back and see where I am with things. What else is going on? Well my dear ex had a visit with his daughter, and it was a nice experience for the both of them I'm sure. He has burns on his feet from the beach (yeah, he's a yellow boy) and my daughter can now pass for being MY daughter (she got a really dark tan). We were in the parade (African Heritage in Montclair) on Saturday with the Church. The Youth Choir sung and it was GREAT. But my already brown behind, got BLACK...I cant even wash it off family...its a REAL tan. ha ha ha. and I have to say this about baby daddy...**THAT MAN SURE LOOKS GOOD. HE REALLY DOES.** You know KJ loves nice arms. That's the one thing I won't compromise. A man has got to have GOOD arms. I want to see some cuts - not too many, but enough to qualify (for lifting - ha hah a) read in between that line if you DARE. So the Female Crush has now been renamed to "Luke" 'cause I'm going to bring her "to the dark side" ha ha ha. What else is going on? Well again, I'm happy with my decision to leave the job because it puts me in a better place to sell books and go on tour. I can't do shit working full time. and there are many other reasons for my departure that include female crush and others. the thing is business and personal. So that's one of the MANY reasons for my departure. What else? Well Life is great. I look good, I feel even better and my daughter is happy and so what else matters? EXACTLY ...nothing. **I'm hoping that this weekend was the END of me and baby daddy having BIG drama...I'm going to let by gones be just that...over and GONE. Today's assignment: Take a chance on yourself. Your girl KJ Moore signing**   **off.**

June 7, Its Tuesday and I'm ok. just trying to make a dollar out of fifteen cents. No one is speaking to me at this job. its funny. Since I am leaving, they are acting funny. Secret Crush ain't speaking... Which I find disturbing especially since she was at my house last night. I'm glad I won't be working here too much longer...'cause this way...I can BE ME. Ok. **so what else is going on? Well life is good and I'm just having a blast. Today's assignment is: Hey better yet...NO assignment for today. Go out and enjoy the weather. Take your shoes off and let the breeze blow through your toes. Love ya! your girl KJ.**

Ah do the Humpty Hump, just doing the Humpty Hump...what's up y'all its your girl KJ coming to you on this fine Wednesday afternoon. Secret Crush is standing in front of me looking like she just swallowed a mouse. We've decided that once I am free of this b.s. I am going to "take her to the dark side" - **JUST KIDDING IT OUR OWN LITTLE JOKE. WE ARE NOT "GETTING TOGETHER"** - What else is going on? Well today I was offered an interview within the company but in a position that offers TWICE what I am making now. I have to tell you people...THIS...I gotta think about. Because you know your girls ass was gonna be on the NEXT thing smoking to North Carolina. This morning I spoke with my cousin LaLa and we laughed and talked about dreams and goals and...family secrets...ha ha ha. You know we went there. and yes, there are a LOT of family secrets or so the **SECRET KEEPERS THINK**. What else is going on? Well my little one is excited about going south and she keeps asking if "daddy can come?" how cute is that...NO daddy ain't coming. He's having the time of his life right now and so are we. So book two drops next week and I'm just saying...I cant wait for your stamp of approval. I'm sure you will find it quite entertaining to say the very least. (taking a deep breath). **I'm just trying to finish up the project that I started the day I stopped getting high and whoring ...ME!** You know I'm a work in progress and I don't mind sharing my past offenses with the world. So today I'm going to take it light and just go home and do nothing...I have to wait for hubby to call me and I have to get to Virginia to see him sometime over the next week or two. **Father's day is approaching and so I have to make sure I'm in North Carolina with my dad for that day. and I have to be ready to re-launch the radio show on artistfirst.com. Well folks, that's my time for now. today's assignment: DO NOTHING. Be a couch potato...you know sometimes you have to just sit back and DO nothing...allow GOD to order your steps and ARE YOU praying? Remember what I told you about the knees thing. Get on your knees and pray. Your girl Kalico over and OUTTTTT!**

Happy Frid....Oops, I mean Thursday y'all. Today I want to share something with you sent to me by secret crush: *BITCHOLOGY* *When I stand up for myself and my beliefs, they call me a bitch. When I stand up for those I love, they call me a bitch. When I speak my mind, think my own thoughts or do things my own way, they call me a bitch. Being a bitch means I won't compromise what's in my heart. It means I live my life MY way. It means I won't allow anyone to step on me. When I refuse to tolerate injustice and speak against it, I am defined as a bitch.*

The same thing happens when I take time for myself instead of being everyone's maid, or when I act a little selfish. It means I have the courage and strength to allow myself to be who I truly am and won't become anyone else's idea of what they think I "should" be. So try to stomp on me, try to douse my inner flame, try to squash every ounce of beauty I hold within me. You won't succeed. And if that makes me a bitch, so be it. I embrace the title and am proud to bear it. **B = Beautiful, I = Individual, T = That, C = Can, H = Handle anything...** *now do me a favor and Pass that along.* What else is going on? Well my little one has a fever. and so she's with my mom this afternoon so that I can get some things done. I am trying to get a vehicle this weekend and I am going to send some things south for me and my daughter to have when we get there. (taking a deep breath)...I'm signing a contract with my cover artist today and my plan is to get these final fifty pages out of "me" this evening. **So the plan thus far is simple: after my little ones graduation we will be going to north carolina for a week or two. and then we will come back and I will think about what I am going to do. because right now...I am just fucking out of it. but I wont get into it today...we'll chat tomorrow. Give me a call if you like...I'm out. Today's assignment: BE A BITCH! your girl kj over and out.....**

Happy Monday - Its June 13, and I'm feeling better about things...Why is secret crush's little girlfriend worried about little ol' me? This "girl" = still in her twenties, works in a bar and from my understanding is a psycho...calls constantly, has "sexual" issues ("no I don't want to sleep with you, and so you assume I'm with someone else...who is NOT interested in me = ME). Now this little white girl thinks she is going to come to my job...to approach me...(taking a deep breath)...over someone of whom I am not the least bit attracted to. This is NUTS. Why me y'all? Why me? So at any rate, because I who I am...(exhaling)...I HOPE she doesn't go there. She's called my house, its like, HOW OLD are you again? OH yeah, well what can you expect, she works in a BAR and only the good LAWD knows what she's into. and If she's anything like secret crush...maybe they can get a TWO for ONE on a psychotropic (medicine for people who hallucinate). ha ha ha. Ok what else is going on? Well I'm on a countdown ladies and gentlemen...to get the heck out of this place. they are so dysfunctional...Oh yesterday I met two women at the pool in Montclair and told them my entire life story...got some advice too...I do that sometimes ONLY because I like to examine the "stranger" factor with regards to how people will have CANDID conversations and expose themselves to total strangers in effort to FREE themselves from whatever is bothering them. and it was going well too...well until one of the kids in my daughters class came running over and his mom said to me, "hey Kalico, is your second book out now and are you still doing the radio show?" OH my goodness,...I was like DAMN...She blew my cover. but after that we laughed about it. it was a nice experience and I hope to see them again. ...What else is going on? Well baby daddy didn't show up as promised to the little one, and so I'm NOT even going to go there, just know I will NOT allow her to call. I will NOT be calling. I am going to act as though he does not exist because in reality...this no show and nine month shit does more HARM than help. So the job sucks, but its my last week. The love life is non existent, but hubby may be on his way home due to a law reversal and so I'm ok. PYT was outside my window screaming at the top of his lungs....He's cut off. walking around with GOLD TEETH y'all. Gold teeth on the bottom but don't have a pot to piss in or a window to throw it through. (shaking my head) he's 26 with no children and so he's in the streets for day to day shit...and so I think that's disgusting...his perception of money and MY perception of money is quite the opposite. and so the beat goes on...So what else is going on? Not a thing. meeting with an attorney today to discuss me exercising "outside" options on a situation that I can't make "go away." and then its home to get myself together for my daughter and her bike riding "thing she likes to do." Oh...I took the weave out and cut my hair short. and it does look good. (don't hate). I saw my ex = Rich, yesterday....can you say, "Fine, fine, fine?" shit...I almost invited him on vacation. (ha ha ha)....**So anyway my dear friends, Old and NEW (BP37) if that's it...I forget and the mother of one of the cutest little boys I've seen in a long** time (the people I met at nishuane pool)...I say **THANK YOU FOR BEING NICE TO ME. BUT NOW THAT MY COVER IS BLOWN...Damn...Ha ha..that's all I have to say. I won't put your names in this so you don't have to worry about me putting your asses on BLAST!!!! :) wink wink...Have a great day and today's assignment is: (drumroll please)....Take a nice hot bath and as my ex mother in law used to say, "take yourself on vacation." and men...you can take a bath too. I know a lot of men who take baths, have a great day! Kj out!**

Do da Humpty Hump...What's up Fam and Happy Wednesdaaaaaaay! Its your girl KJ coming to you on this sunny day in Jersey June 15, So what's the dealy yo? I hope things are good for you because things are looking for me. Friday is my final day here at the Day Job and Sunday is Father's Day and My little one is graduating next week from Pre-K and then My dad will be visiting and taking US back South. We are going on Vacation "peep"le and going to do just that... VACATION... I'm tired and I need a break...QUICK. The second book is dropping and so I've got that to deal with and I'm on the phone with my brother Charlie right now getting some advice on this BIG idea I have to pitch tomorrow morning to a room filled with executives. I am accustomed to handouts but since I am giving a lot of information in the presentation I have designed...my brother says I need to put this in PowerPoint and get it so that I can eliminate the "steal" factor. meaning: No one can steal my idea because they don't have the step by step to get it done. but if I do handouts, then they most surely will have the foundation and everyone knows all you need is a good foundation...shit...you can build anything from a good foundation. It may not be the same EXACT results but you can rest assure, its going to be good just the same...(maybe...lets revisit that statement one day). (taking a deep breath)...I'm just out of it people. Just out of it. **Oh me and secret crush are speaking again. and she is pissed over my psychotropic comment**. ha ha, oh well and fuck it. Ain't nobody (ebonics) tell you to go f with me in the capacity in which you've chosen. and so she's over it. ha ha...that's right kiddies, my way or the motherf'ing STAIRS... **I'm Donald Trumping (firing) people**

left and right and I have to tell you, it feels good. I had to cut the "fat" out of my budget and after a LONG conversation with my ex = Rich... I think I may be headed south for sure. (that is...If these Execs don't buy my "idea" tomorrow). but as always, and as you know...I WILL keep you posted. What else is going on? Well my little one has yet to hear from homeboy aka her father and so as I told y'all on Monday, I will NOT facilitate that relationship anymore. To hell with him too. She is NOT a fucking light switch. **So PYT and I are not in contact and that's a GREAT thing. I left him a msg telling him that he better NOT call my ex again because before I allow him and his friends to "funny style" my ex, I will tell him about our "fling" first and take my "how could you Bitch!! "lumps" and keep it moving.** But neither him NOR his friends better ever reach out to my ex again. ha ha ha. How gangster is that? Y'all know KJ ain't no punk and since I've emancipated myself through quitting the job and firing people, I've been on a "roll" - (exhaling). So I'm sure life has something HUGE in store for me. I hope you guys are sticking to our plan about ceasing to partake in things you have no business so that your blessings won't be blocked. Well with regards to me with that, I've been bad, but not as BAD as I usually am with the things I am suppose to stop...and I'll leave it like that. I'm bad but not TERRIBLE. So, today after school I will be taking my little one out to ride her bike and I'm going to walk alongside, up to the park and then we'll swing for a while and then go home and COOK. yesterday I tried to make chicken salad and it was dry as I don't know what. **I need to call my cousin troubles wife LuLu and get some cooking lessons. Shit her ass be out there in P.A. cooking from scratch.** *(meanwhile I'm thinking scratch is that thing jam master jay used to do on records - r.i.p.)* Anyway, so I called there and she (lu lu) was snapping peas...how REAL Is that? another time I called there She (lulu) was making a cake. I'm like with flour and all that stuff? My cousin sure is lucky, 'cause although KJ can throw down...I ain't fin na (ebonics) snap no peas. God Bless her, but her family is from the south and so you know she knows how to throw down. **Well my dear friends and family...That's my time...I love you and I wish you well. Give me a call sometime: 973-**

342-1039 and if I don't answer, leave me a message. I will get back to ya! For today: Pray and give someone deserving a second chance, but only if the mistake they made was UNINTENTIONAL. 'CAUSE you know WE don't believe in being tortoises here, fuck that...But keep in mind, forgiveness a trait of the strong...Weak people can't forgive. and when you don't forgive, it holds YOU back from reaching YOUR full potential in life because you're mentally and emotionally preoccupied. meanwhile, the "other person" is living their life unaffected. Remember that because it was told to me on numerous occasions and so I want to pass it along to you. That's how WE do, you and ME. luv kj

Its Thursday and I have to tell you...I look and feel GREAT. Like Tony the tiger. So what's up with me? The meeting with the "executive" - singular, just one went for like every bit of TWO hours. and...Hmmmm how do I put this? Ok. I got it, I got it...Its either I'm going to be with these people, or with their completion or THEIR COMPETITION. You figure it out. It would take me less than one WEEK to get that idea off the ground and I mean without a fucking hitch. Off the ground and more Importantly...PAID FOR! **Y'all know how I get down, process...execution and FOLLOW THROUGH> translation: DA BITCH AIN'T PLAYIN'** - Kj coming for that ass and so it was left like this (referring to the meeting) *"lets talk next week after you come back from vacation."* I gotta tell you folks...I don't know about that. During my vacation I am going to THINK...WORK THE NUMBERS...AND THINK... cause if they don't get back to me, I'm not going to get back to them. (exhaling)...some nerve thinking I'm a joke. **But in the "executives" defense...he sure was FINE. and extremely smart. and...REAL so even if it doesn't pan out...I know he's not a fake and so I will deal with and be comfortable with his decision and then...I WILL BE HIS COMPETITION...HEY, "NO BLOOD, NO FOUL." AND I'm SURE HE WILL RESPECT THAT!.** What else is going on? Nothing really. Tomorrow I have TWO more meetings and then once I am done with those, I am going to make an "executive decision" regarding the relocation. Its like this folks...**If people want you...THEY MAKE MOVES QUICK, period and point fucking blank**. We don't have time to allow our lives to pass us by. so in having said that....**the assignment for today is a question: Ask yourself, "Am I making moves?" and if you are NOT, then you better take some time to THINK about what you need to do to change your situation, organize the "process flow" - EXECUTE it and then FOLLOW THE MUTHA FUCKA THROUGH**...See this is the life of Kalico Jones Fam and I never said it was pretty. and this site is straight up with NO chaser. **We're REAL in this arena where corporate thinking meets STREET CREDIBILITY. because when you come from the streets, you take the bulk of what you've learned OUT THERE and flip it for your benefit IN THERE. and trust and believe me when I tell you...** almost EVERYONE I know who has "made it" in corporate America has applied some of the key street principles and therefore attributed their successes "in there" to their EXPERIENCES OUT "THERE" - and don't you EVER get that TWISTED. But its all good fam...to those of you who have had the pleasure of never knowing the meaning of "out there." that's a great thing...but I'm talking to you as well with this because never think because you haven't gotten high, lived in the projects and grew up without a father that you are BETTER than anyone, because even the most treacherous of people were raised by someone and more often than not...the NUTS are raised by two parents, living in suburbia and not wanting for nothing...and you know I'm right. 'cause you see it on the news all the time the neighbors be like, "oh she was such a good kid" or "he was so quiet, he went to work with his father at the doctors office all the time." Shit ...and those be the kids shooting up the school. (taking a deep breath). **so now I am going to resume my radio show on <u>www.artistfirst.com</u> and get that back up you know I'm like 40 thousand strong with my numbers for that one hour on Sundays. so look for me. to get that jumped off again. and let me say this: I have so many things to do next week. the little ones graduation, traveling, etc. and so if you don't hear from me...then YOU give me a shout. 423-200-0261 and don't forget the assignment: Ask yourself, "Am I making moves?" and then** organize the plan, execute it and follow through. I'm your girl and I'm outta here. KJ.

Just got paid...Its Friday night...place is jumping, I'm feeling right...Hey everyone, its your girl Kali coming to you on this fine Friday in the Tri-State area (well I guess since this is the internet...I can say USA and abroad). So what's good Fam, its the 17th of the month and my final day at the day job is done. I gotta tell you, I'm going to miss some of the people there. But I have to get my "ducks in a row" so that I can go forward and I just couldn't do it there. I can't elucidate the details but I can tell you that I'm happy its over. can you say, "peace of mind?" Ok so I just got back from the park with my little one - she rode her bike. and now I'm going to make some calls and try to get in contact with my attorney. What else is going on? Well Mrs. tape recorder (you have to go back to previous posts) has struck again. I told y'all she was going to bigmouth me to someone and she did. This is what I mean about having a stock of chicks hanging around trying to get mentioned in a book. (exhaling). Always in someone else's business 'cause they ain't got (ebonics) business of their own. I'm thinking I have major shit to do. So what's in store for KJ at this point? to be honest, I don't know. All I know is that I am going to try really hard not to allow people to upset me. Its been a lot of hurt feelings for me by way of betrayal, so I know I have to be more careful when choosing someone to confide in and just befriend. I ain't buying peoples kids food and clothing anymore, I can tell you that. and just because I went through the mill, and found my way out doesn't mean I owe everybody going through similar shit...shit. I have to learn how not to be so emotional when it comes to peoples situations because more often than not...my help comes back to bite me in the ass...and y'all know that's a whole lotta biting (ha ha ha). So book two drops on Sunday, Fathers Day and I want to take this time to say, **"Happy Fathers Day!" to all my brothers reading this and to all the step dads and brothers, uncles and grandfathers who are surrogate fathers.** So what else is going on? Absolutely nothing. I'm going to take it light for one week, as my little one is graduating on

Tuesday and We will be vacationing through the south for a few weeks (north carolina, Florida and maybe Atlanta). Then its back to business for me. .. that and continuing to be the best mom I can be. Oh guess who won't be getting a fathers day card? Not even going to go there...just know it AIN'T happening. and don't act like that is shocking news to you (I see the look on your face)...No Card, NO Call and the thing the little one made in school goes in the scrap book for when she gets older. I am NOT going to allow her to continue to be disappointed and hurt by the very person who should be here to protect her...HELL NO. **so y'all I gotta go now. This weekends assignment: "If its on your mind, SAY SOMETHING!" and you know what I mean by that. don't go to bed with things on your mind. Get it off your chest by addressing it. and that doesn't mean be rude. because the person who has offended you may not even know your feelings. So don't go "guns up" - be calm, cool and collected when you step to the person. if you have to, be a "telephone gangster" call them up and just say, "hey, I gotta tell you what you did made me uncomfortable, please don't do it again." If they are your friend, they will say, "Oh, I didn't know that upset you, I'm sorry." and Y'all will be able to move on. So...with having said all of that. I have to say, "Be easy Babe" your girl Kali J Moore, over and out! Enjoy the weekend.**

Tuesday June 21, and I've just returned from the little ones "moving up' ceremony and it was cute. Secret Crush showed up and so that was nice. So this evening is the party and so we're getting stuff together. I just took a quick minute to chat with y'all about Discipline vs. Punishment. I just want to give you a little to grow on today because so many times we can AVOID consequences by being DISCIPLINED. We ask for Mercy and that's fine, nothing wrong with that, but more often than not, we ask for mercy regarding situations we could have AVOIDED had we REMAINED or LIVED with DISCIPLINE... **Can I get an Amen?** So today Family, I want you to THINK about how you are living YOUR life...**ARE YOU DISCIPLINED?** or are you Reckless and then once shit hits the fan, you go to God. You know Jesus is not our spare tire, but our steering wheel and although I don't have as many answers as I sometimes come across as having...I can tell you this (I think I've told you this before)...**THROUGH ALL MY OFFENSES, AS AGGREGIOUS (spell check) AS THEY SEEMED (and rightfully so, cause I was I mess!) I ALWAYS stopped to pray. Even the times when I knew my ass may go out and do whatever I was telling God at that moment I was NEVER going to do again...I was sincere in my prayers and Fam...I gotta keep it REAL, HE (God) has always been there for me.** You know there are a lot of things God wants to give us, but we have to show him that we are Steadfast in not just our Praises, but our way of LIVING and THINKING. and **so today's assignment is simple: Ask yourself, "AM I DISCIPLINED?" for example:** (now here's where the rubber hits the road)...If you are out with someone you really care about and things get "going" and there is no protection aka CONDOM...do you still "go for it" or do you say "as much as I would like to, I can't because we have no protection" DISCIPLINE VS. PUNISHMENT. Discipline is saying, "I can't get down like that, without protection." PUNISHMENT is catching a sexually transmitted disease or maybe an unwanted pregnancy. Discipline is not spending every dime you have on Gucci and Prada when the PUNISHMENT might be, loss of a house, or credit card debt....DISCIPLINE is not going to a party and drinking on a Tuesday when you know you have to be at work the next morning...PUNISHMENT may be, termination of employment or disciplinary action on the job should you be late or call out. So again, today's assignment is to examine your OWN life with respect to **DISCIPLINE VS. PUNISHMENT** and figure out which one of the two is YOU by nature and if you are a discipline person...GREAT and I'm happy for you, keep up the good work...but if your ass is a PUNISHMENT PERSON...I want to give you another question to ask yourself: **IS IT WORTH IT?** what else is going on? Nothing. **I have to call out to P.A. 'cause LULU has to tell me how to season lamb chops, I know she knows.** They made me so jealous on Father's day...I called there and LULU had her foot DOWN in the kitchen. My cousin Trouble was telling me all the stuff she was cooking...She's got the secret sauces and seasonings going on...You know I can honestly say that almost all my conversations to my cousin Trouble start with, "What's LuLu cooking today?" that's a damn shame. I keep saying I'm going to come there, but the truth in the matter is, shit...LULU might f around and have my little one spoiled with this food from scratch shit... ha ha ha. I told my cousin her new name is Cut Creator (LL Cool J's dj - who could scratch), get it...Ha ha ha. I know my sense of humor is nuts. OH...yeah so we're going to try to take it back to 89 and put together some kind of Project family reunion. So if you're from Mt Vernon, NY you will need to be there. This weekend I will be in North Carolina...and then to Florida...Oh that reminds me. I have to call Gina S (from my book) so she can get me and my little one from the airport. Man Unnecessary dropped Sunday and because of a hold up with my printer...you cant get the shit for another week. **Can you say, "throw back?"** 'cause that's EXACTLY what they better do, "throw me back" some of that money I put up. So I've decided to officially run a paper. I will keep you posted, which means, I may not be able to jump up so quickly, but lets just see. What else is going on? Nothing...Just being me and living life without a day job...Ahhh, the peace and tranquility...until I turned to the WB11 and caught about ten minutes of Jerry Springer Show...OH my LAWD, peeples is crazy. and now the audience is fighting the guests and the guests are fighting security...its nuts I tell ya, just plain ol' nuts. So that's my time for today. Later on, I will post a photo of my little one and the people at my house this evening for the celebration and then... I have to do it all over again in three weeks for her birthday...DAMN I CAN HEAR THE SCREAMS COMING FROM MY PURSE NOW...(exhaling)...**so let me get back to cleaning the carpets - rented a machine from home depot in Clifton while I was up there at Costco ordering the cake for the little one...and NO her dad ain't coming...and I HAVE nothing to do with it. She called him, he knows its her graduation. I just have to get used to his ass being on a nonparticipation basis with the kid. Its all good though. and we AIN'T beat. (meaning mad over the bullshit). Ok. so its back to the carpets. I will chat with you tomorrow. I'm YOUR girl....Kali J Moore. over and cleaning carpets and**

cooking for about thirty people. (taking a deep breath and shaking my head)...I'll Hollllaaaaa! Peace.

I know, I know...I missed "hump" day and I'm pissed. Sorry Y'all but yesterday I was whipped after the party - which didn't end until sometime after 1am. My daughter and I just ate and slept ALL day, that is AFTER my "friend" left at 8am. So today I had to go pick up my check from the "day job" and that was quick, good. I have nothing to say to those people in "corporate" = where I had to pick up my check. Ok so me and the little one are about to have breakfast - its 10 am and then we are going to get our nails done and then we are going to do laundry and then come back home and pack for North Carolina. I spoke with Hubby last night who told me to go ahead south. So I think that's what I am going to do. Y'all wish me luck...No screw that...Pray for a sista. So what's up with me otherwise? Nothing. Just living life and doing things I want to do. I'm sick and tired of doing for others, now its time for me to be selfish. Ohhhhh...before I forget, the book printer is going to give me a credit for 600 bucks, to go toward my next print run...I'm like...I don't think so, **CUT ME A CHECK**. ha ha ha. Ok. well that my time for today. **Today's assignment: "Think about what you can do to build your life" now that could be a job thing, a spiritual thing, a getting rid of all those people who are using you thing...a stop drinking and getting high thing...it could be being a better parent thing...whatever the "thing(s)" may be, just think about it. and write it down and put it in your pocket as a reminder of what your goals are.** *My mother told me to put a sign up in my cubical that says, "I made THIS choice" and put my daughters photo next to it. and you know what? It worked. Each day I came in and through the drama and all that b.s. that went on at the "day job" I had that sign up and it reminded me of the **bigger picture**.* I have someone counting on me to provide for them and so I have to do what I need to do **NOW = LIVE IN MY REALITY**, while I do other things on the side to get me to my GOALS and DREAMS. Now, I know I quit the job, but family, that place was dysfunctional to say the VERY least and it was like that prior to me coming on board. and to be quite honest, I just couldn't take it anymore. Now I am not saying to quit your job...I'm saying, **ITS OK TO HAVE A JOB YOU DON'T LIKE TO GO TO, BUT WHAT ARE YOU DOING ABOUT IT? WHAT ARE YOU DOING TO SET YOURSELF UP TO BE FREE OF HAVING TO TAKE JOBS JUST BECAUSE YOU HAVE TO? SO** lets get this assignment right ladies and gentlemen...**"Think about what you can do to build your life" and lets get to it**. and if you have to...shit, put the sign up **"I made THIS choice"** and set yourself so that when you leave, its by your own accord and fuck management, unemployment and severance...just "peace out" 'cause you've got business to handle. (exhaling). **So me and the little one are out y'all. I have to call my girl Val from SPOT TV, the Ying Yang twins are in Greensboro on Friday and she can get me all access so I think I'm leaving tonight. I will keep you posted. and give me a call if you like you know I do pick up the phone 423-200-0261. Your girl Kali J Moore, over and on 95 to 85 south. I'll Holla........Pray for me and my little one. We're going house shopping again.**

Its Saturday and Y'all know KJ don't write on no weekends. June 25, and me and the little one are in North Carolina. Hopefully for good. (exhaling)...So I have things to do. Tomorrow, I have to get the paper and get to getting with regards to Houses. I have one in mind, lets see if goes "through" - I'm out here and I'm going to visit some old friends - my boy Cheesy is out in Laurinburg and Val from SPOT TV is in Greensboro and my old neighbor miss Vanessa is in Raleigh so I'm going to be catching up with them and trying to get a hold of Everlasting (an old friend)...so it goes like this family...Kali is doing HER. We will try to catch up with my daughters Nanna to see if they can hang out over next weekend, but if not...No blood no foul, it ain't like she is used to seeing "them" anyway. and homeboy...well I just got off the phone with him and he ain't even "beat" to speak with his own kid, so its like...HOW LONG do I put up with and FOCUS on their stupidity?

EXACTLY...I should keep it moving. So I tell you what Fam...HE has the number to where his child is staying and so the ball is in HIS court. I WILL NOT nor AM I going to reach out to him, yet again. This is NOT going to be a repeat performance of the shit "they" did to my little one the last time she was south. (taking a deep breath)...so I had a panic attack as soon as we pulled out of Virginia. I almost stopped to see Mike = Hubby, but I will get to that on Thursday. I'm glad my step mom put the pool up 'cause you know that the FIRST thing my daughter did when she got out the car, "Grandma, is the pool ready?" So, I'm here and I will keep you guys posted as far as this move is concerned. I really want to do it. Pray FOR me. I know some of you be hating on the girl (I know my "competition" reads this as well), and truth be told...I ain't mad at y'all for reading 'cause I do make for a nice read. So the old day job wants an exit interview. They are "investigating" my reasons for resigning...I left a msg. "I'm on vacation, when I return, I will give you a call and we can set something up." Now WHEN that is going to happen is another story. **My life right now is contingent upon me doing some MAJOR MOVES and an EXIT interview for a job I QUIT is not a contributory factor to the success of KJ**> I know you guys feel me on that one. What else is going on? Well I ate a sausage, a burger AND hotdog. and now I'm stuffed. My little one acts like she ain't finna (ebonics) get out of the pool. Oh...I had a nice talk with Rich = one of my EX's and a wonderful conversation with Bev = someone from my old job...**Both of them were very encouraging to me in respect to what I need to do for SELF right now. With all the books, the looks, and whatever monies you think I may have...and yeah, I'm a GREAT mom, it takes MORE than that...You have to have that "thing" in you that keeps a smile on your face and although I have NOT found "it" for me as of yet...I** do know what "it" AIN'T = money, dick, pussy, a day job, fake friends aka the clothing borrowers and dinner wanters...It ain't PYT and it AIN'T secret crush (of whom I have not spoken to since the graduation party and that's fine, trust me). **I'm in solitude and I need to be in order to get to where GOD would like to see me go. So faith without works means NOTHING.** Its NOT enough for you to BELIEVE what God has in store for you...YOU have to begin to ACT like its already going down. **So this weekends assignment is: STEP OUT ON FAITH! and I don't mean just saying you BELIEVE something good is going to happen for you or in your life...I MEAN begin to SEE the good things manifest in your life and the lives of your loved ones. BELIEVE its going to happen and then discipline yourself to walk in the FAVOR God has given you. So that's my time for today...I'm a little tired and I just want to walk around...got my shoes off and where I am there are no sidewalks. I love you all, your girl Kali J Moore over and FREE!!!!!!!!!!!!!!!!!!!!!! Be Easy Babe!**

Sunday and I just got up - It's 11:34am and so I'm getting ready to begin my day. My father is a Pastor and so I thought we were going to Church, but not today. He's very tired from all the driving (been up over 24hrs.). My little one just asked if we were going back to Jersey...I'm like why? she said 'cause she doesn't want to. So that's a GOOD sign. I'm getting ready to go to Wal-Mart - Raleigh because I just LOVE those commercials and I don't know where a Wal-Mart is in Jersey, although I'm SURE there is one...its nothing like the hospitality of the Wal-Mart's in the South. Ok and I'm NOT "dissing" Jersey. So what's up? Well yesterday I get a rather strange email from secret crush. She was responding to a voice message I left her, just saying that I had something to tell her face to face and thanking her for her participation with the little ones graduation, etc. Well her response was something like, "time has run out...I made a pact....if I don't hear from you today I may never hear what you have to say..." **What in the WORLD did she "think" I had to say?** My goodness, its only a Thank you card (I have for her)...DRAMA...so I mailed it to the "job" - People, I tell ya. its nuts...Can't even say "thanks" to folk nowadays. (taking a deep breath). I'm so happy to be FREE. My cell phone don't work down here (a blessing in disguise). I forgot to forward my home service down here (you can only do it from your home phone, the company can't do it for me) another blessing in disguise and so I'm checking my home phone and cell phones but to be honest...**I HAVE BUSINESS TO TEND TO AND SO I'M NOT EVEN GOING TO CHECK VOICEMAILS WITH ANY REGULARITY TO TELL YOU THE TRUTH. Well I have to go now. going to see miss Vanessa first, then come back and get ready to see my boy cheesy. that's a one hour drive. and then I have to try to find everlasting..."it" says he may be in Brooklyn. I have to see where he is. If he's in bk, then I have to wait until I get back (obviously). Ok well that's my time for today. Today's assignment: Turn off your phone and see how much rest you get. ha ha ha. KJ over & OUT!!!**

Wednesday June 29 What's up family. I've decided to do this post this way because it gives YOU the opportunity to respond to what I say. So things are good in North Carolina. I'm out every night. I went to see miss Vanessa - my old neighbor, she is living LARGE. and today I'm running around getting things together for my daughter and myself. Its a good chance I will only come back to Tri-State to get my belongings, as I may have all the things I have asked for with this one move. I can't even keep it real with y'all on me meeting someone...yeah...met someone and he's a nice dude. You know ain't nobody (ebonics) from N.C. down here, everyone is from NY or NJ. Met a girl from East Orange and a BUNCH of folks from Brooklyn. Its a different world to say the very least. Ok. so I'm off to do what it is I do when I'm getting it done. (the movie Ray). BET music awards...don't you just love Jada and Will Smith? I thought they did a fantastic job and Lauren hill looked like a black doll. She is gorgeous. The Destiny Child thing was ok. beyonce looks fabulous, but so do kelly and michelle. My return to radio is put on hold (don't panic, just for a moment), as I attempt to put my life together once and for all. I'm having a blast. Take care of you and **today's assignment is more like an english test: "What is the meaning of love?" So many of us use that word loosely and so I would like to take some time to examine the meaning of LOVE. and is it possible to fall in love with the "fairytale" meaning what you perceive love to be and so in search of the fairytale, you don't pay attention to all the "other" things**

you should notice along the way...Hmmmm, makes you think, doesn't it. I say that because I made a list a few weeks ago with everything I want in a person. and **when I find the person, I'm going to be like "Santa" and check the list twice**. I have decided there will be NO more compromising..."he's got these five things...so I can overlook this ONE thing" because that same one thing we overlook may be the "thing" that fucks us up in the end. Now I do believe in love at first sight. I honestly believe this can happen. You look into someone's eyes and feel "something" that makes your stomach ache and your heart race...yeah...I've had those feelings before...too many times to mention and after the "feeling" wears off ...You're calling him a no good mutha blankety blank just like all the rest. Ha ha ha. I don't know where that feeling comes from...but I know there must be something behind it. Maybe...just maybe those stomach jumps and quick heart beats should be interpreted as **"RUN quick, he ain't shit!" hmmmm....just gives you something to think about. like who in the hell wrote the book on love anyway? What's love to me? I'll tell you what I tell Hubby, "Love has NO boundaries"** *There are no walls nor a definitive description of what LOVE encompasses because there are different degrees of love based on situations. The love for my daughter,* **"The highest level of emotion where wrong and negativity cease to exist, pure purity"** *The love for my daughters father, "An interdependent bond that derives from forever coexisting mentally, emotionally and physically (because we have a child together)" The love for my husband, "Unbreakable, because we have watched each other grow and have been there throughout all the phases of each others lives and have YET to skip a beat.* **Respectful in the choices that we make, keeping in mind the effects today may have on tomorrow, a fortress of peace, covered and protected."** *Jump off love? Ha ha ha. "Love for a 'nut' lust for a while, but once you get 'it', 'its' gone." 'Cause we all know that anything that comes forth from a jump-start usually needs a new battery after a while* **TRANSLATION:REPLACEMENT AKA REPLACEABLE. AND NOT WORTH THE EMOTIONAL INVESTMENT.** *Same Sex Love: (y'all know I had to go there) Same Sex Love, while I don't believe in waking up and going to sleep with a* *woman, I can understand and have "played in the park" a time or two...or three...(ok, ok you got me...more times that I would like to share) and I believe there can be love between "lovers" of the same sex, but for me...The love is more of a "friendship" not an in-love, not a "I need to see you right now" love,* **there can be none of that because I still subscribe to the basic principles of life: BE HAPPY and going "there" full force is not my definition of the basic principle of life with respects to MY LIFE...so respect it. What else is going on? Nothing...just taking it slow. I love you and you know you can call me if you like. So don't forget today's assignment: "What is your definition of LOVE?" and holla at your girl. I'm gone...KJ.**

"Thursday June 30th or July 1, - ..." A damn shame family. Well today I want to discuss a little bit of this and a little bit of that...Since my departure (for vacation, etc.) its been really peaceful. The kind of peace that I find so hard to FIND in the tri-state. I don't want to leave and so tomorrow I have a job interview in research triangle park and some other things lined up for next Tuesday. One of the houses I saw yesterday was WAY too small for me. If I'm going to do it fam...its gotta be a "statement maker" and so I'm in search of that. The day job thing is just so I don't have to rely on the book money and I can save more, that's all. and besides, I don't want to ever feel as though life is just me chillin' and signing a book. When I wrote these books it was not to become a millionaire. As many of you know I am educated and have an outstanding professional background and so I don't want to lose the skill set I've obtained over the years by holding down good ass jobs. Ya feel me? Ok so today there will be no assignment only because I have something planned for you guys for the end of the Summer, and until I get things situated, I will be back and forth from NY, NJ and NC - that may be for about a month or two. Its amazing just how many people come out of the damn woodwork once you make a decision to be OUT. I tried to contact Luke formerly known as secret crush, she was unavailable. I guess I have to get this bracelet fixed by another jeweler, oh well...or maybe just buy the little one, another one...its that simple. What else? Well nothing. Enjoying life. getting ready to finish making lunch for my little cousin and my daughter so they can get in the pool. and I have a lunch date. Yeah...I said it...a lunch DATE. I have to try to catch up with my girl Pudda today and Pam and Val and all the others who are in this general area. (taking a deep breath) there are things I waited purposely to do on Friday so that I would be good when I get there. changed my addy with CSE (child support). **It ain't like I'm beat for the checks...lets see if they come...maybe they will now that homeboy doesn't have to worry about his child calling him and wanting to see him now that we are going to move. ha ha ha. Its funny I tell ya, just funny. Hubby co-signed the move from "in there" and WHAT...he sure did and so have all the "others" and so what's left to decided? EXACTLY...NOTHING. Well Seize the Day my friends...and live in the moment but don't be reckless with it...just enjoy whatever life is giving you at the very second you're getting it. I love you, you love me and lets talk again real soon. Comments? holla, this is a forum now and you can do just that. Your girl Kali J Moore over and loving NC!**

July 1, - Friday" What's up everyone and happy Friday. I know most of you are headed out of town or to some grocery store to get the food for the bbq. As for me? Today I registered with an employment agency. and went by my fathers office to see him in action and he turned around and introduced me to what seemed like EVERYONE in the company. I'm going to view houses later this afternoon and tomorrow I'm going to hang out with cheesy - Reggie b. from mt. Vernon and his friends and family. After that. I have to catch up with my mail and some private issues with hubby so I will be headed for V.A. sometime over the weekend. Oh that reminds me. I have to make a call to the facility to make sure my arrival is on par with their regulations. Uhhh, I cant stand it, but it is what it is and its almost over - hubby on his way out. That's right. Ok so in the mean time and in between time, I'm doing ME! I'm having so much fun in North Carolina that Miami is seeming like it may not get done. But I can't lose my loot, so me and the little one are going to be traveling for another two weeks, at least. Which is good because we both needed a break. She's in the pool now and just having a blast. So you guys are shy, huh? I made this into a forum so we can chat back and forth and YOU can also add topics to chat about but I see that may not have been a good idea. **hmmm. let me see what I can do about changing it back. I better not lose the diary, or...I'm going to have to begin again. But nevertheless, I'm good and I hope you are as well. Notice how the dramatics in my life has SLOWED down since I left? Usually y'all know I be (ebonics) off the hook with the personal and social life. I love the peace down here. I have to tell you. Well today's assignment is: (drumroll please) Enjoy the background of your life, pick and flower and SMELL it. Wish on a star, say a silent prayer for someone you haven't seen since the day you met. You know the person I am talking about...the person who left a lasting Impression and for whatever reason you didn't exchange numbers or you lost contact...pray for that person. I love you. KJ. Man Unnecessary!**

"Its Saturday July 2, " Hey you guys!!!!! How are you? How are things going for you? Well I'm ok, just being me. today I want to talk about "Summer Love" - summer love happened so fast...met a boy cute as can be...(exhaling) the whirlwind that is one week. Have you ever slept walk? aka: Summer Infatuation "relations" - Well that's what I want to talk about today. You know the saying, "What goes on while you're on vacation...STAYS on vacation" and I'm living by that rule ladies and gentlemen. Met someone, had a few nice times and now I'm done. (exhaling trying to figure out if I'm going to Keep it REAL) ha ha ha. Nah, but he's a nice guy. Works really hard, cutie pie son (today is his bday) and Mr. Man is a cutie himself. Nice setup for himself that goes BEYOND the house, vehicles and business. Just an all around nice person and I'm happy we met and I'm sure he feels the same. You know despite the fact that KJ leaves A LASTING IMPRESSION, your girl souvenirs when I "dash" - this time Love Spell scented Frankie

B's - - - Just a little something to keep the mind fresh, not that he will need them, but its just my way of saying, "I had a nice time, take care!" How real is that? Well I'm leaving this message early because I am on my way to Laurinburg to see Cheesy and his family. I have to put myself together for what is going to be a two hour ride. and I can't stay long because I want to make it back before it gets dark. So I'm only going to stay for a few hours. And besides that...the highways out here make me nervous...shit these country folks drive way too fast for me. So when am I leaving NC? Well to tell the truth, I don't know. I have a million and ONE things to do and I can't get some of them done until Tuesday because of the Independence Day Holiday on Monday. Today I want you to think about your first Summer Love experience (unless it was bad, then move on to your second, or third, or fourth...or....) you get my drift...just think back to it. Did you and the person keep in touch? Did it amount to anything? Where is he/she now? I ask that because its been YEARS since your girl has been "out like that" and I just want to know the "standard operating procedure" when it comes to future communication. I left it limbo by hanging up while on hold. I just didn't want the "moment" that was inevitable and although it was brief...IT WAS REAL aka A really nice time. what else is going on? Well I have to catch up with my girl Terri. **her and I are on the check in with regards to landing time back in NJ. she has been in Miami and Atlanta and I believe she may be going somewhere else, but the girl lives the life (hanging out, and doing her) We talked about being sexually active as women in our mid thirties aka "DATING HARD" and We've come to the decision that whatever we do as women is OUR business. If you want to "take it there" with whomever you are with...then be responsible aka Use protection. Its YOUR body and YOUR life and so respecting yourself should always be first thought, unless you are living out some kind of fantasy...and then still...YOU ARE respecting yourself because that's what YOU WANT to do. Now run and play my friends, the WORLD awaits you. Today's assignment: Stop lying to yourself. Lets face our realities. and I'm not going to elucidate the particulars TRANSLATION: ELLABORATE...'Cause you know**

EXACTLY what I'm talking about. Your girl Kali J Moore over and loving' summer. One yourself!

It's Monday July 4th and I just got back from Cheesy's house. We had a nice time. ate, drank and was merry. I met his cousin - a cutie and hey...I've uploaded new photos to my site, go check out the photo album. Ok. so my date today was right on the money. My Vacations Relations Jump off and I spoke very briefly. He is "entertaining" and ex - or trying to be ex, someone he dealt with who is apparently having a hard time dealing with the break up...YEAH right. now please pass my head so I can screw it back on. **Listen...the beauty of a Jump off during a vacation is NO EXPLANATIONS and NO REGRETS and so therefore I am really NOT amused by the excuse he tried to throw at me. Not interested.** Please BE GONE and those Frankie b's...He can hold those 'cause they ain't the only 30-dollar pair of thongs I own. ha ha ha. Y'all know how it goes down, scented with Love Spell by Vickie Secrets mixed with the limited edition fragrance and NO I ain't sharing that...'cause the freaks reading this may go out and grab 'em up and be running around faking the funk with my signature smell. So...No more information for you...it ain't going down. **So my friends...I'm outta here, its about eleven at night and I have to go take care of big business in the morning. Love you kj.**

Back in the day they didn't want me...now I'm hot they all on me...(mike jones). but who am I kidding...I was HOT back in the day...Wuzzup Family its your girl KJ on the check in getting ready to pull out of North Cackalack, down to Miami and back to the tri-state. I've got a whole lotta of people to see and a whole lotta of money to get. (taking a deep breath). This weave is still strong y'all. You know your girl gets nervous about the hair after a few days, but I must admit...The curly joint stayed proper the entire time. I'm good for another couple of weeks, it seems. (exhaling)...So. I've had a great time in N.C. and I'm headed out sometime today or tomorrow morning. Trying to see what's smoking out of Raleigh and I have to look at another place this afternoon about 2pm. My daughter is like, "you go and I'll stay here" but you know how it is when you are in someone else's house. Its just not the same. Now don't get me wrong...my father and his wife are cool, but I like the comforts and FREEDOMS of my OWN HOME. Ok. so I'm waiting for the mail to come through. Had something shipped to me and I hope it gets here today, otherwise, they (pops and his wife) are going to have to mail it to me. So its Tuesday the day after the fourth of July and I hope everyone said a prayer for the soldiers defending our civil liberties...You know we are truly NOT independent. and so we should NOT take things for granted. Ok. well today I have to make this entry short and sweet...so I'm going to say, "I love you and wish the best for you all." **Today's assignment is (drumroll please): 'Keep your word" if you say your going to do something...DO IT. If you feel as though you cannot, then don't say you can to appease the person you are promising whatever it is that your ass know you can't follow through on. So many times we fuck the "game up" by not keeping it real as to what is feasible for us to accomplish and what just ain't gonna go down. and its that "black eye" that causes relationships to suffer. I subscribe to my belief that "Once you reach a certain age, all that lying shit should be OVER!" I just can't cosign someone lying to avoid telling the truth. Its bullshit. That's my time for today, I'm outta here. Your girl Kali J Moore. One yourself!**

"Lil Kim ... 20 Years, say it ain't so!" Oh Lawd...why did someone call me talking about Lil Kim got 20 joints and she ain't even been sentenced yet. Now I know y'all like KJ what does that have to do with you, but let me break it down for you...KJ is the Original Queen B. just ask Big Wes and them from White Plains. That was way back when "water was free" - I would call up and be like, "Tell Big Wes his presence is being requested back at the hive" We had all types of nicknames and shit like that. You name it...I had it...at one point I was referred to as S.H. (Superhead) the first Female Super Hero niggas liked behind wonder woman. ha ha ha. That shit is funny. **Ok. but on the real...Its Hump Day and you**

guys know how much I love Hump Day...now back to lil Kim...so I'm told she got twenty joints and I'm pissed because I know lil kim must have hit the f'ing floor when they spit that at her. **But ... my information was incorrect and you know your girl don't like being rude, wrong or obnoxious...**(exhaling...well two out of three - you can trade off rude for obnoxious) depending on what mood I'm in. Ok. so I'm happy she hasn't been sentence yet...stay tuned and thank goodness I wasn't on some breaking news shit, 'cause I would have caused chaos and mass confusion all over the place. ha ha. Ok. **so secret crush...I called her today just to say hello and I think I had something to ask her, but damn was she ever the Beeyach!** So to hell AND back with her. I know why she's upset and I can't do anything about it. **In life we have to make the best of whatever is thrown at us and most people cant handle my "abruptness" and my "emotionless moves." aka I do things without instituting the opinions and thoughts of others...fuck 'em and I don't consider the emotions of anyone but myself when making moves.** meaning: **You love me?** *Not gonna stop me from making a decision...***You LIKE me**...*not going to hold back whatever decision I have to make because of it...***You'll miss me**...*Sorry Dog, but I gotta do this and maybe you'll be around when I'm done, maybe you won't but don't hold up your life for KJ...* Hey, its REAL life and so **BE all you can be...**that slogan ain't just for the army, you know. What else is going on? Me and N.C. Jump off had a nice time last night (got in around 8:30 this morning). He's a good dude, just a little confused with regards to shit he needs to be doing right now...but its all good. This morning we took my little brother and my daughter to breakfast at the Waffle House - there are a million of them down here and he dropped me off. I will be using one of his vehicles to get around in for a little while. Oh that reminds me...I'm cooking dinner for him tonight (taking a deep breath)...Oh...so we looked at a flat...NOT a house, an apt. not too far from my father's house and tomorrow morning is the appointment and so I will be able to tell you guys something about that then. Well, I have to head out 'cause I'm behind schedule with the shit I'm supposed to be doing. **THIS IN JUST ....LITTLE KI'M SENTENCED TO ONE YEAR AND A**

DAY...I JUST SPOKE WITH SOMEONE WHO WANTED TO KICK MY ASS FOR TELLING HIM LIL KIM GOT TWENTY JOINTS...HE TOLD SOMEONE WHO TOLD SOMEONE ELSE, WHO TOLD SOMEONE ELSE AND NOW HE HAS TO "FIX IT" OH LAWD... SOURCE IS NOT CREDIBLE. KJ CAN'T EVEN MESS WITH THE SOURCE OF THAT TWENTY JOINTS "RUMOR" NO MORE. so now I'm off to get my tire fixed. triple A had to come put a donut on it because I didn't have a REAL spare tire. **That's the thing WE all need to keep in our cars, REAL spare tires because a donut is only good for a few miles.** (taking a deep breath)...I wanted to talk about something, but this lil kim potential rumor got beneath my skin y'all 4real because I repeated it to someone, and based on my "cloth" they repeated it and now we're ALL wrong...its the ultimate "diss" to be wrong like that, 'cause its embarrassing. ok so let me go and cuss his (the source) ass out again for playing like that...talking about, "I ain't know you was gonna tell somebody kj"...nah lil scrappy, it ain't that easy...You're cut off, but you know what...**as a WRITER...I KNOW BETTER...YOU NEED THREE SOURCES... CAUSE ONE IS GONNA LIE, ONE IS GOING TO TELL THE TRUTH AND ONE IS GOING TO SORT THEM OUT. today's assignment (drumroll please): Listen and Listen and Verify three times...Use the KJ hearsay verifying procedure (H.V.P.)...hear, confirm what you heard, get the story from two more sources and then....DO WHAT YOU WISH WITH THE INFORMATION...UNLESS ITS ABOUT ME, 'CAUSE ITS PROBABLY TRUE AND YOU WONT NEED ADDITIONAL SOURCES... Enjoy your day! Kali**

What's good Family? Its your girl Big Kali on the check in, Thursday July, 7th and I'm feeling like "Whoa...Who in the hell left the gate open?" I just got a few calls about ME by someone I used to work with...Ok. so let me get this straight...You're into my life because....(fill in the blank). Its going down ladies and gentlemen and I mean its going to be a corporate fist fight...but unlucky for them I got the Mike

Tyson of Corporate litigation and I'm NOT talking about the Mike Tyson of now...I'm talking about the pre-Robin Givens Tyson, where bouts didn't last more than 2 rounds. I can't believe someone is fucking with me like this. (taking a deep breath), Oh well and screw them. They just f'd up the kids vacation because now I have to get back to the Tri-State and meet with my attorney face to face. (exhaling). What else is going on with me? Well lets see. me and the little one were out with **Vacation Relations Jump Off last** night and this morning. He gave me full usage of one of his vehicles and that was nice...full tank of gas and $$$$...That was sweet. But really, **I rarely have problems with men because I am VERY honest:** *I'm spoiled, I like nice things, my kid is spoiled and we both throw temper tantrums, I need to have my way all the time and I don't like to compromise unless I'm going to get a "treat" for doing it...****TRANSLATION: SOMETHING BIGGER OR BETTER IN THE LONG RUN...****I rarely ever go three days without attending to my fine dining habit or the salons and the shoe collection is never on freeze. I have pretty things around me and on standby for when / if I ever lose these pounds off my ass.* **Not that its a hindrance (my ass), because I'm a brick house (yeah, I'm obnoxious...but you knew that already),** *I just love to have people and things at my disposal. I'm a handful and although I will cook, clean and pay my OWN bills, I don't want you to get used to it aka **THINK I MAY CHANGE.*** So, in having said all of that...he's like **"So I need another hustle for you, huh?"** Listen...**"you're the MAN Manage it!"** That's all. I wasn't here for women's lib. I didn't fight for women's rights...if I were here, I would have been protesting against those beeyaches the entire time....**Its my PERSONAL OPINION** that men should take care of women. Women are here to smell good, look pretty, cook, clean (lightly, 'cause men should work harder to get additional domestic help) and raise the kids. We should keep ourselves together (shapes on point, hair, nails, etc.) and most of all, **When we LAY DOWN OUR TOPS AND BOTTOMS SHOULD MATCH! I can't stand to know that some of my sisters are running around here on mismatch. What part of the game is that when your panty and bra do not coincide?** Ok. so now I'm sure I will get the "fuck you KJ" mail behind the women's lib comment, but again...**ITS MY PERSONAL OPINION AND IF YOU DON'T LIKE IT...OH WELL AND SO WHAT...DON'T LIKE IT.** This is the life of Kalico Jones and in THIS arena, I speak my mind by allowing MY mind to speak. **If you have to hold it back, then you are a fake.** Even the Bible has rules about withholding, *"if you know someone is lying and you allow them to lie, you've just lied yourself."* Really, its in the Bible, of course not worded like that, but its in there. What else is going on? Well today I had an appointment for a flat out this way (Raleigh, nc) and someone had an appointment before me and they've shown interest and so basically that means if their references turn to shit, I will get the place. (exhaling...damn I feel a little exhausted). I tried to get a post office box. Trying to get one of those is like, trying to get a "wetter" (box cutter) on a plane...it's a 50/50 chance dunn, if you know what I mean. They ask you for all types of shit and you know I didn't have any of the requirements. you **should have seen me in the post office clutching my NY Drivers License and a credit card, like PLEASE I need an address. lol. They didn't give me one. Oh well. Oh. the weave...its coming out in about thirty minutes and I'm getting someone that's going to drop on the sides and come across the front. Hair in the south is EXPENSIVE. like double of what I pay in NY. Ok. well that's my time, I'm tired, but I'm 4Eva Your girl...Kj-Moore over and NO assignment for today! Enjoy your life...LIVE!!!**

Freaky Friday? It must be, because I just left V.R.J. = Vacation Relations Jump off and it was NOT a good departure. I don't know why the Ruckus that is I, couldn't just walk away...Ok. so we're talking on the phone and he asked me to come to his house. I guess he wanted to see me before I left N.C. = Tomorrow night (Saturday). So I get there and his phone is constantly ringing. Its home girl calling and this is the very SAME young lady...(taking a deep breath) Who am I kidding, I want so very much to call her a "minor" (Does this make me a hater?).. Ok. so I'm over there and they are on the phone and based on his portion of the conversation...he lied to me, ONCE AGAIN. That is NOT good Family. I don't have time for that and so I politely grabbed my belongings and left. and so ends the V.R.J. ha ha ha. What else is going on? *Well due to a financial "f" up, I couldn't get back to see my mother off on her trip to St. Marteen.* (taking a deep breath)...I know she is upset, I could tell in her voice she wanted to see her grand-daughter. and with my little one turning FIVE years old next week, I know she is a bit pissed by my not having all my banking stuff in order before I left. (I left behind cards because I had enough cash and then I shopped and spent it all and so then I had to wait on a Western Union and that was late, and then...it just snowballed from there)...(exhaling)...So I have a new WEAVE...**V.R.J.** says its *"a good look"* for me and I said to him, *"U don't have to tell me that, I already know"* - I saw the look on his face when I walked in (sizing me up and having a flashback)..he tried to play "hard" but nah...I KNOW...it was ALL over his face. Ok enough about him, not going to revisit that. Like I told him, **"I am a TREAT to men"** - **expensive, but worth it**. and so it is unlikely that I would put up with home girl and him going back and forth because **I am not going to allow anyone to make me "common"** - period and point fucking blank. its just that simple with me. and I don't compromise. and **NO REAL man** would want me to. That's why ladies, I have to tell you...**Since I've enlisted the Kalico Jones Keeping It Real Relationship Rules** (KJKRRR), I've been just fine...Trust and OH PLEASE BELIEVE. I'm like *"I don't do shit but look pretty and smell good"* **I let them know right from the gate that I am not having another kid, I am not meeting your mother...Don't introduce me to your friends, unless we are in a SOCIAL setting (so I can mingle with others) and you can knock off the movies, dinners and trips...I do those with my little one and my girls...**That's it. **But you can please feel free to bankroll any portion of my life**. ha ha ha. and I have to be honest...My **KRRR's** are working. People are not getting KJ confused with "girl Tuesday" or "winky" "twinky" and "pinky" - and so I'm good with the honesty is the BEST policy when it comes to relationships. The ONLY thing that is off limits is **"how many bed partners I have had"** THAT IS NONE OF YOUR MUTHA F'ING

BUSINESS! **I WILL NOT ENTERTAIN THAT QUESTION AT ALL. ALL YOU NEED TO KNOW IS THAT I AM HEALTHY AND I PROTECT MYSELF AND I AM NOT EASY.** With regards to Bed Partners, **its off limits because with all this disease, ONE bed partner can be the death of you...**Feel me? So it is what it is and that's NONE OF YOUR BUSINESS...**YOU DON'T LIKE IT...DON'T LIKE IT!** What else is going on? (deep sigh)...nothing really, just trying to figure out how I am going to manage all the stuff I am taking back to the tri-state with me, that's it. and I'm about to go and take care of my mailbox = mailbox etc. that's a good look for me because it gives a physical street address for any and all packages and so that's what's up. **When I touch down the first thing I am going to do is get a sea salt body scrub, a steam bath and bleaching cream to make sure these every bit of 20 mosquito bites don't blemish my skin.** Ok. so enough about me for today. **Today's assignment is: Safe Sex. If anyone tries to have unprotected sex with you, you should take that as they are trying to pass something off to you (like an STD)...If you are in a situation where there is no protection, do not proceed. Enforce the Kalico Jones Stop, Drop and Roll Evacuation procedure (KJSTRep), STOP the foreplay (kissing, touching, etc), don't DROP your pants, panties, dress to the floor, etc. and ROLL aka LEAVE I'MMEDIATELY. Folks please pass that along. Have a great weekend and if you are one of my readers in North Carolina, "Thanks for having me, I had a blast...and I WILL see you again!" Your girl KJ Moore. B Easy Babe!**

Wuzzup Fam? Its me, the one and only Kalico Jones bringing the Truth to you on this pretty Saturday morning. I just got off the phone with Amtrak, I will have to go there and pay for my train tickets because I don't have any credit cards, banking cards, NOTHING here with me. Shit...I messed up y'all. At any rate, (taking a deep breath), I have to drive into Raleigh and pay for my departure tickets. That's crazy. My little brother wants to come back with me...I'm thinking about it. I think yeah, that would be nice for him...anyway, so I attempted to get the bus back, anything BUT a plane because I just can't deal with heights right now...must be something relating to my Anxiety and Panic attacks...whatever the case, the heights...just cant do it right now. So...Train it is and believe it or not, the TRAIN was MORE expensive than the plane. and so I will be leaving early in the week. I need a day for business out here. Which is good because my ex has to come and meet me to let me in the house - forgot my keys. Uhhh...and the other one with my keys, well, I don't know what's going on with him. Maybe I will try to call him about the keys...lets see...hold on, let me try him now (cell phone ringing...cell phone ringing...) Ok. so I think I'm going to voicemail (his wife must be around). Ok. so its back to my ex letting me in the house (exhale). I'm changing the locks for the time I'm in jersey. I really am. I have to pack up a lot of stuff and get things together for what may just be me moving in a week or two...Ok. so I just spoke with my ex, he's going to be at the house waiting on us to touch down. Shit...and that day is his birthday...Damn, I don't like messing with folks bday night, but (shrugging my shoulder) Oh well, it has to be done. he's a man and therefore its his duty to Manage it. So let me jump off this computer and get my ass washed and prepped for the drive into downtown Raleigh for these tickets. Oh...I have to go to western union too....I almost forgot. What else is going on? Well I have to do my little ones hair because it took the cornrows out and she's running around this house with her "wig out" (hair a mess)- ha ha ha. So Let me do her hair first, curl this weave up (took out the rollers and I have "bends" where the clips were and that CANNOT happen. Maybe we'll go shopping once we get into Raleigh, who knows and its NOT like we need to. I know I know, just SAVE the money KJ, Just save the money...(exhaling)...**Today's assignment: Open up another bank account and don't get an atm card. Just open it up and put 10 bucks in it per week. lets holla back in one year to see if you have your 520.00 - that can go toward vacation, xmas shopping for your loved ones, a bill (if you are me) or a "treat" for yourself. That's my time folks, I'm outta here, your girl KJ (aka "mommy the hair dresser"). Oh. I'm told there are thongs on Ebay that once belonged to me. (taking a deep breath) WHAT'S NEXT PEOPLE, WHAT IS NEXT?**

HA HA HA. Lets see where the bidding ends, I would be Impressed to see that. kj moore over and moving out.

(singing) "And the mirror says you, must love you, because nothing comes easy...me, myself and I " (Shirley Pepsi Riley) I just love that song, don't you? So today is Monday and I have to pack up. Last night I made lasagna for V.R.J and his son and nephew. I had a nice time with them. It was special 4real. Had to spend time with them before I leave (tomorrow morning). I'm going to miss them, I really am (*singing* "yes I'm leaving you again, and I thought I'd tell you when...I know how you must feel, but if your loves 4real, you'll try to understand that I'm in popular demand...") -new edition I don't even remember the year...that was a hot joint ...So I'm outta here tomorrow. I may have the apt. I looked at the other day, lets see what happens. Its Monday and I'm feeling a little hung up and over. . I spoke with and OLD friend the other day: Janine Crump-Singleton and I am proud of her. She and her family are doing great works with regards to her brother's ministry and I am going to support them by going out there to visit the Church. They are in the south as well. It was a great conversation and again, I can't wait to see them and support their efforts. Me and my father had a conversation about expanding his Church. He's thinking BIG and that's good because God has BIG things in store for his people. (I miss VRJ -thinking aloud). (exhaling and shaking my head)...DAMN and WHY? I'm back home tomorrow to see Mel (its his bday), clean up, open all the windows, close out my lease and pack up. I am moving Y'all - yes, its going down and I can't wait to begin again. My daughter is excited and that's about it. I am bringing my radio show down here. I am doing some promotions for my books and my diary is going to be published. **Well I really don't have much to say today. Just LOVE yourself. We have to begin to act as though we are IN LOVE with OURSELVES. OUR minds, our bodies, our souls, The Lord, Our children, just be so full of love and respect for our FIRST business, FIRST. Well that's all I have to say. I love you and I may not write tomorrow because I will be traveling, but** *you can* *always get in touch with me baby, call on me anytime...*(that was a song as well) 973-342-1039 Act like ya know! Your girl, Kali J-Moore over and busting loose.

I like it when you do that right thurrr...What's up Family its your girl KJ on the check in. Its Friday July 15th and I'm feeling like "Whoa" Things are really looking good for your girl. Since I've been speaking with a LONGTIME friend, I've been feeling better about "certain" things. Rest assure, the road to FREEDOM is narrow, but nevertheless, MUST be traveled. So what's up y'all? What's on YOUR agenda for the weekend? As for me, I'm doing a pizza party for my little one tomorrow - its her Birthday - FIVE years old already...damn, time surely flies. Oh I lost my cell phone. Actually I believe its in my car in North Carolina or in my room at my Dad's house. I have to see if I can get the number transferred to another phone tomorrow. So if you call 423-200-0261 you will hear my LONG message about losing the phone. ha ha ha. So VRJ (vacation relations jump off) and I have been speaking a lot over these past few days, since my tri-state "touch down" and the conversations have been good to say the very least. Oh...that reminds me...I'm waiting for Hubby to give me a call. That should be sometime tomorrow. I sent him a message about the cell phone, I hope he gets it today or tomorrow - in time for his step daughter's bday, or else he is going to be pissed with me. Ok enough about that. Today I had to come to grips with something - homeboy possibly being more of a deadbeat than I initially thought. I fucked it up by calling him to REMIND him of his daughter's birthday, I should NOT have done that. I should have waited to see if his bum ass was going to remember. What else is going on? Well I have to tell you guys all about my Amtrak ride back to jersey from Raleigh, NC...Can you say "Off the mutha trucking hook?" Oh my goodness. They had to stop the train because this lady started an altercation with two young girls, threatening to beat their asses and EVERYTHING...and guess what? The GIRLS got put off Amtrak in Wilson, NC. Then the lady and the girl I was talking to, **Stephanie C from Brooklyn, NY** = very attractive girl, I believe she is 29, has a kid, etc. Yeah your girl gets all the info, that's the WRITER in me. We exchanged stories about our lives, it was a nice ride. but anyway, the lady began to direct Stephanie to shut up and Stephanie was so GROWN about the way she handled the lady...it was GREAT to witness a young lady handling herself like a WOMAN, not yelling and cussing and just being Ghetto. But after while, the lady left her alone and we continued to trade secrets. THEN they had to stop the train again 'cause a man got drunk and he left in handcuffs, I don't know what he did. And THEN, we hear about how people were screwing in the bathroom and were put off the train.. YUCK, do you know how FILTHY an Amtrak train is after Virginia? Disgusting, I tell you. Oh and we were LATE to the tune of TWO hours. Terrible I tell you, just terrible. Needless to say, I am happy to be back, but its only for a minute cause I am moving by the end of the month. I will keep you posted. **I will begin packing on Monday and then I have to transfer things over and out of Jersey and I have book business to handle and then...well...its a WRAP...there is no assignment because I cant think of one...Oh I got it. Drumroll please.....today's assignment is to READ the Bible. Read James, Chapter 1. Just read the entire chapter. It talks about having unwavering FAITH in God. We have to have that you know...I'm stepping out on Faith with this move. I know its hard relocating, but its something I must do for myself and my daughter, WE need FREEDOM. I love you, you love me...Stay FREE, Kali J Moore.**

Its been a long time, I shouldn't left you...what's up Family!!!!!!!!!!!!!!!! Its me, the one and only Kalico Jones sending some luv your way. I missed you guys...I really did. Ok. so lets get ON with it, shall we? So today is Wednesday, July 20th and I'm gathering boxes to begin my packing. wait a second...I know y'all don't want to hear about that...Y'all want to know if Baby Daddy = "homeboy" showed for his daughters party, right? NOPE...he is the deadbeat that I feared he was...A true DEADBEAT in every SENSE of the word combo...Not even a fucking phone call. and y'all remember

I reminded him the day before and his response was, "I know. I know" and NOTHING. So what in fuck do I want with him? I don't! and that's why I don't entertain shit like that. But then again, my "taste in men" has EVOLVED since my newfound FREEDOM. NO ONE should be "hanging" with this jerk off, he should have NO friends and that's my personal opinion and I AM entitled to it. So how did your girl KJ handle it? I waited until my little one was asleep and left him a message, *"I don't know what part of the game this is, but I am no longer playing. Today is your daughters birthday and you couldn't even give her a call, but when you needed me to lookout for you...it was DONE...I made a promise to myself that today, enough is enough and so therefore I am NOT calling you again. You have her numbers, you call HER when you find yourself. I am not mad, actually I am going to pray for you and you need to pray for yourself because wherever you are right now in your life where you cannot be a dad, is NOT a good place to be. I wish you well, take care of yourself."* and I hung up. I have no plans on ever calling him again...Oh I almost forgot...I did mention that he BETTER pay his child support ON TIME and IN FULL or else I would be filing a violation every chance I got. ...THEN ...I HUNG UP. I'm done with that. I don't deserve to be put through that and so you know I am NOT going to allow this ass, to f with my daughter, no way and its NOT going to happen. What else is going on? Well the party was a success. It was like Christmas in my house. She had a bunch of Kids and **lots of gifts. in all, she had a GREAT fifth birthday. and truth be told...SHE DIDNT EVEN ASK ABOUT HOMEBOY SO FUCK HIM. Ok. now lets get off him, I'm sure he's being rode hard by his conscious. What else? Well I spoke with someone named Erica, she's from Louisiana and she is very nice. She reads the diary every day. There is no assignment, just LOVE YOURSELF.** KJ

Friday, July 22nd - Wuzup "peep"le? I hope you are okay. As for me...well, today I have decided to put my list of "friends and associates" on the chopping block. Its a done deal family because I have learned something today about myself that I wish I did not have to learned the hard way...I

GIVE TOO MUCH OF ME. MY TIME, MY MONEY, MY EMOTION, THE PHYSICAL KJ, THE MENTAL KJ AND JUST ALL AROUND...ALL OF ME. I am tired of it. When KJ needs someone to "come through" for her...**AIN'T NOBODY AROUND**. No one returns my calls, EVERYONE is busy or in the midst of a "situation" themselves. And so its like this, I'm going to have to not only subscribe to, but Implement **the Kalico Jones "LOVE THOSE WHO LOVE YOU" rule**, where **no one is a taker**. Its better that way because I get so disappointed by people just not following through on shit they said they were going to do, etc. But the thing that bothers me most...is people tend to say they are going to do something for me ONLY BECAUSE THEY ARE LOOKING FOR SOMETHING IN RETURN. Now WHAT they expect in return is another thing, but for the most part, things are **ALMOST ALWAYS DONE FOR ME WITH A MOTIVE**. Kind of like the way I lived, ONCE UPON A TIME, OF COURSE! (SMILE). (taking a deep breath)...Someone once told me, *"you can tell what a person has, by what the person WANTS."* I am here to say that is not always true. What I can say is "be careful of what you ask for, because should you get it, it may have ulterior motives attached to it." People are just so fucking fake nowadays, **NOTHING TO ME IS REAL ANYMORE. People are just walking around lying to themselves, NO ONE IS "KEEPING IT REAL."** And so today I must admit, I have witnessed the death of the phrase, "Keeping it real." (exhaling)...What else is going on ? Hmmm, nothing much. V.R.J. is not giving me whatever it is I am looking for in a person. I mean he's nice and all, and I may see him tomorrow, he's coming this way...but for the most part...its like, "nice place to visit, but wouldn't want to live there" with respects to him. He's worn out my "sweetness" already with some of the things he does when I try to have a conversation with him. NOW don't get me wrong...he is a GREAT listener **WHEN OR IF I CAN CAPTURE HIS ATTENTION.** But its - our conversations - are almost ALWAYS interrupted by other calls coming in on HIS end. He is NON-STOP and so I have to understand that should I feel like proceeding. Hmmm, another thing for me to think about...**NOT...KALICO JONES IS NOT EVEN GOING**

THERE. LETS CALL V.R.J. "TEMPORARY INSANITY" but at this stage in my life...I REFUSE TO COMPROMISE. What else? Oh last night we had a girl's night out at my friends Ruby's house. . . it was so nice I toured her building today and put that on the list of options with regards to moving...I just ain't staying here. That ain't going to happen. I'm tired of paying money to people who don't respect money...Anyway, we had a great time, pina coladas and a few glasses of wine. Her husband is a song writer and has been in the music industry for YEARS. The other girl in attendance, has just completed an off Broadway play...she's very "actress-sy" if that's a word...Well I know it ain't...but its a NEW word now...I wanted to say "animated" but that would not be accurate...Nice looking woman and well versed. I'm proud of my sisters. we're out here doing it for ourselves. What else? Nothing much. Have the boxes, have the bags, going to finish this packing thing...call v.r.j. and find out if he is coming my way tomorrow, if not I am going to make plans for myself and my little one. **Monday we will be in Mt. Vernon - where I am from. My sister is graduating from her sobriety class - TWO YEARS CLEAN...I'm proud of her. So we - the family - will be there in Centennial Church on Monday evening... showing her some support**. I've decided to change my numbers. That will go down sometime over the next few days. Other than that...All is well. Oh...me and my little one went swimming today, it was a great time, but NEXT time I'm going to wear my swimsuit so I can get in the water...CAN YOU SAY HOT AS HELL? Whew, it was HOT. **So...we need an assignment right? Today's assignment is (drumroll please)....ask yourself... "Am I happy?" A lot of us, including myself, equate happiness to having money or having a nice car...or no bills, but I am proof you can have "things" or what people perceive to being a "nice life" and be unhappy to some degree.** *Now before you go crying for me, ARGENTINA (remember that song? I love that song),* I'm not going to jump off a bridge or anything. **I'm just talking about need for REAL and TRUE love and REAL and TRUE friendships...**That's all. second question for you is, **"Who are my REAL friends?"** and make a list...if your list is missing people of whom you let your children play with, people you go out with, people you lend money to, people whose kids you watch, then **THEY SHOULD BE CUT OFF IMMEDIATELY - because you didn't think enough of them to label them a true friend!** and you don't have to cut them off by telling them they are cut off...just stop calling. **Stop being available for chats and babysitting...STOP being their personal ATM...just stop...they will look up soon enough and ask themselves, "Damn, what happened to (fill in blank with your name)...I haven't heard from (fill in black with your name) in a long time..." that's all. Association severed and they didn't even know you were keeping it moving on their asses...Well that's my time family. I love you and I hope we are friends 4REAL...Your girl Kali J Moore over and OUT!!!!!! Be true 2 U.**

Its Tuesday my friends and we are all the way LIVE in this arena...So y'all this weekend was GREAT!!! Ok. so Friday night I think I chilled. Just had my mom over and then Saturday...OH MY GOODNESS...My peeps came through from N.C. = VRJ and his friend and my friends were there...we had a nice little party...Had a lot of fun and it went on until Sunday afternoon. Once the party came to an end, I took a few fleet laxatives - YEAH I'm offering too much information, I know, but your girl had to fit in a tight chocolate skirt yesterday and I needed to lose the water weight... and IT WORKED. JUST WATER AND FRUIT...AND ONE OF THOSE FIVE DOLLAR BLUE ELASTIC WORK OUT JOINTS FROM KMART...I was in the tight skirt - classy, but a little on the sexy side...and we had a GREAT time at my sisters anniversary...Sobriety is a great thing you know...WE should try it one day. lol, and that's NOT really funny. Ok. so that was Monday aka yesterday. and then this morning...I woke up to my daughter's father - FIGURE THAT ONE OUT... Nah...We spoke on the phone...that's what I mean for all you nosey asses reading this like I'm really going to tell you if I Jayed my baby daddy...ha ha, you can get a smidget, but you cant get a lot. (taking a deep breath)...Its HOT today. Ok. so me and baby daddy had the "talk" and I've decided that between this dumb ass bitch getting on my final nerve Friday...I'm not even going to dignify her behavior by spitting her name...all you need to know is that people tend to WANT to do things for your child and you sometimes because they have some kind of sick fantasy of what they THINK their life SHOULD BE. or what they really want it to be, but NO ONE says to me, "but you let her father take her" after I tell them they cannot take my daughter with them for the weekend. Like how in the hell do you even play yourself by comparing her father to you? and more so, **If I vent to you ... then that's because I want to get it off my chest, NOT FOR YOU TO TAKE WHAT I HAVE SAID AND JUDGE ME OR WHAT YOU THINK MY SITUATION MAY BE WITH IT....** and the beeyach did all that acting while I was in the presence of my mother, like she didn't even respect the fact that she KNEW my mother was sitting right next to me. I asked her for a favor, she said yeah...then she took that as a "sign" to say to herself, "ok let me fuck with her now 'cause she needs me" I DON'T THINK SO...She was wrong, wrong, wrong and I'm NOT mad at her, but she tried to act as though things wouldn't get done if she didn't help me and That's ALL WRONG...Wrong, Wrong, Wrong yet again... I can't even go into the particulars, what I will say is that ...I'M DONE WITH HER. And I will NOT entertain any correspondence...What else? Nothing much...I have to go now, because I have to clean my apartment and cook so that I can have company later...**today's assignment is (drumroll please): RE-Do your resume...I know some of us - me included, are looking for gainful employment and some of us are not,...but if an opportunity should come your way, don't you want to be prepared? so lets prepare ourselves for what may come our way...UPDATE YOUR RESUME... I love you and I'm gone...my daughter just scraped her knee...Have a great day and stay cool. Kj**

Today is Thursday...Damn, these days are going fast. In just a few more days, it will be August. Thank goodness I've already completed my daughters school shopping - IN JUNE! I want to talk about something that happened to me last night. Ok...so I'm sleeping...and I have this "dream" that I

am up, but can't get off the bed. I see my daughter, I'm tossing, turning and screaming for whatever was holding me down to get off of me and I reach out to my daughter to grab her to protect her and this "thing" is holding me down to the bed, and just as I get my hand on her shoulder I yelled, "Jesus where are you!" and I woke up...THIS IS NOT AN EXAGGERATION...IT WENT DOWN JUST LIKE THAT. I was so afraid. I got up and ran to my Bible and read James, first chapter. I wanted to call my dad, the Pastor, but it was a little past midnight and I didn't want to disrupt his sleep. I was praying y'all and yelling, "Devil, I don't know how you got into my house, but you are leaving!" and I just kept on praying. That was really an experience I don't want to revisit. **Sunday you know where you can find your girl...CHURCH! AND I'M NOT PLAYING AND I'M ASKING THE PASTOR FOR THE HOLY OIL.** (taking a deep breath)...So I make a final decision about what I am going to do with regard to the move on Saturday. I just have to see where I am with things. I found a GREAT apt. in the next town over and I want to move there. Luxury hi-rise with a pool, gym, decks. etc. its nice. 24hr doorman and it really looks like a luxury hotel, but its not...its LIVING folks. What else is going on? Well baby daddy is supposed to be coming to get the little one for a family reunion...lets see what happens with that. and I am going on a few job interviews next week. I'm just tired ladies and gentlemen, just tired of being home. I've decided that although I am "dating hard" as I like to refer to it...I am cutting EVERYONE off and just sticking with ONE...that's right you heard it from me FIRST, just one. he's nice, cutie pie and everything about him shows and TELLS me that he can handle the woman that is I. ha ha ha. What else...just living. don't watch TV. because the day time shows are dumb or my mentality is too high for me to enjoy that kind of silly banter. I'm losing weight...and its coming off nice, might I add...it must be because your girls OVEN DOESNT WORK. fucking landlords asking me for rent and they ain't done shit to fix my oven...I guess that's a good thing in some sorts because you know I have the smothered chicken, mac and cheese, lasagna, etc. your girl gets DOWN in the kitchen. Anyway...I am not going to change my telephone number if I move because too many people have it that are Important and more Important than that...I can't get in touch with them, so I'm leaving it the same. Well...I have to go now...have some freelance work to do...**today's assignment is simple: Narrow down the crew. This is for my freaks...Ha ha ha. Its not worth the headache and the reputation you will get should anyone of them big mouth you to their friends.** Oh... pyt is in jail...bail is set at 25 grand and that's a damn shame...Secret crush is going on vacation and other than that...WE have no contact with each other...just not interested in her antics, especially after what she did to me the other day. Won't go into details because some of her friends read this diary and I don't want to put her ass on "blast" like that. I'm sure it would be embarrassing for her and for them as well. When you have someone's heart...its hard for the other people in their lives to LIVE because they know deep down inside the person they are with, would give anything to be with SOMEONE ELSE. if you are in a situation like that...you better get it together...go to the other person and express yourself, but don't cry and scream because then you look like a psycho to them and that won't get you anywhere. just state your feelings and ask if they are interested...if they say yes, then go for it...but if they say no, or have others in their life that you would have to share them with...DON'T DO IT...you know the saying **"COMPROMISE TO GET...COMPROMISE TO KEEP" AND WE AIN'T GOING OUT LIKE THAT HERE IN THE KALICO JONES ARENA. AND TRUTH BE TOLD...NO ONE WHO REALLY LOVES OR LIKES YOU WOULD WANT YOU TO COMPROMISE YOURSELF AND YOUR BELIEFS...ITS NOT WORTH IT, TRUST ME AND you will be hurt in the end. so its best to just let it "burn" now and move on. Because you won't be in a position to recognize someone who really loves you and wants to be with you if you continue to hold onto someone who has let you go a long time ago...BE BLESSED AND UNSTRESSED. Your girl, Kali J Moore over and out!**

Monday, August 1, (singing) *"My milkshake brings all the boys to the yard and they're like its better than yours, damn right, it's better than yours I could teach you...but I'd have to charge..."* **What's up Fam, its Milkshake Monday here at <u>www.kalicojones.biz</u> So what's good y'all? What did you do this weekend? (taking a deep breath 'cause I've got some shit to get off my chest)... As for me...wel**l I sent my daughter out of town after getting a call from homeboy's family asking for her presence at a family picnic...Sorry no dice. **At first, I was with it. I was actually going to send my little one with people of whom have NOT checked for her in two years. Have NEVER called to say happy birthday, HAVE yet to send a card, gift, or place a "how ya doing" phone call her way since the day I got us up out of that condo in Spring Valley in 2001.** And NOW...THEY reach out and don't even have the decency to say, "Tell her happy belated birthday" or even ask to speak with her... just "We're in town and we want to come get her late tonight, and by the way...can you meet us off the turnpike at an exit so that we don't have to come out the way to get her." Ha ha ha. Who bumped their fucking head? **Family ...and with THIS ...I kid you NOT. I was with it**. I took my daughter back to the salon. Got her hair done up nice. Picked out the clothing and got her polish touched up on her feet and hands. It was set to go down and then... I get another call stating that it was either going to be REALLY late, or I would have to drop her off in Mt. Misery...oops I mean MT. VERNON, NY. in the morning... sorry no dice. I'm not waking my daughter out of her sleep to travel to be with people who until they called my house... I didn't even think had the number. but I was told that not only did they have it...but they BEEN had it. OH HELL NO. and then. . . It dawned on me... "where were these same motherfuckers two weeks ago on my little ones fifth bday" and "where were these same motherfuckers three weeks before that on her graduation day" and "six months before that on Christmas" and five months before that on her bday and so forth and so on, I'm sure you get my drift. This is a family picnic, which was PLANNED...so why am I getting a call the night before the jump off? How disrespectful is that? I just don't have time to continue to allow the inconsistency. So like I told homeboy who uses his probation when it's convenient for him 'cause when he needs something from me, that probation DOES NOT STOP HIM FROM COMING ACROSS THE G.W. FOR IT. ok....so this lame and I are on the phone Thursday and I straight say to him, **"You are going to look up one day and realize the calls to you have stopped."** he was silent. **NEVER ONCE ASKING HOW HIS DAUGHTER WAS DOING. HE NEVER DOES.** I CAN PROBABLY COUNT ON ONE HAND HOW MANY TIMES HE HAS ACTUALLY ASKED ABOUT HER AND THAT IS ONLY **AFTER** I BRING IT TO HIS ATTENTION. So really fam...There are NO more excuses left for him . I can't justify the bullshit any longer. I am NOT going to allow my daughter to continue to be hurt by the very PERSON who should be protecting her. Its a done deal. and they can say what they want...I have paperwork to prove EVERYTHING I say is FACT. He's a liar who has told his family whatever the fuck and they fell for it. **and again AND FOR THE RECORD...I don't care what goes down WITH HIM OR ANYONE IN HIS FAMILY... my daughter won't be there.** The only thing he can do is make sure the child support is on time and in full. That's it. if not, I will file the violation because paying his little bit of support is the very least he can do for a kid that doesn't deserve the way she has been tossed to the side and LIED TO by everyone in his arena. I'm getting ready to be on some Remy Ma shit.. like I really cant stand men shit... like what person is co-signing this kind of behavior? He should have no friends and his family should be disgusted. But I'm sure he used me not sending my child as a "see I told y'all she was a bitch." But that AIN'T IT. I AIN'T A BITCH WHEN THE CHILD SUPPORT ARREARS NEED TO BE FORGIVEN. OR THE COURT ORDER LOWERED OR A LOAN OR GAS, ETC. So there is more to the story than he has told them. **and NOT ONLY DID I ERASE HIS NUMBERS, BUT HIS MOMMAS, HIS AUNTS AND ALL THE 404 AND 410 NUMBERS IN MY CALLER I.D. AND THEN I WENT INTO MY VOICEMAIL AND DELETED ALL THE VOICE MESSAGES THEY LEFT** *(WITHOUT CALL BACK NUMBERS MIGHT I ADD - SO THEY REALLY DIDNT WANT TO SEE THE LITTLE GIRL)* **BECAUSE ITS LIKE THIS FAM...NOT ONLY DO I HAVE**

SELF CONTROL ,BUT I'M TOTALLY RELAXED WITH MY DECISION. They need to start off slow with a call or card. NO GIFTS, NO MONEY... SHE DON'T NEED IT. just a call maybe and then follow through when they say something...Now back to me and my little one. So anyways... she went with friends. had a blast and I finished up the packing. I'm looking at the F150 today, I love that truck. My friend said he has some nice shoes for it for me (rims). Lets see. Oh. I should be in two places by the end of the week (n.c. and n.j.). . . I told y'all I found a place a few towns over and so I'm going there today to give the deposit. then I will be south for a few because I am taping a show. I can't wait. I have this curly hair like Kelly from Destiny child - the SAME hair style, but I'm not feeling it anymore and I want something a little different FOR THE SHOW. Lets see. Something with a china bang and dropped past the shoulder. or I may just do a pony tail and bang. You know what? That's what's up...ponytail it is with a bang. something like 20 inches. Lets see. (exhaling). today I have a bunch of stuff to do and my daughter got her hair straightened. It looks so cute. She says, "mommy I like it better this way and not puffy" I'm like it was cute like that - PUFFY-...but the curls were so tight at the ends . . . it stayed tangled and I just couldn't continue to watch her suffer through what should be a pleasant experience...GETTING YOUR HAIR DONE. So its a little straight and it looks cute on her. OK so remember I told y'all I was cutting off everyone except for one...well now that has changed....EVERYONE IS CUT OFF. I'm chilling. The months that I have "dated hard" are over. I am done. The legend that is I...is retired ONCE AGAIN. SO LONG MY DEAR FRIENDS OF THE PAST few months...I'VE HAD A BLAST. Now its back to business and your girl is going back into the Church...**today's assignment (drumroll please).....Pray! Get on your knees and pray! That's the assignment for today. It works. Let me see, its about 1pm and I am going to pray every hour until I go to bed today. Join me. Lets pray and ask God to forgive our transgressions and what we've done to others. Even if you think you may not have done anything wrong to anyone. You never know what the person is thinking. You may have offended them and not know it.**

So lets ask God to forgive our transgressions today. Let's be free of the past. I know you guys always hear me talk about mercy and being here by Gods Mercy and that is true...and based on all the crap with baby daddy, I need to live as long as I possibly can so that I can be here to raise this little girl 'cause he damn sure ain't trying to help out...Ok. enough about him. that's not Godly and I've gotten it off my chest already....(see how quick you can get sidetracked when your thoughts and actions are NOT grounded in the Lord)...Ok. **So yeah family...Lets pray today. If you are going through something and need Gods assistance... BE SPECIFIC WHEN YOU TALK TO HIM...Lets ask him directly and specifically for what we need. don't be afraid to take it to the Lord in prayer. So that's the assignment. and if you are awake at 9pm EST. you can pray with me. Get on your knees at that time and lets ALL pray...Asking God to answer the prayers of each other...our sisters and brothers...** You know in the Bible it makes references to each one praying for the other...and that we SHOULD pray for each other. So lets do that. **and if you are in a position where you can't get on your knees or be at peace to pray at 9pm...just say it in your mind. "God please forgive me of my transgressions and those who have hurt me" ask God to give you a forgiving heart and to keep you protected and covered... DON'T FORGET TO ASK FOR WHATEVER IT IS YOU LONG FOR. be specific and make sure you WANT it, 'cause you just might get it. remember that once we pray, we must forgive ourselves for whatever it is we are asking God to forgive us for. We must also forgive whomever has hurt us because that's a part of growing and the dislike will consume you eventually - take it from me. So remember, Pray, Release and LET IT GO. Cry if you feel like crying... I love you and if you can't catch me during the day, you can catch me at 9pm when I pray... for YOU! K.J. peace Man Unnecessary is almost out of the printer. I will keep you posted.**

Tuesday August 2, and I have to tell you, today has been going GREAT! First let me just say, I'm in the new place. I

will let you know what date - looks like the first of Sept. I'm getting hits on my resume...I told y'all I didn't want to be home. I'm trying only for part time jobs, five hours per day. like 10 to 3pm. (taking a deep breath). I'm on my way to Nishuane Pool - taking my daughter for a swim. Mommy ain't built like she once was...so you know my ASS is out! lol. What else is going on with me? Oh...yeah the place I am moving is straight luxury...and I ain't mad at no one. Its about time for me and my daughter to do what we need to do. aka LIVE LARGE! I have so many things going on and for the life of me, I WILL get rich or Die trying - 50Cent. Well that's my time for today...I know it short, but hey...it is what IT is. **Today's assignment is: Do laundry! lol. ha ha ha, I just told on myself. Why does your girl have like FIVE damn bags of laundry waiting for me in the hallway? and why is the landlord going around telling people how I have not paid my rent? he's bugging and that won't help him one bit. I'm moving and so that's it that. No assignment for today. Just be true to yourself. I love you, I'm ghost! Kj**

***"Do the humpty hump, just doing the humpty hump...What's good Family.....Its Wednesday aka Hump Day and for all my freaks reading this ...that does not mean for y'all to be out there giving up da goods (humping folks). (taking a deep breath) Well today has been a little rough for me, I can't front. First the luxury apt. bldg may not have room for me and my little one and so the "six and six" I assumed would go down (we live six months in N.C. and six months in Jersey) may not happen.** I've been on the phone all day trying to put shit in order. Figuring out if N.C. is just what will be at this point. I put in calls to schools down there and I've got to get there soon because school begins the last week in August and I have a job interview down there next week, so regardless, your girl is leaving the tri-state. As far as the apt. EVERYTHING is packed up. and I spoke with V.R.J. and he will meet me on the other end to get me settled in. I just don't have time for this any longer. this flip flop shit. The F150 made me feel as though I was going to flip over each time I turned a corner and so I'm thinking that's OUT. I guess I'm not made for BIG WHIPS....ha ha ha. So I have to check into things a little "sedan-ish" to get me going. With my credit score, I should be good for whatever, but its the PAYMENTS that I absolutely cannot stand. (exhaling). . . I spoke with my attorney today in regards to a potential lawsuit and so that's on standby. I have to make a final decision on whether or not I am going to put the fire to their asses or not. Sometimes you know...you just sooner walk away with nothing than to deal with turmoil and confusion. My little one is visiting my friend and she should be back either tonight or sometime tomorrow, lets see. **I may just take my ass out to Diva Lounge - Montclair - New Jersey...**if you haven't been there...SHAME ON YOU! THE PLACE NOT ONLY LOOKS NICE, BUT THE CROWD ON WEDNESDAYS IS OFF THE CHAIN. What else is going on? Nothing. Just can't wait to get outta here. I'm tired of living in a flat filled with packed boxes. I almost bounced my ass to Pennsylvania, but my cousin has YET to call me with the information. I will be calling his wife 'cause that's who you need to call when you want things done (keep that on the hush). Nah, but you have to call LuLu 'cause she is really the ONE in the house if you know what I mean. Oh...damn, I forgot...they are traveling and so of course he can't get to me. Oh well. Ok so my girl is having a BBQ at her house and in effort to avoid being around baby daddy, I may not ride through. Just don't want to be in the same space as him. and NO I ain't finna (ebonics) talk about his ass, so lets move on... My curly weave is still holding up and I have to admit, it was a good look for the summer, but as soon as the weather cools down a bit, I can get the china bangs and straight drops – can't do that now with the humidity, not cost effective for my lifestyle. I think I'm going to reach out to "boss man" and get him to drop some paper on this move...calling it **the Kalico Jones begin again relocation fund**. ha ha ha. Nah, but seriously...I am outta here. I told ya I had this show jumping off and there are just so many things I have on my plate, but nothing is getting completed out because I have either enlisted the advice of people who are stupid or I have solicited the services of vendors who are just plain ass dumb. and so now I will be doing things for myself for a little while and see how far I get. (exhaling). **So VRJ will be** up here again this weekend and I believe my girl Tiff may **come through for a moment. She grabbed up the new ML (Benz) and its a good look for her. My other girl snatched up a house and so I'm the only one left who ain't done shit with her dough.** I have to fix that. I just absolutely can't stand a car note. I **see these one and two income families who APPEAR to be Kobe and Shaq (ballers) on the outside, but the credit is crazy and they're eating chicken and spaghetti every other night. I just don't want to be part of that crew**. I'd rather live nice, SAVE money for my daughter and be able to travel and not on a discount. **If you ain't got shit to leave your children...then what's all the car notes and house payments for?** TO I'MPRESS OTHERS. I have so many people who try that shit so they can showboat and GRANDSTAND and yet...they have nothing. Their lives are filled with talks about other folks and who they know. meanwhile...ain't nobody talking about them. **That's why I don't go to peoples houses...they want me there just to let me "see" how they are living because people - WOMEN have always been that way when it comes to me, always having to prove themselves to me one way or the other ...** like I'm really going to make calls and tell my REAL circle how they are doing. HA, that's laughable. Always on top of whatever drama is going on if they ain't part of it. I left that shit alone a LONG time ago. You got drama, then trust and believe...YOU need to have other friends...other than me that is because I ain't commenting and I don't care. I have come to realize that people tell me shit because they want to hear my comments, but again...**KJ AIN'T NEVER BEEN NO HATER.** I don't care who it is. If you are doing YOU...and **if you are happy for YOURSELF...then I am happy for you**. But to tell me shit when you know you are only telling me for commentary purposes, won't get you anywhere because I'm bigger than that. (ugh) and that's why when I bounce...the only way most of these bitches are going to be able to reach out to me and know what's going on with me is by viewing this diary and then **AND STILL I'M GOING TO HOLD BACK ON SOME SHIT, AS TO NOT GIVE THEM ANYTHING TO DISCUSS BETWEEN THEM. ha ha ha.** When you reach thirty...Nah, let me take that back...When you become a mother...

you should really have BETTER things to do than to discuss other chicks and try to chicken fuck ME into commenting on people, places and things that I could give a shit less about. Its like, I don't even give a damn about my daughters father, and so you KNOW I could give a damn less about what the next bitch is doing...I'm out here on a paper chase... and what are YOU doing? Can't go anywhere, can't work anywhere, and can't be nowhere without the dramatics following your asses around. I don't live my life like that. My daughter is a ten, I'm a twenty and so there you have it. Nothing else left to say. Things are good. and each time one of you bitches try to chicken fuck me into saying anything ELSE that is not GENERAL knowledge... you can FORGET ABOUT IT. 'Cause I'm bigger than that and I'm on to you. **Family...I just had to get that off my chest, because chicks be around your girl for what?** To get a name drop in a book. To be able to say I called them last night to others. Ain't shit I do or say between these bitches sacred and so I give up. Its over. Number changed and they are getting the SAME number you got 423-200-0261 and not to say that number ain't Important because I do return calls and I DO answer the phone, **but as far as MY HOME NUMBER AND BUSINESS NUMBERS...OH HELL NO. if YOU AIN'T WENDY WILLIAMS you ain't calling me direct**. If you ain't a producer for Oprah, you ain't calling me direct...If your name isn't affiliated with Ingram, then you damn sure ain't calling me direct. Its over for that after being fed up by the behaviors of chicks who less than a week ago were fucked up in the game. how soon do we forget. and I ain't writing no books about it 'cause the diary will be published and so it will be ready and available in print for ya! Yesterday me and the little one went swimming and I can't say enough about how men act when they see a big ass. I took off my jeans and they lost it. aka their minds...what is going on men? It was just a damn shame, I had to actually say, **"I'm with my daughter, can you please leave me alone"** then some other nigglet walking a pit bull in the CHILDRENS park, might I add stopped to ask me about that damn When Gucci Came First, and I'm like yeah, that's me... Ugh, just one interruption after the other and I suppose that once my TV. show goes through, that will happen again. Oh well and

I guess that's the price of all THIS. anyway, I'm outta here. **Today's assignment: CUT OFF ALL THE FAKE CHICKS IN YOUR LIFE - IF YOU ARE FEMALE. CUT THEM OFF. ALL THE ONES WHO CALL YOU AND DON'T SAY HELLO FIRST, JUST STRAIGHT TO THE GOSSIP...LET THEIR ASSES GO. ALL THOSE FRONTING ON YOU AND EVERYONE ELSE...SAY BYE BYE AND JUST KNOW that just because someone invites you to their house, that doesn't mean you have to go. learn to stay in your OWN house sometimes. that's MY TIME AND I'M GONE. Oh I spoke with hubby today...he's ok. just waiting on me to decide on the move and I believe I may have done that today. Stay sweet. Your girl Kal over and OUT!**

It's Tuesday "Peep"le and I have to say, I'm having a good day! Its damn near September and I haven't decided what in the world I am going to do... Ok. so lets see, today is the 9th of August and my little brothers bday. (taking deep breath)... So lets see, I haven't spoke with you guys for like a week and so I have much ground to cover....First, I did go to Diva Lounge last Wednesday and I had FUN, FUN, FUN... On the mic and doing my thang...then Thursday, Friday and Saturday I was at my girl's house helping her mom out with the decorations for the bridal shower we had there on Saturday. **Nicole is getting married THIS Saturday and HER bridal shower was nice** . Wonderful conversation and I was just pleased with seeing young ladies (they are in their mid twenties) doing there thing. Big jobs at that age. Educated, pretty and ALL handling their respective business. Very good. My little one is one of the flower girls and I am, of course, the helper of everyone...so wish me luck! The astronauts came home safe this morning. I was up watching the landing and I did pray for their safe return. It must be something to realize you may not make it. Like...we all know we are going to leave "here" one day, but to be up there, in outer space with the drama (foam and tiles falling off), that must wear on your nerves. **You know they - NASA - couldn't send your girl up there because I would be yelling, for them to bring my ass back. and besides...I don't think you could have acute**

anxiety disorder and be in space...its just something about not being able to calm down that leads me to believe I would NOT be a good candidate ha ha ha. Ok. so the apt. in jersey is a done deal. paying for it tomorrow. so it's "six and six" and I can't wait. I should be out of this flat before next week and thank GOODNESS. I began a job search and have some things lined up for this week and so lets see what happens. (exhaling). . . VRJ and all the rest have been out of my life for a week now and I've been getting more sleep. **You know SLEEP is a GOOD thing...** Today I am doing the laundry and I'm taking appointments to view a leather living room set I am in the process of selling. At first, I was going to put it on the sidewalk, but then I thought... I paid too much money for that and so if I sell it cheap, it would STILL be a blessing to someone and I could use the money to put in my daughters account. So that is being sold... and so is a new fridge. Where I am going, I don't need the one I have. the apt is all stainless and for that fact, so it the house. I think I'm going to do the first "six" here in the tri-state and do latter six in North Carolina... at any rate, it is what it is and has to be done = a MOVE. Oh that reminds me. I have to drop the official change of addy forms tomorrow morning. (ugh)...don't you just despise moving? You never know how much stuff you have until you move. I'm hoping I find my damn cell phone. But you know yesterday I got two, so that makes four. One business, one pleasure, one for family and one just for my daughter AKA "the bat phone). Only her, her school and anything relating to contacting me in regards to her. and yes, she does have a cell phone. I gave it to her only because I felt it was a necessity. Ok. so today we are going to take it light. I have so much laundry to accomplish and I have to go back to my friends house to help with some last minute preparations for her daughters wedding and I need to take this weave out - pick up my dress, pick up a pair of shoes for my daughter and hair and just the little things that are needed in order to be "together" for this coming Saturday....then my daughter is off to the hamptons and Martha's vineyard...she goes every year and its cheap - free...'cause she goes with family, but I don't go. **THEY DON'T ALLOW ME TO GO... :(** They say when I am around the little girl don't listen and expects everything. I think that may be true. Ok...so today we are doing laundry and getting some book stuff done. This diary is going to be taken down and restarted because I am going from one year to the next and so after I believe next Saturday... the entries will be new. I don't know if I am going to have it available on this site, since its being published in volumes. So this would constitute volume ONE. **Ok family... HOW are you? let me know...hit me up... 973-342-1039 and that's the ONLY way you can get the new number...**because remember I lost that cell phone and had to replace it, but its still on but it serves as a voicemail only. **Today's assignment is : Begin a relationship with yourself. If you are searching for answers, its said to "look within yourself" but if you do not know yourself then how can you expect any answers? that's right... YOU CAN'T. So lets start being kind to ourselves (body, mind and spirit)...lets renew our faith in our OWN ability to love thyself. and I mean truly love thyself. Lets stop drinking, drugging, smoking, fighting, and all the rest of the self destructive things we tend to entangle OURSELVES up in because we don't HAVE A RELATIONSHIP WITH OURSELVES. I love you and don't forget it. now love yourself! You girl KJ Moore over and beginning again! Peace**

Wuzzup Family? Its HUMP day and yes, I am going BACK to Diva Lounge tonight. I'm trying to get a sitter as we speak. ha ha ha. Today was filled with shopping, lounging and just being FREE. Oh. I realized something last night...something I wanted to share with you guys, but I think it would be best left unsaid. So when I get up the courage...YOU KNOW IF ITS SOMETHING I CAN'T SHARE, THEN IT MUST BE HUGE.. give me a few days, possibly by the end of the week. Ugh... life is a nice thing to participate in, isn't it? Ok. well today I don't have much to say. I did the laundry this afternoon and it was not as bad as I thought. I really only had like four bags, but they were mostly towels and bedding...clothing, of course, but the reason why I needed to so many bags was because of the bedding. My daughter is testing my patience with her behavior and I think it may be time for me to have a talk with her about interrupting me while doing business. and **SHE KNOWS BETTER!** Trust me, the child knows better. Everyone keeps asking me about the modeling again, but to tell you the truth...I just don't want that for her again. She had fun and that's it. got a little dough and that made it better, but its time to focus on the main studies aka READING, WRITING, MATH, etc. and so that's that with THAT. **Well I have a secret and I don't mean "crush" ha ha ha. I just mean I have something I could share with you, but I don't want the hate that comes with having something really nice happen for you. Y'all know what I'm talking about, don't act like y'all don't know what I mean. ok. so there is NO assignment for today...just sit back, relax and have a cognac.... I'm your girl and I'm good as GONE!**

Thursday, August 11 & Legal action it is...How dare they try to f with me! Ok so today I get served with a court summons regarding someone I used to work with. I hope she has all her paperwork in order because I am going to have this case eaten quickly. Ugh, this is why you don't mingle with bums. First of all. I fed this chick. her and her daughter. Gave her clothing, money, brought her breakfast and I'm sure she is still rocking the earrings and sunglasses I gave her upon my leave from the job. Ok. so why is she filing charges against me? (taking a deep breath)... well lets see. I finally gave the company an exit interview via telephone and her behavior and skill set came into question and now I guess, she believes by bringing charges against me, she is going to do what? Ha. this is a joke. I know because my attorney said so. I can't even get into it with you family because its not worth it, just know I have to be in court to address something I didn't even do. But that's ok. like I said, the paperwork better be in order and the company... I have been advised not to discuss what is going to occur, but you can REST assure, I have documents and statements that go back almost TWO YEARS...can you say, "Pattern?" be ready 'cause EVERYONE is going to court, and I mean everyone. Can't be serious interrupting my move with needless drama. What else is going on? Well I'm just trying to get through the day. Not going to discuss this with family because it will "excite" them and I'm sure they don't need another KJ thing in their lives. But I have to make sure my daughter is ok. She spent the night out and is not home as of yet. Oh I met the author of **"the dog's on the porch"** he's from Jersey. I have to read his book and y'all know I don't read anyone else's books. Ok. so family be careful of who you befriend because you never know how it is going to come back to bite you in the ass. When you meet people who are literally burned down, you cant just give you friendship to them because you feel sorry their boyfriend gave them an STD. or you feel bad because they have no clothes and they can't take care of their children properly. **Sometimes we have to stop trying to be SUPER SAVE-A-HO because some people just don't deserve to have someone look out for them. and its nothing you can do about that. and to top that off...most of the time that very same person can't go to their family...WANNA KNOW WHY?** because their family is sick of them. Exhausted by the constant dependency and so they are like "f" if, let them be on their way and that's how that person usually comes to you..."**Me and my family are not tight" "we don't get along" "my mother does not like me" etc. and you fall for it and then BAM!!!! state of nj vs. your ass. ha ha ha. This is dumb and provable and so I'm good. Well let me get ready to go swimming. I have to take the little one, but first...I HAVE TO GET SOME FOOD IN MY STOMACH, DIDNT REALLY EAT ALL DAY, BEEN RUNNING AROUND TRYING TO GET MY SHIT TOGETHER FOR MY MOVE. Have a great day and lets stop trying to be SUPER SAVE-A-HO..... Shit sometimes we gotta just save ourselves. I'm gone...KJ.**

Friday, August 12th, - and I have to tell you going to court is not as bad as I thought. I have to return next week for trial and I'm sure this trial thing will go away as quickly as the suit against me. (exhaling)...so what else is up family? DRAMA...right? I know but hey...It is what it is. So today I give a public statement to the press regarding my lawsuit. I'm sure you guys will understand once the developments come out as to why this was necessary. Sometimes you have to know when its time to stand up for yourself and NOW is the time for me to do that, so in having said that...I am not

going to discuss it. However, next Thursday I will keep you guys posted as to the outcome of the case against me, as far as me with company...YOU CAN WATCH THE NEWS FOR THAT ONE. Its hot out and I'm a little tired. I have to entertain this evening and so I must try to get some things in order. I have put in several calls with respect to movers to get my ass outta here Immediately and this court B>S. is just an example of why. That was my final straw with people in this town and just people in general. Remember yesterday I talked about not being super save-a-ho and that's what I meant. you cant go around trying to help people. this is the reason why my ass is going to court now. trying to help someone down pick herself up. No education, Baby father burning her every chance he gets (STD), had to do her resume (not smart at all), buy her food, loan her money (of which I never got back) and lets not forget the clothing and on one occasion she took the shirt right off my back... boy oh boy I tell you... you just cant befriend everyone folks, you just cant. So... I wish her no ill wills, just to get her life together and know that when you sign an affidavit for court...that it is a LEGAL document and when there is proof you have LIED on the document...you can be found guilty of perjury - a criminal offense - Ok. so I guess someone put her up to this...I wonder who the jackass was... hmmm, there are so many of them, its like...where do start? Enough about that. I'm sure time will have my back. Now onto me... I look great. In court today with a tailored suit - nice gray with a baby blue wife beater underneath. kind of sexy. mostly professional, definitely RESPECTFUL. I'm going to get ready to get my little one who hasn't been home in TWO days. Tomorrow she will be on vacation and I will join her next week after the movers are done. and this dumb court crap is over. So what else? hmmmm, well I have a lunch date and its a little after noon and so I have to go and doll myself up. I will chat with you later. Have a great weekend. I have a wedding and some shopping to do. My daughter is in need of a couple pairs of shoes for school and I think I saw a pair of Kenneth Coles on sale for twenty bucks. I have to re-read the pull out from the paper. **This weekend's assignment is : (drumroll please) Find some "me" time. that's right you heard me. Find time for YOURSELF. Take time out to take a bath, spray Perfume on**

you, and do something that will make you feel good. No matter what that entails. Maybe its taking a walk in the park by yourself. Picking a flower and smelling it. Go to Church, Pray, Whatever the "me" time is, Do it. Ladies, give yourself a pedicure or a manicure. do something that would constitute you having time with yourself. and if that means pulling out the magic wand (if you know what I mean)... then do it. Pull it out and KNOCK YOUR SOCKS OFF! HA HA HA. Ok. well that's my time, I'm outta here your girl Kali J over and NOT GUILTY....

Its Tuesday AUGUST 16TH and I'm a little tired. My little one is on vacation : Hamptons, etc. she goes every year. I'm just tired family, just tired. Between my lawsuit and this jackass trying to jam me up in court...I have had it. But nevertheless, I'm good and again...I can handle it. So... I have court on Thursday, my corporate attorney is on vacation and so he will not accompany me, but he says he doesn't have to. Retaliation is a mutha...Let me tell you. People need to think prior to proceeding on dumb ass Impulses aka CONSEQUENTIAL THINKING. Ok. so I know there are many of you of whom I no longer communicate with reading this and so I just need to say that I am ok. My little one is fine and I hope things are fine with you. but unfortunately when a lawsuit is present, you can't keep in contact...it compromises the integrity of the entire case. I'm sure you understand. But I miss some of you guys and I know some of you have gone on vacation and I guess I will never get my postcards, but that's ok. I understand. Hopefully when this case is over, I can get my postcards and you can see my little one. What else? Nothing much. Getting ready to go to the hair salon. Get this curly weave taken out and I'm getting something else, but something a little SKIP TRACK-ISH if you know what I mean...just don't want the whole process with sitting for a head of cornrows and then the sewing...just too much. (exhaling)...so I got a royalty check and can you say, "WOWEE" yes family its going down. but I have so many bills to pay...ugh...I can't tell you...the BILLS and the moving and the packing and the six and six dream...its just a lot so my daughter is vacationing while I am moving and the address is going to be a post office box...I'm sure you understand why... just don't want people to have direct access to me any longer. trying to live my life and I cant do it with people constantly around me and on my back. I want FREEDOM. Ok. so this weekend was my girlfriends wedding. and we were all TWISTED. If I never see a long island ice tea again....Whew! I don't even want to GO to long island... I caught the bridal bouquet...I don't know why, cause my ass ain't no where NEAR doing the marriage thing AGAIN. I already have that... LOL. but since people don't know...Oh well...DOES THAT MEAN I HAVE TO RETURN IT? ha ha. Well let me get out of here, its a little after two pm and my appointment was at two and so I'm sure Tye is using the "f" word right about now because I am NOT respecting her schedule. Let me get cracking. Oh... there will be no assignment for today because I cannot think of one. **Just pray folks. and remember that Jesus Loves YOU for YOU and despite what you may have done in the past, if you ask him...HE WILL FORGET IT. SO WHO GIVES A SHIT IF OTHERS DO NOT. Don't live your live waiting for people to stop talking about past transgressions because people never forget those. They are too busy in need of things to talk about. . . just keep your head up and stay focused and you will make it through. I should be moved in less than a week. its my goal that when I join my daughter on vacation that I am completely moved and unpacked in our new home and just MOVING FORWARD. that's IT. just moving forward. So fam...YOU MOVE FORWARD TOO! Screw those who are not in your best interest. So what you got drunk at a party and fell down the steps. So what you did whatever it is you have done that people just won't stop f'ing talking about... Let it go (in the words of a long time friend) LET IT GO. Well that's my time and so I have to bounce, take care of you and remember.... If NO one else cares and knows...I DO... and so here we are, almost at the end of kj's diary volume 1. I figure that after I go to court on Thursday I will officially end the diary Vol. 1. "Damn, Time flies" BE EASY! KJ.**

Wednesday and I'm ready for my court date tomorrow. Today I went out and had a nice time with a "friend" we ran a few errands and had lunch. Tonight I will be at Rascals comedy club in Montclair to show support for my office girl, Shayna's brother. He is performing tonight and I promised I would be there. Oh...last night I met a group of young ladies. I have to shout them out. They are from Paris... (bless me...I just sneezed)... Ok so that's about it for today. I will surely tell you guys what happened in court tomorrow. and my hair is in a ponytail. Its timeless and so that's what I decided to do with it. Its growing out nice. But until it gets out of this "middle length" stage, I am going to be weaving and pony tailing it up. Have a great evening and if you are in the area...drop by Rascals. **OHHHH...before I forget. I am going to be hosting a monthly event there. I will let you know when the first day is going to be. Stay focused. Your girl KJ. bye bye.**

08/18 - CASE DISMISSED! Bitch! trying to jam me up. Lying on me. Fake charges, Lying on a police document = PURGERY. Can't be serious, trying to assassinate my character... What a JOKE, but its over and now its time for me to move on. Its a damn shame though because the few hours I spent in **Montclair Court today, WITH THE NJ STATE VS. ME** BULLSHIT, I could have been making moves on behalf of me and my daughter. But I'm over it. Paid the 100 dollar public defender fee because my attorney is on vacation and someone had to seek a dismissal on my behalf... **SO HERE ENDS THE SAGA THAT IS THAT BITCH!** Just being a straight menace to me and everyone involved. (Ugh...). So that's it for today. Its Laverne's Bday and I'm responsible for the cake. So I'm getting ready to go pick it up. We are having cake and champagne. Oh. last night at rascal's I had a great time. it was a nice evening and I looked great - might I add. I had the whole Celebrity chillin' look. Like it was what I would like to refer to as "relaxed glam" full make up, nice jewels, high heels and army colored (green) knickers and a t-shirt with the sleeves rolled up over my shoulder, nice belt and bag. Like a side line at the Lakers look. Just chillin' --- Ok. but enough about that...The comedy was good. Mitch was good for a first timer. Ok. well I **have to go, but I just want to say something to you about life and life in general. In the Bible it talks about being unevenly "yoked" - don't be unevenly yoked. this could be a friendship, association, an intimate relationship, fiancé, etc. because when you are unevenly yoked, you allow for the situation I was just in.** I had NO business, based on ALL the things I have heard about this young lady - **ALL FROM RELIABLE SOURCES, INCLUDING THINGS SHE HAS SHARED WITH ME ABOUT HERSELF..... I should have NEVER befriended her. There were too many red flags letting me know this young lady and I had absolutely NO business being anything more than hello and goodbye.** Had I listened to half the people who told me to stay away from her...OR MORE IMPORTANT...had I LISTENED AND CAREFULLY PAID ATTENTION TO THE THINGS SHE HAS TOLD ME ABOUT HERSELF...I would have run in the opposite direction. and not attempted to be "super save-a-ho" So please, don't be unevenly yoked. Its just not worth it. Oh Hubby called me this morning about the case and just to see how I was feeling because despite the "I'm kalico, I'm this and all that" blah blah blah, I am STILL a person with FEELINGS and although it takes a lot for me to show them....I do have feelings and my feelings get hurt sometimes too. I just wish people would understand that one thing about me. That there is a REAL person behind Kalico Jones and she needs hugs and love too. **Oh well, that's how I am feeling today, very emotional - I'm learning how to have feelings (ha ha ha)...But seriously... Can I get a "how are you today?" Shit...no ONE asks me that, NO ONE. I only get the "what's poppin' kali" and that's ok, but damn...SOMETI'MES I DON'T WANT TO BE KALICO JONES. I WANNA JUST BE ME! Well that's my time. I'm your girl, I'm gone and MOST I'MPORTANT... DISMISSED!**

08/19 - this is the final entry of Kj's Diary - I know, I know...YOURE HURT. HA HA HA. But seriously. Its been ONE year since I began this segment of my site and I must

say, its the most enjoyed - this and the books of course. Ok. so today began early. Since I've stopped the champagne habit and late night newports, I've been feeling GREAT. Yesterday I made a Rocky Road Cake laced with Hennessey (spell check) for Laverne's party in the store. Can you say, "Twisted?" People loved the henny cake. and of course there was the "regular" cake for the candles. and then there was the champagne...and since I do NOT drink... I couldn't partake in that portion of the festivities. But I had a nice time decorating and just being the hostess with the MOSTess. Ha ha and Laverne was happy and so that's always a plus. (taking a deep breath). Well my little one is still away enjoying the remnants of her summer vacation and I as well. I'm going to relax now, have a Lunch date and I don't want to be late. My life seems to be on "relax" right now and that's great. This weekend I believe I am going to look at a few properties. I may fly out to Florida, have to see if the seller is going to pay for the flight...if so, then I'm out. OH...damn...I can't go NO Where. My girl Pudda is having a BIG bbq tomorrow. I have to be there. Ok so South Jersey it is. She has a pool so your girl will be bringing her bathing suit. and I'm not eating today so that I can make sure I get my belly filled. Her and her husband ...I'm very proud of them. Doing their thing...making it happen for the family...its a great look. Well... **Today's assignment is: Pray for someone other than yourself. and if I may share a secret...** I came this close (putting my pointy finger and thumb very close together without actually touching) to smoking a Newport. Notice how I say Newport instead of CIGARETTE...that's because that would be an admission on my part and I don't want to claim that nasty ass habit. **So if you smoke...JOIN ME IN QUITTING.** Everyone says I'm a closet smoker - because I am. Never smoke in public or during the day time. People can't say they have seen me smoke unless you were at my ex co-workers bday party at Bens some months back and then ... maybe someone else will believe you when you tell them I smoke. Ahhhh. I'm in the mood for Gladys Knight... *(singing)"he said he's going back to find... a simpler place in time....I'd rather live in his world, than live without him in mine..."* We had a great time that night at D's party. Ok. enough with the sentimental shit... So your girl has been smoking but only at night and only with a glass of champagne. it doesn't sit well on my stomach without it. so that means I had to quit the champagne as well. and I'm doing well with that. So LETS QUIT SOMETHING TOGETHER. Remember when I told y'all about God blocking my blessings because of two things I have not been able to shake...? Well there they are: Champagne & Newports. But NOT during the day, NOT in public, NOT in front of others, NOT in front of my daughter...ONLY when she is sleeping and NOT any where near her room, etc. (thinking aloud), "those oxtails I just ate are laying on my stomach, yuck!" Ok. **let me leave you with this: I've had a great time speaking with you and sharing my life with you for this past year and I just want to say to you that YOU can accomplish anything you set your mind on. You have to remain focused and it can and WILL be done. God loves you and so do I... Its been a hell of a ride and its been MY pleasure... and so ends Volume ONE of KJ's Diary. This will be published ... AS IS. You can stay tuned for Volume TWO beginning soon. Take care of yourself and remember: I'm happy for you if YOU are happy for yourself. (lets see the character changes going forward). Your girl Kali J Moore over and out... (one year later) Love ya!**

*******Volume 1.5 ************* A BONUS FOR YOU ******

Monday, August 22, - What's up everyone? Just checking in on this fine Monday. Tired as shit. Went out last night to Rascals comedy club and "grill" - after the "Silver Foxes" Event, which was very nice might I add. Met the Mayor of East Orange and his wife, she's from Mt. Vernon, NY as well (I believe). Very nice couple and the wife is gorgeous! It was a successful event put on by the God Parents Inc (in Christ = inc.). they give scholarships to adults and send children to camp. What else? Nothing. Just trying to get some stuff out of my apt. so that my move can go easy. My little one is still on vacation and I miss her terribly. I tried to call her today, but there was no answer. This is why she should have taken a cell phone with her. Damn! Oh well and at any rate, Secret Crush called me the other day, TWICE. and I saw PYT's father last night - who told me to "stay away from my son" ha ha ha. Just that his son is at a place in his life where he wants to be treated like a little kid (feed me, f me and put up with my shit - oh and most Important - don't question me or complain) ha ha...MEN they truly think they have it going on... NOT. **Oh I saw my friend Fred on Friday - he is married to Michelle and they are doing well. I absolutely adored the wedding band. - about four carats. Nice job Fred and WAY to go Michelle!** What else is going on? Nothing much. I have a afternoon snack date with Boss Man and then after that its just me trying to find a Sunday paper. Usually I get one from a spot on my block, but she ran out and so I have nothing from yesterday. I could check it out on the internet, but I like the good old fashion way (turning pages). Today I want to talk about how I missed Church yesterday because Boss Man needed to talk. I don't know what I'm doing with him, but he's nice. and before you ask, **NO SEX. Its NOT a sexual thing.** Its a mental thing and I guess that can be more addictive... we just talk about life. his life my life and where we want to be within ourselves. he's into Church and I'm into God and so we talk about religion and just our beliefs, its strictly that kind of a relationship. The reason why I call him Boss Man? Hmmmm wouldn't you like to know. But you can rest assure you will find him in the next book. and speaking of books. I know you are tired of me and this damn Man Unnecessary is a pain in the ass. Its still NOT out in stores and It's not on the internet yet because of an outstanding distribution bill on my part. But the thing is "when was someone going to tell me?" (taking a deep breath) and so I have to send the money in so that my shit can be released, just one thing after another, I tell ya. But as usual, I'm going to handle my business and get my shit in order quick so that I can bring it to you sometime this week. **What else is going on? Nothing really just missing my daughter, having some fun, and just loving God and being very appreciative of everything HE has given me and brought me through. I don't know if there is an assignment for today. I'm thinking we should just have a MOMENT OF SILENCE for our OLD selves as we transition from caterpillar to butterfly. Say goodbye to our old SKIN and hello to a NEW beginning and a beautiful beginning at that.**

Enjoy the day and don't forget to pray! KJ.

8/23 – Wild Wild West....Wild Wild West, I used to live downtown, 129th and Convent...Remember that rap song by Cool Mo Dee? He's got to be like 50 years old now. Dayum... Well Today I am getting ready for an interview. Begins at 2:30pm and so I had to fix my OWN pony tail. ha ha ha. But y'all do know I can do some hair. Yes, I can. Just ask anyone from where I am from... KJ can put in a weave, cut, perm, press and curl and now... Pony Tail. ha ha ha. and it came out better than when I went to the hair salon. Can you say, "Saving some money?" Oh hell yes. and I need every dime I can get. So I spent 640 bucks on nothing over the past three weeks. Its terrible. I was counting up all the dinners and lunches and the cheap pair of Reebok classics I purchased for myself - 35 bucks. I don't spend money on sneakers anymore after the Louis Vuitton fiasco .Just too much money and I've had those sneakers for what... THREE years now. I just refuse to let them go. My little one is still on vacation. I called this morning and I was told she was "resting" - I'm glad. Mommy can do some running around while she is away. I know she has to come back soon because school begins shortly and I have to make so many arrangements for her with regards to before and aftercare. I'm thinking that I have to purchase a car really soon and its going to be something for like 2 grand. **AND I DON'T CARE WHAT PEOPLE THINK**. and If I can find one for 500 bucks I'm going to purchase it. I'm not Impressed with the whips and shit. Because as soon as you drive it off the lot, you're down about ten grand. So... a hoopty it is (spell check, its ebonics anyway so I'm sure it doesn't count). Oh. I had the nerve to watch **Banging in the hood part three**... Yes its an adult video... can you say.. **WICK WICK WACK? Oh my goodness. Remember back in the day when porn stars did their hair? (I'm laughing).** and the sound affects were pretty decent and so were the places (mansions, nice houses, pools, etc.). Now... they're just on a cheap pleather couch, with no nothing - hair a mess, looking like crack head and babies trying to be big girls... and this is what pissed me off... **WHERE WERE THE CONDOMS? NONE**...NO condoms y'all. Oh my goodness. Someone needs to come out with a SAFE SEX porn movie. **Protection IS sexy!... THERE IS NOTHING SEXIER THAN A MAN PUTTING ON A CONDOM...** Y'all hold that thought... I see hood t-shirts on that one. and don't try to jack my shit... **Protection is sexy**. I can market that... Let me call Puff...excuse me... I mean Diddy... I think we can jump off some kind of AIDS / HIV awareness campaign with that one. **AND AGAIN, DON'T TRY TO JACK MY SHIT.** 'CAUSE I WILL SUE. Ok. so yeah... there weren't any condoms and I was a little disturbed by that. As you can see, your girl is BIG on protection. and for all my ladies out there on shots, pills and patches... BE CLEAR those things cannot help you if you are exposed to an STD. So you must use a condom each and every time you have sex. IT'S THE LAW. Like those commercials for buckling your seatbelt..."Its the LAW" Hold that thought y'all. **Let me get Diddy on the phone while my flow is on. I see an AIDS/HIV campaign jumping off. Y'all be ready for that.** You know I have so many ideas and just things in my head that are constantly rolling...constantly rocking sometimes I can't even sleep because of it. My "friend" Boss Man, says I'm "crazy" and that's ok. he says its the author in me... I'm like its the "urgency" in me to get my messages out. So I went out. Had a few glasses of wine. I'm down y'all. Broke my champagne habit ... FINALLY. and your girl had the nerve to get A MARRIAGE PROPOSAL ON SATURDAY. (taking a deep breath). I'm like... I am with someone already and I've been neglecting him. aka Hubby. He knows I'm doing my thing, trying to make things happen and so he respects that, but I know he is hurting because I haven't had any time for him lately. **The marriage proposal... well that came as a shock, as I didn't even know he and I were still on that "level" but I guess we are. He's a sweetheart, but your girl has to get it together. I've got a lot of shit I have to do and I cant do it the way I've been doing it, 'cause that way ain't working. Ok. So let me get outta here. I have to get ready to pull out my "A" game if I am going to sound and LOOK good for this interview. I will holla at you tomorrow. Until then... Lets be careful out here. Kali J Moore, over and OUT!** 1

Its Wednesday and I think I just want to chill tonight. Went out last evening to "celebrate" my latest accomplishment. We went to rascal's and then from there we went to Diva Lounge - both in my new hometown - Montclair. Ok. so last night was "gay" night at Diva and I have to be honest... me and my friend had a great time. Met a lot of nice people and so it is. I tried to call my little one, but she was enroute to the poconos. Damn she's having fun. I'm like "does she even want to talk with mommy?" ha ha ha. I'm glad she's having a good time because in just two short weeks, she is going to be in school FULL time and its back to dance and books and karate and everything else. I'm getting a car tomorrow. Boss Man made the call for me and so I'm getting a little something to get back and forth from things until I make up my mind on just what kind of vehicle I would like to whip around in. Y'all know I'm against payments so ... (exhaling). Tonight its back to Diva Lounge for hip hop & r&b night and I'm going to meet up with my friend GARCIA for a quick one = drink. I've been good with regards to that although last night we did pop one bottle of champagne. Well let me get ready to eat. Having smothered chicken, collard greens and sautéed spinach and I think potato salad is in the bag as well, courtesy of Smokey's American BBQ. Its in Montclair as well and the food is DELICIOUS. **Well that's my time for today. I'm going now. Want to read the Bible for a bit and just relax with God for a moment. You guys be careful   out   there.   1   KJ.**

What's good, its Thursday Y'all and I'm having a ball. Went to Diva lounge last night. Stayed until it closed. Boss Man met me there, looking handsome as ever. GARCIA and I went round for round last night on the drinks and then... guess who walks in? "James" from my book Man Unnecessary. I was SHOCKED! He was looking Good y'all and I was happy to see him. he said he came by my house and saw the lights on but knew I wasn't home. I guess he was a little bored last night. I was happy to see him... Did I mention that already? Hmmmm, so you know it was on! That's my baby. We worked together for a time and he and I had a great relationship. GARCIA drove me home , he and his brother. I like

Garcia's car - LEXUS, WHITE with nice tires. (thinking aloud) "who in the f is banging on the wall like that? Ugh, it sounds like they may be banging in a nail, but its gone on too long for that to be what is making so much damn noise" - just another day living in the hood. That's what I call this place, the HOOD because LAWD knows me and Ivana's dad have always lived in palaces. I miss spring Valley and our North Side addy (address). What else is going on? well its eleven a.m. and I have to go back to bed. I just wanted to give you guys a quick shout and thank you for being you. Lets thank God for waking us up this morning and bringing us to our destination safely. **We have to pray a little more folks. I know I will be in Church on Sunday. But don't think you have to go to Church in order to get your blessings from God because you don't. Church is for fellowship. But I listen to Different television preachers and I especially enjoy Joel Osteen (not the right way to spell his name I know) But its the tall white guy. He has good messages and then there is Creflo Dollar. I enjoy him as well, but the other guy is my personal favorite. Ok. well I have to go now. Need to get in the shower and back in the bed. I wish you well, your girl Kali   J   Moore.**

Saturday and I'm chillin' - Actually I just got in the house from last night. Went out to my girl Laverne's house. She had a private Bday party. But before that it was me and my mother at Rascals and then off to Egan & Sons on Walnut. Had a nice time. Damn, I'm not even tired. Like not one bit. I fell asleep on Laverne's couch round about 2am and woke up at 9 then went back to sleep until 11. So now I'm just getting back into town... Its 4:30pm and I stopped off to get my hair because I'm sick of the ponytail and I want to get something a little skip trackish for a month or so. I think I may have to re-perm my hair before I get it done so that the hair can lay right. I cant stand to see a weave that is all laid out wrong. What else? Well my little one has yet to return home. She is in the Poconos and just having all the fun she can have at this point. I've decided to put myself on a Salad diet. Just back to live veggies and fruits for a few weeks because my 34 bday is coming - October - and I have to make sure I am a six. Or at least an 8. Oh...I have pictures to upload to this site and I will do that but it wont be today. **Tomorrow I will be in Church. Going to try to get some Soul in my Spirit. Ok. well that my time. Just take it light for today. and enjoy yourself. Its beautiful outside and hopefully we will continue to have great weather over the next week. Have a great day! kj.**

Hey Everyone, its Tuesday August 30th and I've been busy. My little one isn't home still and so I've been out and about. Oh that reminds me, I have to go food shopping. and purchase a lunch box for my daughter. Ok. so that's about it. Just trying to be me and FREE. **You have a great day and remember: Do YOU.** **kj.**

Friday, its Friday, Friday, its Friday... What's up Y'all its KJ on the check in today, Friday September 2nd. Well my daughter will be home tomorrow and I'm excited. She begins school on Wednesday and so I will be taking her to school, well not to school, but to the bus stop. with her lunchbox and all. ha ha ha. Its the BIG league now y'all and I'm ready. Tonight I am going to clean, food shop and sort laundry. and get my little ones school clothing out for the week. and yes, before you ask, I LACED her. I didn't go to the school mixer on Wednesday only because she wasn't home, but I am going to the next one, which is sometime over the next two weeks. I have to do before and aftercare. I am putting her back in karate. she will go back into dance and we are going to do our thang. Mommy is working again during the day ...I forgot to tell you guys, yes...I took a FULL TIME JOB. my vacation from work has ended. and I like the place. the money is nice and the income potential is unlimited and so that's wonderful. **ok. so today I want to talk about something family...I want to talk about DRESS CODE FOR AN INTERVIEW: THE DO'S, THE Don'ts AND THE BITCH I KNOW YOU AIN'T EVEN SERIOUS ABOUT WEARING THAT! This is because this week as part of my position,** I am interviewing candidates for a customer service position and in the midst of me interviewing a host of people - all from different walks of life, I have come to the conclusion that "WE" are out of pocket = aka = DEAD WRONG when we go on interviews. The big HOOP nose ring = WRONG. The sunglasses on AFTER you've entered the premises, during your conversation with the receptionist and up until you shake the hand of the interviewer = WRONG . How about losing the paperwork given to you to fax back (and you call and say you left it at your boyfriends house) = WRONG. The tight skirt (one I've been guilty of) = WRONG. if your boobs are hanging out = YOU AIN'T RIGHT. and Please leave the bright red lipstick home, OH>>> I'm sorry and the jean suit with the open toe high heels that look like you brought them from Buttercup and 'em at the strip club = WRONG. and did I mention her jeans were TIGHT...we have to stop this because it makes people not want to even give you a chance. Ugh. . **Lets pray for our people in New Orleans and tell the news to go F themselves putting all that shit about looting on TV. and then had the NERVE to say, "shoot 'em" like we are animals. They're breaking into stores to take FOOD and PAMPERS for goodness sake, not a damn TV.** What is this world coming to when we have to beg for things this country so willingly GIVES TO OTHERS. the shit reminds me of Tupac, who was clearly ahead of his time, "We got money for wars, but can't feed the poor." Shit makes you wanna holla. President Bush is sitting in air force one canvassing the scene. THERE is no scene...these people have been displaced. there are dead bodies all over the place. no water, no electricity and no food and all the national guards you got out there ain't doing a damn thing but making sure they don't "loot" stores. shouldn't they be concentrating on other things like, hmmm let me see... EVACUATION PROCEDURES. these people have no homes, no jobs, no nothing. they literally have to begin again. It's going to be YEARS before anything moves in that town...and to be honest...it may NEVER happen. If you are in a position to give money...give it to a reputable place. make sure they are going to get whatever you send to them right away. **USA for Africa, USA for Iraq, USA for everyone but Americans, this is a damn shame. Lets be thankful for today 'cause tomorrow is not promised and if it is, it may not be what you want. Have a great weekend. its the END of the Summer. Say a prayer for our brothers and sisters in New**

Orleans and try to remember them at your cookouts and other things. Lets be kind to one another. New Orleans, I love you and I am praying for you. kj.

Hey Y'all its Wednesday, September 7th and I'm happy to be here. Today was my little ones FIRST DAY OF SCHOOL - KINDERGARTEN - and I took her this morning and NO I didn't cry, almost...but no. And my little one was just so mature about going to school. She's getting big... I look at her and realize time flies. and oh...She's losing a tooth too! WOW. I'm excited. You know the tooth fairy is going to bring her gifts and money. Its going to be like Christmas if I can help it... But I'm going to leave a note saying that the first tooth gets all the gifts and money, any tooth after that and its just money. Like the first tooth is saying "welcome to the big kids world" something like that. I will think of it when I happens. What else is going on? Well we still haven't heard from her father. I feel sorry for him. and this is NOT me talking about him. this is just me saying that "its a damn shame" like...today the first day of school, a tooth and what's next? I hope he gets it together before its too late. But in the meantime... WE pray for him and I teach her that although he is NOT checking for her, he still loves her and besides that...She has a whole bunch of people who love her and that's that. Ok well that's my time. I hope you guys are well. Love ya. Kali J moore.

What's up Peeple!!! How are you on this fine Saturday afternoon. As for me, well I'm doing GREAT!. Its the 10th of September and me and the little one are getting ready to go to Nicole's Cafe in Bloomfield, NJ for salmon and salad - and champagne for mommy - and a nice spritzer for her. (sprite and cranberry juice). She loves that. I'm waiting for her tooth to come out...IT WON'T MOVE Y'ALL. At any rate...she is going to love the tooth fairy when it does go down. ha ha ha. So I'm trying to get Buffy the Body to host a party for me. My bday slash talent showcase. I got the numbers. and she ain't cheap...but its worth it. I have to see what the venue is going to do for me. I'm meeting with Mr. S. Williams today (producer) and we are going to go over the details with cost vs. door & bar...**'CAUSE IF IT DON'T MAKE NO DOLLARS, THEN IT DOESNT MAKE SENSE**. I'm sure you understand. Ok. so my little one and me are getting ready to be out (its a quarter to four). . . The Job is going well. I'm hiring sales staff and stuff. Its challenging in the fact that I am back in corporate America and I don't think the corporate world is all that. what else is going on? Trying to get representation on a project. Looking for Kevin Ghee (movie maker) lol. Have to see if I can get a Kite out to him. (taking a deep breath). Well I look good and feel great. Oh the weave was coming out that was until this morning. I greased the shit, brushed it and then took my time and drop curled it... KINDA SEXY If I may say so myself. Boss Man loved it. and the shoes. . . CAN YOU SAY, "MEAN" YES the shoe game of today is CRAZY. I've been stepping my "game" up over the past two weeks, just trying to feel a little better about things. There are some things I can't discuss with the public. Not that I ain't giving it all to y'all already, but the really deep deep shit that keeps me up at night...I won't go into. (exhaling)...so I haven't been feeling 100 percent each and every day and that's because I'm in turmoil. Have some personal issues that are bothering the hell out of me. Been going to Church more and just seeking God's infinite wisdom. I have to move before the first of October. I need another car. I have so many things I have to do in like three weeks. I don't know where to begin. I really don't. Well. Let me not bother y'all with that. **OH>>> if you want to donate clothing to the people of Louisiana, please send them to me and I will forward off to someone I know who is out there on the front line , helping out. send me an email to: <u>kalicojones@yahoo.com</u> and I will send you the address to send the clothing or food or whatever you wish to donate. It could be school supplies, etc. Well that's my time. Don't forget to pray for our sisters and brothers in the gulf. they need OUR prayers. So "throw one up" for them AKA... PRAY. and I'll see YOU when I see YOU and if I don't, you can always holla at your girl 423-200-0261 Be easy Babe! Mrs. "Gadget"** **ONE!**

09/14 - and the beat goes on....WHAT'S UP EVERYONE, ITS YOUR GIRL KJ ON DA CHECK IN, JUST giving you a quick holla. I'm a little tired today. Had company last night and just really didn't get a good nights sleep after that. My little ones tooth has yet to fall out, but she's enjoying Kindergarten. As for me, I'm just trying to live and let live. I have to be back in court the first week in Oct. Being sued ...AGAIN. lol. Its like, damn if you do, damn if you don't and to be honest... I am not letting it get to me. I know what I have to do and so there it is. **At any rate, I hope you are fine and please don't forget to pray for our brothers and sisters affected by hurricane Katrina. God Bless you, good night. kj.**

09/16 - HAPPY FRIDAY Y'ALL What's up? How are you doing today? I hope fine. Well I know I haven't had much time to spend with you lately and that is my fault. I am having a hard time with TIME MANAGEMENT. translation: KJ ain't keeping up with her schedule and so I want to apologize to you. So many things are going on right now beginning with and including the fact that I MUST move. **my lease is up and I've overstayed, which now means the new landlords are attempting to EVICT me via court order and so I have to be out and so I'm trying to find a place.** And all the places I WANTED to go keep falling through for one reason or another. (taking a deep breath). At any rate, I am confident I will be able to get this off by months end. I will keep you posted. What else is going on? My daughter loves school. But she's having a hard time getting up in the morning and to tell you the truth, so am I. Ha ha ha. But rest assure, this weekend we are going to get plenty of rest and get our butts on a schedule with respect to our coming and goings. **I think she robbed me this morning y'all (still talking about my little one)...** Because she asked me for 5 dollars for lunch today. I'm like Lunch is five bucks little girl? She's like yeah mommy. just like her mother...hustler. So I guess she got "it" honest. What else is going on? **Don't you know my dear ex cursed me out for 12 minutes yesterday?** I have the recording to prove it. I should link it to my site and let the entire world see how he gets down four years **AFTER THE FACT**. Had the nerve to ask me why I didn't let my daughter participate in their family reunion... HA, 'cause y'all don't treat her like family. No calls, no cards and lets not talk about gifts **'cause they can't do SHIT FOR MY CHILD, NOTHING and everyone who knows me will attest to that statement as being FACTUAL.** Calling the night before the jump off asking for a little girl who does not see (three years) or hear (the same amount) from anyone, including him. Ok so how did I end up speaking to him. Well I don't know, stupidity on my part I guess 'cause for some reason I was compelled to call him to ask if he would like to contribute to the karate uniform. **WE DO NOT NEED THE MONEY FOLKS...** so again, I guess that was me just being needy on some level. I DON'T KNOW. maybe I should take my black ass back to Dr. Wiener - therapist. **At any rate, I called him at 10:23am yesterday and for TWELVE, COUNT 'EM...1,2,3,4,5,6,7,8,9,10,11,12 Fucking minutes he cursed me OUT!** I have it too y'all as a .wav file just in case a beeyach needs it for court - to prove my restraining order should be continued beyond his parole, probation or whatever its called in the county nowadays. Ok. so he cursed me like I stole his chicken (y'all knew I was going to say that, right - refer to my book When Gucci Came First) Ok. so he's yelling and cursing and mentioning his mother wanted to take my daughter shopping... **FOR WHAT? YOU THINK SHE NEEDS CLOTHING? get the fuck outta here. Ha ha ha.** He's talking about my books and asking why don't I have money if I'm supposed to be (with emphasis on supposed) doing so damn well. I'm like listen...why are you so angry with me? What in the world did I do to you. He was like, "this is how I talk to everyone...I don't give a fuck" I'm like, you sound so bitter...I'm going to pray for you. "he told me to go fuck myself" and I said that maybe its best that he is NOT in our daughters life. and before I could hear his next curse, I disconnected the call. WHO HAS TIME FOR THAT? **Men, if you are out there...PLEASE DO NOT DISRESPECT THE MOTHER OF YOUR CHILDREN AS HE HAS DONE...its not a nice thing to do.** If you don't get along with the mother of your child, then just limit your conversations to those that are on par with whatever is going on with your children. NOT who she (the mother of your child) is fucking. NOT her job, NOT her books (my case), NOT an old ass champagne habit (my case), like that shit was going to BREAK Me. FUCK Him. I'm doing me and I'm a GREAT mother. For him to be so damn disrespectful was simply unnecessary and so its back to the way it has been...**HE'S A BUSINESS TRANSACTION AND please BELIEVE I will enlist the CONSEQUENTIAL THINKING I'M ALWAYS TELLING YOU GUYS ABOUT. its when you THINK OF THE AFFECTS OF YOUR ACTIONS PRIOR TO ACTING ON DUMB ASS IMPULSES...'cause had I thought this one out and weighed the past bullshit with the current bullshit, I would not have called him.** I would have kept it the way it's been. (exhaling) But from me to you once again fam...I'm going to say that IF he gets a call from me or my daughter....**It will be a cold day in HELL and I am not going to feel sorry for him.** Ok so on to other THINGS. .. **Boss Man and I are getting along great, but that's easy to say because He's a great man and just an all around sweetie pie.** and I'm not talking about SEX so get your mind out of the gutter. I'm talking about just conversation and personality. The only thing is he has a wall up and I guess that's ok. I have one up to. What else? **Well today I get my hair done. YES I am getting my hair done. another Kelly from Destiny child weave. LONG just like that too.** I had this other look for about one month and I have to say...I'm keeping my hair in longer now. I wonder why. **and my little one will have full services executed as well (hair, manicure, pedicure and mini facial - which is only a deep wash, no chems (chemicals), now I on the other hand will get the full facial, deep cleaning because my face broke out.** I think it had something to do with the grease in the hair. Razac. Oh well Its doing better now and the Proactiv...still haven't used it. I should. Hell I'm paying for it on my credit card every month. and lets not forget that ab lounge too. that is on my credit card...and now its a hanger. lol. Have a bunch of clothing on it. (taking a deep breath). Well I'm getting ready to go now. I will be changing my site soon. Giving a new look to it. lets see how that works out. anyway today's **assignment is (drumroll please): IF THERE IS SOMEONE WHO YOU HAVE WRONGED, APOLOGIZE TO THEM. If there is someone who has** wronged you, go to them and tell them, don't hold it inside because when we hold things in...we become bitter and angry at the world and that's not fair to those who we meet who want nothing more than to love us. Lets not let that love pass us by. Allow yourself to feel by not holding onto stuff that really in all honesty don't even belong to us. If you have that friend who is in need all the time, learn how to say no. If there is someone who is a mental and emotional drain to you, lets break away from them. Lets make a conscious decision to say so long to pain and hurt so we can not only RECOGNIZE but FEEL LOVE WHEN IT COMES OUR WAY. I love you, you love me, and lets enjoy our weekend. I will talk with you soon. Take care of you! Respectfully, your girl Kali   J   Moore.   ONE!

Just another Manic Monday, *(singing) I wish it Sunday, my I don't   have   to   run   day...just   another   manic Monday....*(exhaling) What's good family? Its Monday September 19th and I'm doing better than yesterday. I am cooking tonight for Boss Man and my daughter. I got my weave put in yesterday and I missed Church to do it (LORD PLEASE FORGIVE ME). Y'ALL KNOW I don't play with Church. So what's up with you? My little one is doing the share and learn today in front of the class - she is bringing in her tooth that fell out Friday. The tooth fairy brought her 12 bucks and a bird. Yes a bird. but I f'd up y'all and left the tooth. So excited about leaving the money...that your girl left the damn tooth. someone told me that I have to do it again. I told my daughter that the fairy left it so that she can keep it for when she gets bigger. (dumb I know, but I couldn't think of shit to say). How do you forget to take the tooth KJ? I know y'all. Oh. and whomever is leaving me the msgs about my sisters praying for me...LEAVE YOUR NUMBER. I wanted to call you back. I appreciate the message. You left it at the time when I really needed something the lean on. I saved it too. See I do listen to the hotline number. 973-342-1039 and y'all know there is another number right? yep,,, there IS but I cant give it out to you as of yet. but just know I listen and I return calls. "cause I'm down like that." Anyhow. so I have to move. Went to look at a place the other day - Saturday and it was a damn shack. they SHOULD BE OFFERING TO PAY ME FOR LIVING THERE! 1200 bucks per month to live like that UGH! awful I tell ya, just awful. Ok so any way. I'm getting ready to go and before you ask or in case you are wondering...my daughter put in a call to her pops the other day. he didn't pick up the phone. she did leave a message. I didn't stop her, **but I AM NOT GOING TO ENCOURAGE IT EITHER. ok. so enough about his ass. this ain't about him, its about ME, kj and he ain't got nothing on me. so what else is going on? had a panic attack right before I was set to go out to meet my ex coworker and secret crush. shit. I couldn't believe it. I honestly got sick. thought I was going to need emergency assistance. but I took my meds and felt a little better. this panic shit ain't no joke. well I gotta go. I love you and lets MOVE ON TODAY...today assignment is to MOVE ON! Peace, your girl kali j moore.**

DO THE HUMPTY HUMP, JUST DOING THE HUMPTY HUMP...What's up "peep"le, its Wednesday, "Hump" day and once again to all the freaks reading...this does not mean to go out and HUMP people. ha ha ha. So I just got off the phone with Boss Man. Who has never been exposed to the DIARY (surprised look on my face) . . . my cover is blow y'all and he said I HAVE NOT KEPT IT REAL WITH YOU, THE PEOPLE, MY FANS AND FAMILY SO ON THIS DAY... September 21, I am going to make a confession to you...well a few confessions...hmmm, (taking a deep breath) just put it like this, we've got a lot to talk about. so here it goes: Boss Man and I have been in a "thing" for a few months now. He is my rainbow of the moment if you know what I mean. ha ha ha. So we hang out and most of the time its me on him...literally. he does something to me that has not been moved since baby daddy. y'all know I don't even front when it comes to the way I feel about my little ones father. its just a damn shame it didn't last. but lets not go there. hmmm, what else can I say? I have something for him. is it love? hmmm, I don't know. Is it lust...definitely. am I going to tell you that my heart beats fast when I see him...I SURE AM. Can I tell you that I have sensations when I think of him...Of course, I keep it real and since I am the REALEST...I can and WILL go there. (taking a deep breath, 'cause I cant believe I'm actually saying this to you). Have I told him how I am feeling? Nah, I'm too much of a punk... Can you believe that? KJ is a punk! I've been examining my feelings because I don't want to confuse attraction for something else. Also, he's the type that won't tell me how he feels. He's got a brick wall up and it bothers me a lot. There is also an additional "factor" in our whatever you want to call it (fill in the blank) RELATIONSHIP and I can't go into what it is, but there is another element that was prior to me. Now...what could that be you may ask? I can't keep it THAT real with you guys...I really can't because its a "sensitive" issue. But just know...my time is my time and I'm cool with that. At this point I have to be honest...I'm just having fun. and you know my favorite saying, "no blood, no foul" and that's how I live my life. But to be quite honest with you...I may have to depart from the situation shortly because I am not getting what I want out of this. Meaning: He is not into me the way he should be. and since I have it going on - and that's not an "I'm all that" comment, its just factual. I'm not going to be "with" someone who can't be "with" me and since I don't ask for much, I think whatever I ask for should be given...**WHATEVER IT IS. and there is no way in hell I am going to compromise myself for a little fluttering of the heart. I like him, yeah I do, but if I don't see something soon, my ass it out. and I don't really know what that "something" is...all I know is at this point. I need him to show me he cares. (exhaling)...when I'm not with him, I miss him. when I don't speak to him, I'm thinking of him and the times we spend together are endless to me. Its like touching a rainbow...its beautiful, and pure but overwhelming all at once and I don't like to feel helpless...Love should not render you helpless...OH SNAP...DID I SAY LOVE? damn, I got it bad and that's about it. that's all about boss man, well not ALL, but enough to hold ya! ha ha ha. hopefully he will show me something soon. I'm gone. have a great day. kj.**

******BONUS ENTRY *** 09/21...U R NOT READY** OK, so I'm sitting here in front of the computer reading my entry of today and I'm saying to myself, "KJ, what in the world**

are you doing?" - We're talking about my "thing" with Boss Man. and for the life of me I cannot figure it out. I can't and I'm saying to myself, **"Kj...is this what YOU really want to do with yourself?"** and the answer I'm getting is "no" I don't want to be what I am right now in his life. and so I have to fix it. Shit! another one bites the dust, ya think? Nah...I just need to express myself and I haven't really been able to do that **because he's so HARSH**. LIKE HOW you ask? Like if I should I discontinue my end of this "thing" he wont be affected. and that bothers me. which makes no sense, because I sound so fucking needy and lost... YUCK! its like why should I continue to give myself to someone ...ANYONE for that matter who is really unOBTAINABLE? He is. Its like...what's the end result of this? **WHAT COULD THE END RESULT POSSIBLY BE?** Just fuck with me until he makes BIG decisions on his personal life? I don't think so and that's the way I'm feeling right now because when I went back and read my entry I sound like dumb ass school girl and lets face it...**34 is FAR from being a teen, now a TEN...that...I may be, but a TEEN, NOT AT ALL AND SO I HAVE TO STOP ACTING LIKE IT.** and besides...my husband once told me "Men do what they want" so if I'm something he "wants" then he will step up and act accordingly, if not...then thanks for KEEPING IT REAL, BUT I'M GONE. these two to three months is long enough to know if I am someone he misses at night. and check this out y'all. I don't ask for much. I'm EASY on him, but I have to keep it real with MYSELF. . . and I'm going to "Date" and that's it. See what's out there. But not like "that" with the sex part. THERE IS no S-E-X in DATE. That ain't gonna happen, but lets face it. I can't be out here with someone who obviously does not feel the same about me. and if he did / does, whatever word you want to use...he's not man enough to SHOW ME? what's up with that? Not good family, not good. I wonder....(putting my pointy finger on my temple and saying hmmm), what is it about ME where I ALWAYS fall fast for these kinds of men? Like is it that I am the one who truly does not wish to be in a relationship with someone on a serious level. MAYBE and how can I if I keep going down this same WACK ass road? **EXACTLY, I CAN'T! SO ITS DECISION TIME MY FRIENDS. IS THIS THE**

END OF BOSS MAN? I don't know. But I can tell you this...**I'm not going to continue to FRONT ON MYSELF.** maybe I'm just a past time to him until he figures out what he is going to do with his situation. That could be my role. which makes this all the more stupid on my part, just all the more stupid I tell ya. Like am I just here to wait around for that? (exhaling). Poor little ol kj, getting involved with someone who is really only involved in himself and above all and at this point UNOBTAINABLE.. here's the part where I'm accused of "cackling" (boss man's favorite terminology when I get long winded). ha ha. Oh. so back onto me...last night was my little ones back to school night. I saw her classroom and met her teacher and the other parents. the school is very nice. I'm Impressed and the only reason I'm Impressed is because its free. **NEVER BE IMPRESSED BY SOMETHING YOU ARE PAYING FOR...I learned that from Miss Vanessa, my old neighbor. when you are paying for something**...its not an Impress, its a standard, a mandatory, etc. you know what I mean. ok. so I went to that and I enjoyed my time with the other parents. if only they knew who I am. LOL. what else? well nothing. Tomorrow I will be taking it light. and returning a few calls. its time for me to give someone nice a chance. I can't keep preaching to you guys about living life and not settling if I'm doing EXACTLY the opposite (settling and not living my life to its full potential). and **If I don't stop this thing now, I may miss out on someone who is going to love me and miss me at night. so...I guess there's my answer. Keep Boss man, but don't stop my life. So its back to DATING HARD and making people EARN MY LOVE. PERIOD AND POINT BLANK. So today's assignment is: (drumroll please)....DON'T BE EASY! LET PEOPLE EARN YOUR LOVE, YOUR TRUST, YOUR FRIENDSHIP, ETC. THIS WAY THEY WILL RESPECT "IT" AND YOU. I'm your girl and I'm out. bonus entry over! Kali J-Moore**

What's up Y'all. Lets talk today. Its Thursday and I'm feeling some type of way. BM in my guest book is "Boss Man" he read the diary y'all. Oh my goodness. Well he

didn't quite get to the bonus entry. Thank goodness. But we did have a talk. I know he's feeling me. and that's what's up. but I changed the rules in the ninth inning and that is something that is NOT fair. I approached the "situation" all wrong and so I am trying to fix what I Implemented. "Sixty seconds is a long time if you REALLY want to get it IN" ha ha ha. I'm thinking out loud. I almost slept in after that. Boss Man ...(exhaling). I'm feeling him and he knows it. Its just that WE collectively know ONE OF US IS GOING TO BE HURT in the "end" whatever that means and whenever that happens. Ugh! don't you just hate that? I know I do. What else is going on? Nothing much. didn't go to Rascals last night because I didn't feel like being bothered with the show. and I wanted to try to be home to have some time with Boss Man and just express myself to him and try to allow him the opportunity to tell me what is on his mind. Its a damn shame though, because he thinks sharing emotions equals "vulnerability" (spell check that please) but it does not. It takes a STRONG man to do that. Share his emotions...that's sexy. Makes you wanna really do that thing you only do on Birthdays...if you know what I mean. ha ha. So today I am going to say to you, "DON'T SHY AWAY FROM YOUR EMOTIONS" you may be cheating yourself out of a wonderful experience. take it from me, I've done that many many times. What else is going on? **Nothing, just taking life one day at a time. "I'm tolerable"(as my dear friend Boss Man says). I wonder, when do you tell someone you love them? Just thinking and asking for direction. I mean, do you do it when you feel it or do you just say fuck it. He ain't gonna really be mine anyway...so why bother? Holla at your girl if you have the answer 973-342-1039 the hotline is up and running. I love you all. and don't shy away from your emotions. Be easy!**

Happy Friday everyone! How are you today? What's going on for the weekend? How was your week? Well mine was great. Started off a little rough on the job front, but for the most part, I'm learning...back doing t-1's and shit like that. Framing and line coding - its a telecommunications company and so things are good. I'm thinking of moving to hillside. that should go down any minute now. I think hillside would be best for me and the little one because its close to my job and out of the way of all things that bug the shit out of me. Oh so let me tell y'all what happened last night...DRAMA! so I get home. speak with one of my girlfriends and my other girlfriend - or so I thought was there. When I went to speak to her, she was yelling and cursing at me like an animal. I could not believe what I was hearing. When I approached her to shut the f up, she became more hostile and at that point, I, **your girl KJ ...LOST IT! THAT'S RIGHT FOLKS. I LOST MY MIND.** I called her all kinds of crack head drug addicts and this is a woman old enough to be my mother...she's like 59 and I dated her son for a minute. then the other friend...I just lost it with her as well because the both of them separate are their own mess - individually, so collectively... **YOU KNOW HOW ITS GOING DOWN. Ok. so between the pills: Oxycontin, Xanax, Percacet (spell check) and the weed and the coke and the drinking...I'm dealing with Junkies.** Like when I was out there (read my book, **"when gucci came first"),** I had a drug of choice...COCAINE. I was a "sniffer" didn't smoke it, didn't shoot up, never smoked weed, I didn't do all those things. and that's not to diminish my "offenses" this is just to say, damn...**DON'T DO EVERYTHING!** (taking a deep breath)... that's just being a glut for punishment and it causes havoc (spell check) on your body. Like what is going on. So at any rate. the person who witness this go down was upset. **These are two women of whom I have lent money to, purchased clothing for, given things to. Furniture, etc. you name it and they get down like that. and I told them both...when they come down off that shit...DO NOT CALL ME BECAUSE I AM NOT GOING TO WANT TO HEAR IT** . and rest assure fam...I got a total of **SEVEN,** count em **1,2,3,4,5,6,7 fucking calls and every last one of them began with an apology...**WELL I'M NOT SYMPATHETIC. and I cant wait to move. leave these bitches right where they are **and I have to stop thinking that since God has brought me through so much that I owe the world my soul. I am NOT SUPER SAVE-A-HO.** I'm going back to my **"don't bring your problems to me, take 'em to the Jesus"** 'cause he's the only one who can help these beeyaches anyway. and the saying is **"God bless the child who has his OWN"** Get your own beeyaches!

Please 'cause right now I don't have anymore time to deal with this. I have given bday parties for these beeyaches, fully equipped with champagne and my famous henny cake (on the order of a rum cake, but sub the rum with Hennessey) Its yummy and the cake has to be rocky road. 'cause its something about the chocolate and nuts that compliments the Hennessey. Ok but that was my night. I was so upset, I cried to one of their sons, who told me to leave his mother alone. don't deal with her anymore. she's too far gone and that's that. I have gotten all the apologies, but I refuse to entertain the dumb shit. I can't wait to move. what else is going on? Nothing its Friday. I have a date tomorrow and I'm going to see a few apartments. **I will keep you posted and before you ask, my little one is doing just fine. have a great weekend. and please whatever you do, DON'T BE A SUPER SAVE-A-HO. Some people you can't save with kindness and gifts. It's all we can do as humans to SAVE OURSELVES. don't get caught up in believing or thinking that you have to save the world because of your own past transgressions. Just live your life to the best of your abilities and keep God first. This weekend...lets all go to Church. At 9:30am on Sunday I want all of you to pray with me. lets pray for each other. Ask God to protect our comings and goings and just keep us grounded in his word. Love ya! Your girl Kali J Moore**

Hey you guys!!!! Today is Saturday and its a lovely day out to say the very least. God woke us up this morning and so we should have a great day because to experience another day is GREAT in itself...HOLLA IF YA HEAR ME. Ok. so today I am going to get my mani / pedi combo and my little one is getting her hair done and all that stuff as well. Tomorrow is her fathers birthday and SHE will NOT be calling his ass. Hey it is what it is and so please don't say shit to me about it. Two wrongs may not make it right, but it damn sure makes it even. ha ha ha. What else is going on? I found a place to move and so I'm doing that this weekend. trying to get things out and done rather quickly. I have a post office box and that's where ALL my mail will go from here on out, including those wack ass child support checks. I am not going to divulge my whereabouts, but I will give you one clue: It ain't no where close to where I am now. Thank goodness. Having my cell phone number changed and the home number is being changed as well. Its just a new beginning with my new place and my NICE job. What else is going on? Nothing...Boss Man and I are having a midnight rendezvous (spell check that)...Its going to be nice. We have a lot of ground to cover and I have some things to show him. Oh...that reminds me...My newspaper is going to be off the ground finally...and my cover artist is working on some stuff for me as we speak for the next few books. getting all that out of the way so I can do my thang. Well I got a good nights sleep and right now I'm keeping the mindset like fuck every body (FEB 108&Madison). That's how we got down back in the day when water was free. Ok. so I'm outta here, I have to drop off something to boss man, I have to get to the salon, I have to wash clothes, I have to get the boxes from Hertz and I have to finish reading a book on telecommunications. So I'm swamped. Oh and I have to food shop and prep something nice for dinner tomorrow - after Church. and I have to cook for my little one and Boss Man. So you see folks. . . its a bit hectic, but all in a days work. Oh...before I forget, I saw one of the old beeyaches I was telling y'all about the other day. I saw her last night and she had the nerve to speak. I didn't even look her in the face. I said hello and kept it moving. **So today is here, WE are here and so lets be happy today. Take advantage of your life...DO SOMETHING WITH IT. Lets pray for our sisters and brothers getting hit with another storm.** They need our prayers and if you want to send something you can send it to **kalico jones c/o Universe Multi-Services 310 orange road, Montclair, nj 07042** - we - **my online networking group <u>thekalicojonesproject@yahoogroups.com</u> are sending things down there. We have a direct connect to a few Churches in Louisiana and we know for a FACT its going to get right to the people.** So if you want to join in on that, send whatever you can. NO CHECKS, NO CASH, NOTHING LIKE THAT, JUST Send clothing. We're doing a clothing drive so don't send food or money. and if you want to promote your book, event, business, or whatever, feel free to go online and join our group again its called: **<u>thekalicojonesproject@yahoogroups.com</u> we've been around for two years now and its going great.**

You get daily updates on things that are going on. its an African American business resource group and so if you have things you want to share, promote, if you need advise, there is someone in the group who can and WILL help you. and you can get tickets for the Ebony fashion show, its just a whole bunch of stuff and membership has its privileges. So that's about it. its almost noon and I have to get myself together. Enjoy your day and remember those less fortunate. OHHHHH BEFORE I FORGET...KENYA...THANK YOU FOR LEAVING SUCH A BEAUTIFUL MESSAGE FOR ME. BUT YOU DIDNT LEAVE YOUR NUMBER AND THAT'S OK. I WOULD HAVE CALLED TO THANK YOU PERSONALLY. I listened to it again this morning...So thanks for the kind words. I love you, you love me and if God is for US, then who can be against us? EXACTLY NO ONE. I'm gone...your girl, KJ. peace.

Just another Manic Monday...What's up Family? Its me, the ONE and only kj coming to you on this rainy afternoon in September (26th). So lets get right to it. Yesterday was Homeboy's Bday = my little one's father and before you EVEN think about going there...NO I DID NOT HAVE HER CALL. Shit, she didn't even ask and she knew. So the way I look at it...Yesterday his bday, next month Halloween, then thanksgiving and Christmas and by the time new years rolls around, I should be good and rid of his ass being on my mind and hers by then. and besides...he DIDNT call her on HER bday or graduation, or Christmas, or ....etc. so please ...I am NOT the bad guy in this and if you think I am screw U ! Now what? and don't think that means I don't love you...that just means I don't care if you disagree with me on that (how's that for keeping it REAL) What else is going on? Nuttin much, me and Boss Man had a nice Sunday afternoon ... can you say TERRIFIC? (his words not mine y'all) your girl holds it DOWN. ha ha ha. Ok so I cooked yesterday and had to cook twice because my little one wanted something else after I completed her first request for King Whiting fish, mashed potatoes and veggies. Then it was Beef Stew and Spanish rice (yellow with olives, and peppers. she loves it. Ok.

so I have decided to get this weave out of my hair today. I am going to get a pony tail because my face is all broke out. and I can't understand why and I have this thing in my chest going on. The acid reflux is bothering me daily now and my eating habits are not helping (plus the newports, plus the champagne at night). So ...my friend tells me to stop the madness or ELSE. she is what I would like to call my "therapist" but she doesn't charge. ha ha ha. We talked about everything and I have to do a little bit better than what I am doing now with respects to just allowing certain things to occur in my life. Well I just wanted to give you a quick shout. I have to get ready to go I have a friend coming to pick me up and I have lots of things to do before I go to bed tonight. ONE being this damn hair. I look like a frizz ball...and that ain't what's up. So I haven't called Boss Man today and its almost five...there must be a miracle in there somewhere and you know what...He AIN'T called me so I guess Terrific...It may not have been. **Oh well and so what...I know what I have in ME with regards to a deadline and what I have chosen to remain silent on and so lets see what happens. At any rate, I have places to look at today and so I have to get ready to get out of here. Holla at your girl... kj. 973-342-1039 over and Out...OH... today's assignment: Lets read Jeremiah chapt. 23 (the BIBLE) Ugh, I hope I didn't have to tell you that.... UGH! Lets read that. and I Hope you guys prayed with me yesterday morning at 930. have a nice evening.**

Hello my friends, its Tuesday and I'm feeling some type of way... I have to get this off my mind family and since I have no one to turn to at this point...I have to turn to you. Its about Boss Man...Yeah, I know, I know...why am I so concerned about someone who is unOBTAINABLE, right? (taking a deep breath). but really, I am worried. He's been ok with me lately but there is something going on with him. Something I wish I could help him get beyond, but I don't think I can. Its definitely something he has to get through / over / beyond on his own. I just hope he is ok. what else is going on? Well nothing. I'm getting ready to get some "work" done to myself. Trying to move and just set myself up for what is to come. I'm feeling like I'm doing something right and I don't know what it is. Oh...the weave is cut short, not out and it looks better. I think I may keep it in for a little while. My bday is approaching - Oct. 10th and I STILL have yet to get the party situation under control. I have to move and there are so many little things I have to attend to. but I'm thinking...I have to wait until after Thursday to get some things jumped off. I have a friend who is going to take me to the furniture place on route 46, I'm going to trick out the entire new place. found a place in Bloomfield that sells the kind of furniture I want in my living room. You know that very Italian princess shit w/ gold crests in the fabric, camel back and wood carvings sofas with footstools and human size replicas of Greek Goddesses and Globes and shit... that's my taste . lol. I like stuff like that. Very Tony Montana...scarface-ish...So what's up with y'all today? how are things with you? I hope your day is going well. I'm leaving this at 11am and so I'm already pumped for today. My plan is to go home and cook. spend some time with my little one and possibly see if I get a visit from the man of the moment...lol. Nah, he may be the "one" I gave him something I haven't given anyone in a long time. since my daughters father...I'll let you guess. at any rate. I had a nice time giving it to him. But I don't think he noticed. Hmmm, he laughed about it yesterday when I told him. so did my girl in cali, Hannunah...who will be visiting me for my bday. You know my girls come every year for me. We have a great time. Oh...I did miss Britt's bday - my friend Yolanda from Atlanta by way of Texas. I just can't find her number and so I didn't call. Britt is 18 and just a sweet young lady.. I miss her and her mother. even though me and Yolanda had a big argument before she went back to atl. I have to try to find her email addy. **Ok well that's about it for me today. Just try to be nice to someone. you never know how your kind words will make them feel. that could be a turning point for them. Lets make it a habit to extend kindness to others. I love you...You love me, and WE love others. In the Bible it makes mention of "how can you love me , for whom you cannot see, and not love your brethren of whom you see every day" its something like that. So lets continue to love God and Respect Him by loving ourselves and our brothers and sisters. Y'all** be   easy   out   there.   **Kali**

SEPTEMBER 28, Is it hump day already? Damn the weeks are going fast aren't they? (SINGING) Ah do it baby, do tha humpty hump, just doing tha humpty hump...What's up "peep" le its me, the woman behind the madness, your girl Kali....WUZZZZUP? How are things? (taking a deep breath)...the deep breath right off the top means I have some things to say...So I've learned over the past 18 hours that with Life and love specifically, you can't compromise your standards. You just can't. Now compromising standards is TOTALLY different from COMPROMISING little things because they don't matter like: Not putting the top on the toothpaste or not drying the dishes right after you're done washing them...those things...are things that don't breach our standards (hopefully or else your just plain ol f'ing ANAL)...lol. but if there are things about a person, place or situation that you feel your participation goes against your personal standards (which means they go far beyond leaving the cap off the toothpaste and drying dishes), got it? good. Well that's where I am right now, just trying to figure out when I am going to say "enough is enough" and move on. I would have to do this in effort to keep the love for THYSELF FIRST, and the love for him second. Now when I say love for "him" I don't mean in a way where Oh I'm so in love blah blah blah...I mean it in a learning love type of way. learning to love someone. learning to be there for someone other than myself and my daughter, sharing space, sharing laughter, and yes...sharing LOVE. but what is the true definition of love: Remember I spoke of this before...It went something like this: **TAKEN FROM JUNE 29TH 2005:**
What's love to me? I'll tell you what I tell Hubby, "Love has NO boundaries" There are no walls nor a definitive description of what LOVE encompasses because there are different degrees of love based on situations. The love for my daughter, "The highest level of emotion where wrong and negativity cease to exist, pure purity" The love for my daughters father, "An interdependent bond that derives from forever coexisting mentally and physically (because we have a child together)" The love for my husband,

"Unbreakable, because we have watched each other grow and have been there throughout all the phases of each others lives and have YET to skip a beat. Respectful in the choices that we make, keeping in mind the effects today may have on tomorrow, a fortress of peace, covered and protected." Jump off love? Ha ha ha. "Love for a 'nut' lust for a while, but once you get 'it', 'its' gone." 'Cause we all know that anything that comes forth from a jump start usually needs a new battery after a while TRANSLATION:REPLACEMENT AKA REPLACEABLE. AND NOT WORTH THE EMOTIONAL INVESTMENT. Same Sex Love: (y'all know I had to go there) Same Sex Love, while I don't believe in waking up and going to sleep with a woman, I can understand and have "played in the park" a time or two...or three...(ok, ok you got me...more times that I would like to share) and I believe there can be love between "lovers" of the same sex, but for me...The love is more of a "friendship" not an in-love, not a "I need to see you right now" love, there can be none of that because I still subscribe to the basic principle of life: BE HAPPY and going "there" full force is not my definition of the basic principle of life with respects to MY LIFE...so respect it. o.K. SO there went my quote with respects to love and just how I feel in general about love and lust for that matter as well. Lets revisit that...WHAT'S YOUR DEFINITION OF LOVE? AND LETS TAKE IT A STEP FURTHER...WHAT WAS YOUR DEFINING MOMENT OF LOVE WITH RESPECTS TO YOUR MATE? Like...when did you know for sure, you were not only in love but really LOVED the person you are with? Holla at me if you wanna talk. Your girl Kj I'm gone!

Its Thursday and I'm feeling some type of way...So let me make myself absolutely, positively, 100 PERCENT CLEAR...I AM NOT GAY! I am tired of getting these dumb ass emails about me possibly being into women. Well let me set the record straight (no pun intended) once and for ALL. I have played in that park a few times and so therefore I would think I would know if I were into women. Please stop sending me emails asking to "take me out" that ain't happening. **Are you NOT reading my diary? I said, I cannot see myself waking up and going to sleep with another woman.** Its not going to happen, just ask all the men I've jayed over the years. Now don't get me wrong…Women are beautiful creatures and I enjoy seeing my sisters all dolled up and handling their business, but that's does not TRANSLATE into sexual attraction. Listen…the ONLY times I have done ANYTHING with a woman I WAS DRUNK OR HIGH. So please stop it. I am tired of having to screen through my emails because of these types of dumb ass questions. Don't I give you enough in this…MY PERSON DIARY? I'm sure I do. Also, let me set the record straight on another thing because I feel its time for me to share something with the people who read this **who THINK THEY FUCKING KNOW ME**…Ok so you THINK you know someone I slept with? Bring it on! I'm sick and tired of people asking me if I know someone, like I screwed them or something. Case in point: I called Boss Man this morning to ask him about an apt. He had the nerve to say, "don't you know (blah blah)? I think he lives over there, call him." **WHAT THE FUCK DID HE JUST INSINUATE?** I'm like, I don't know that dude like that. I've only seen him in bars and shit. And like last night I saw him out front (of where I live and is the reason why I want to move outta that area)…Ok. So he asked me again, like he knows I can reach out to this joker…WHY? AND AGAIN…I stated, "I don't know him like that" and then we ended the conversation with him saying something to the effect like, "well you won't see me if you move over there" **DON'T TEMPT ME! I'm** moving where I want to move and I'm not worried about the personal feelings of **ANYONE AROUND ME** anymore 'cause they ain't helping me pay my fucking rent / mortgage, etc. So whatever and so what! How dare he. You know **everyday something ELSE happens to make my transgressions CLEAR TO ME!** EVERY DAY I TELL YOU, EVERY DAY. Ok. . . so now I'm going to take the place SITE UNSEEN. **YOU KNOW WHAT THAT MEANS?** It means I take the place since I'm down to the wire, and I deal with it for one year or until I find another place, period end of story. **And TO HELL WITH WHOMEVER does not like the movement because I personally can't** continue to base my life decisions on the feelings / perceptions and opinions of others who are unobtainable, unreasonable, uninvolved and quite frankly NOT PAYING ONE OF THESE DAMN BILLS ON MY ASS. Hell, I can't even get a ride to work! So...let me call the realtor on this...HOLD ON...CALLING NOW. . . shit...no answer. Hold on let me call my girl ruby and find out where this place is. Ok. She's saying its ok. But now here come yet another f'ing obstacle...I need proof of income! UGH...who has that? I'm an author / personality / where am I going to get that from? These people don't want to hear that I can't show them this in the manner in which they need. **WHAT A F'ING HEADACHE**. This is what I'm telling you. Its always something, always and when its not something...**ITS SOMETHING ELSE.** LOL. BUT TRUE. Ok. So I just have to wait a minute and see what happens with this other thing. At any rate, I'll be fine 'cause I just put in a call to North Carolina and if I feel it, I'm out. Its just a simple as that. **I gotta start taking all these "things" as "hints" to get my black ass out of dodge. ha ha ha. 'cause really everything I'm involved in is transmitted electronically - fax, internet, etc. and so I can pretty much bounce out to anywhere. (deep breath)...So family...lets wait and see what happens on the court date - Tuesday and I will get back to you as to what I am going to do. No more calling people about houses and apts. that's over. I'm just going to wait and see on Tuesday what a go on (Jamaican accent) and go from there. I gotta go now, calling car service for my daughter...she is coming to meet me - taking her to toys r us on a shopping spree and then to chuck e cheeses. I'll holla. tonight...take care of YOU. don't let the shit that is going to be here tomorrow fuck with your mental. take care! and read   the   Bible.**

Tuesday October 4th and damn how does time fly? So what's up Guys? Sorry I haven't reached out to you in a while, but things are ...well...HECTIC. I've been all over the dag on place, doing so much in little time. So I've been shopping like a mad woman = feeling down...My bday is Monday the 10th and I've decided NO PARTY! If I have something, it will be

in North Carolina. That's all I'm saying for now. (taking a deep breath)...so I just got off the phone with my crew: mother, ruby, and Mr. big and we've collectively decided that I have to regain my focus. Oh...that reminds me...where in the world is my invoice from Candace? I have to reach out to her again and just remind her to send it to me. Erica...HOW ARE YOU? and your family? I knew there was someone else I knew in Louisiana...I hope you are ok. and you never did send me the list of bookstores. Call me and leave your number: 973-783-0720. (shit I just left my HOME number) ooops. Ok. so Last week, PSEG cut off my electricity. I was supposed to be out of the place by the 15th and I am NOT. so they came there and turned the shit off. I got a call from the Nanny stating the house was dark. I had to leave work early and get that handled. and they didn't cut the shit back on until Friday - **RIGHT AFTER I LEFT FOR WORK**. where was my little one? with her grandmother...don't be stupid...of COURSE I wouldn't let her stay with me in the dark.... Oh and before I forget...the Beeyach over at PSEG who I had to speak with to resolve the issue was a hot fucking mess. She was rude, she was abrasive ...**but ...SHE WAS OVER THE PHONE**... thank goodness, 'cause I would have "checked" (punching my left fist into my right hand) her ass. **It must feel oh so nice to be a "telephone gangster" that way...YOU KEEP ALL YOUR TEETH.** HA HA HA . I even asked her like why are you so rude? and she was like, miss, you're asking me questions I cannot answer...I'm like and you need to be rude? may I have a supervisor? NO...but my direct extension is #### if you don't like it. I'm like it must be nice to give an **EXTENSION** and NOT an **address**...and then I told her to look both ways before she crossed the street. and so that's our lesson for the day: **LOOK BOTH WAYS BEFORE YOU CROSS THE STREET. NOW YOU CAN APPLY THAT TO ANYTHING. because you never know which way your shit will come back to haunt that ass.** Now take this beeyach from pseg for instance... She doesn't know me from Adam (and by the way...who is Adam...if you know, holla at your girl)...Ok. so this heffa don't know me from Adam... and she's steadfast on being a telephone gangster and that's cool, but now let me catch her in the street...and then what? **EXACTLY... NOTHING.** She probably won't even remember the conversation. **That's why its Important for us NOT to play in the street...'cause you don't want to end up getting your ass hit. YA FEEL ME?** Damn I miss **V.R.J.** (vacation relations jump off) ...thinking aloud...Its not a miss like I have to see him, he just crossed my mind that very second...I will give him a holla one day... Ok so now back to playing in the street...DON'T...so that's the first thing I want to say today... next...So that was Thursday...**and then today was COURT AGAIN...UGH...Its like. DAMN, GIVE ME A BREAK.** So I go to court and just like when the girl took me for "whatever" "cause I chew strawberry bubble gum" the PLANTIFF didn't show... **BOTH CASES CIVIL AND THE OTHER...dismissed...yeah I had to cases on the same day..in the same building, just different floors...and so I'm not feeling NEWARK right now, lol..** So again I guess I will have to play the wait by the mailbox for the NEXT summons game. which is bullshit if you ask me. But again...whatever. Ok...so now its time to talk about what I did over the weekend...SHOPPED...that's its. I spent a lot of money. Purchased a pair of Rocket Dog sneakers w/ the bling. Brought some jewelry. My daughter Ralph Lauren sneakers and Hilfiger school shoes. I Purchased a new weave of which I am taking out as we speak. getting a short hair cut and my eyebrows done and I'm going to keep it moving for a minute. don't want to be bothered with the longness for awhile and besides...its not the style I wanted and so I am having it removed. What else, just a lot of different stuff to try to make me feel better, which did not work. so its like, what's it all for in the end if it doesn't mean shit? I know you feel me on that one. Ok. Oh and before I forget...an old acquaintance (sp?) has a hair salon. Me and this young lady (Tina) grew up in the same projects in Mt. Vernon...and as I was getting my hair done, flipping through the pages of a magazine, I saw her name and a midtown Manhattan address and I called and sure enough...it was her...I just congratulated her and wished her well, she did the same for me. That was nice. I'm happy for her and its truly a great feeling when you see people rise up out of whatever they thought their situation was growing up...if you know what I mean because we all think our stuff was the absolute worse of it all and then when you look back...you see that it wasn't AS bad...unless you are me, then you think...**WHERE IN THE FUCK WAS MY FAMILY?** Oh well and I'm not going to talk about that either. Waste of typing energy...I just don't have time...So today I am going to take it light. do some laundry...get my hair done and just be a mom. I am going to pray. **Thank God for today and just ask him for his continued love and protection. I miss my husband**. I'm going to see him soon, thank goodness. its just been uphill with the communication. either I'm not home, or he can't call, or he calls but I'm sleep and don't get the call...just stuff like that. But my bday is coming and so I know I can expect some "bling" last year I wanted a CAR ---- oh that was Valentine's day or was that Mothers day...I think it was mothers day...but at any rate, I have to move first and then get the whip and so that's the order of operations in the Jones household. **So on that note, I will say, " I love you & I'm praying for you and IF YOU ARE HAPPY FOR YOURSELF, THEN I AM HAPPY FOR YOU TOO!" lets give GOD some personal time today and if you are feeling a little down, for whatever reason, just know to look to Jesus because in HIM lies our strength to proceed...LETS LOVE OURSELVES AND EACHOTHER AND LEAN BACK AND LET GOD MAKE OUR ENEMIES OUR FOOTSTOOL. Your girl, KJ....over and OUT...CASE DISMISSED! I'm gone!**

Its Thursday, October 6th - dag, yesterday was my sister Lisa's 40th bday - I think - maybe she's 39...I don't know, but I do know she is up there. lol. (taking a deep breath)...so I'm moving Y'all...and I can't tell you where. The only thing I can say is if you want to see me...you better holla at your girl 'cause I'm out and I ain't leaving a forwarding address. what else is going on? Well just like I told you...I was playing the "wait by the mailbox for the next court summons" game, low and mother fucking behold...yesterday I check the box and sure enough...there's a motion by the plaintiff to have the dismissal vacated and the case reinstated. I have ten days to get a rebuttal on file. I'm waiting until the 8th day and then I'm going to send a letter stating my claim's. Ah...the beauty of it all...what can I tell you. People are a mess. Oh I don't like the job anymore.

That's another reason why I've decided to do what I am doing. I don't know family, its just like its not meant for me to have to deal with people on a regular basis. Like...they get on my nerves really quick. I don't know. **Oh I called VRJ and he's pissed with me. I suppose I should have called him with some regularity...Oh well.** I ended the conversation with a hang up. I just didn't feel like listening at that point. and speaking of listening...don't you know the phones are tapped at my job? they sure are. and today I gave them something to listen to...I returned a call to an employment agency. I'm sure they won't like that. That's how the other guy was let go...They heard him talking about going to another company and BAM...they got him out before he could leave. I guess that's the nature of the game. **MOVE IN SILENCE.** like that call I just made, I could have made later on from home or from my cell, but really...when its over...its over and since I've made a BIG decision and its the final ANSWER...It makes no sense for me to make anyone think I'm sprouting roots. I took my daughters photo down. and so you know what that means. I'm sure they noticed . Its such a shame when you are so paranoid that you feel as though you have to monitor EVERYTHING. I don't ever want to be like that. (exhaling)...At any rate, it is what it is...Oh I have to get my camera from T...I will go over there today. That's a must do, 'cause I have a lot of photos on the disk and I need it. its been there for almost two months. I will do that today, this evening. **What else is going on? well nothing. Just living life. and trying to do what I have to do. I hope you are doing the same and WELL for that matter. Take care of YOU! I'm gone...today's assignment: MAKE A FINAL DECISION. Make your mind up regarding that one "thing" you keep flip flopping on and STICK WITH IT. That's my time family...my bday is Monday and so I'm just doing some early CLEANSING of the spirit if you know what I mean...You know, it doesn't have to be NEW YEARS to make a resolution.**   kj.   423-200-0261.

Freaky Friday and I'm feeling "the same" so what's good Fam? Its me the one and only Kali J Moore checking in with ya on this dreary Friday October 7th. Ok so lets get right to

it. **This morning I get on the bus…and about ten minutes from my "stop" (yes, kj takes nj transit and WHAT?) …Ok so about ten minutes before I am to remove myself from the bus, this man gets on…Older black man, you could see time all in his face, he was a little hunched over, and almost fragile looking, neatly dressed and you can tell back in his day…he was " a looker" – well just as you begin to think the bumpy ride is getting to him, his voice resonates like a trumpet beyond the tone of the passengers,** *"Let's thank God for waking us up this morning and ask him for his protection as we go on our way…."* **And he goes on like this praying and just prayerful if I may say so myself. I had a lump in my throat. It made me emotional. It really did. I was thanking Jesus in my mind and I'm sure I was not the only one.** People were looking at each other and smiling and just being "silently nice" to each other. Its like we were praying and just being thankful to God for His Grace and Mercy. It was a surreal experience. One I did enjoy. And the man on the bus…I prayed for him as well. I hope he knows his words are not falling on deaf ears and his efforts are appreciated. His prayer / sermon…**VERY MUCH NEEDED THIS MORNING. May God Bless Him.** What's up with me? Ok. So today is picture day at my little ones school and of course I forgot to send the money. So …she will take her individual photo on "retake" day…yeah, they have a photo retake day y'all. So that's good and she still got to be in the class photo…thank goodness or else I would have been very upset and just felt terrible about forgetting. Today I found out what was going on at work and I cannot tell you how disappointed I am in one of my coworkers. It's a damn shame, but nevertheless, I go on. So my bday party is tomorrow and I may do a no show IF I get my way…Ooops did I say that? Well it is what it is…it's that I have asked for something special and I think my husband is going to make sure I get it so I may be tied up. I will be there though, but I will have to leave early or come late. At any rate, I will see you if you are one of those who have obtained a spot on the guest list. I think we're going to have about 200 people which is fine by me. Its easier for me to mingle that way. Ok. So what else is going on? Nothing, just working and I have some things to do today. I will chat with you tomorrow. I have to get my house in order, do laundry and food shop and do all that kind of stuff. I was going to send for my little one and her friend for an evening of bowling today, but its going to rain, and Monday she has off and so I am going to wait until then and have her come up here to my place of work and take her bowling and then home. I also have to wash her hair (its long and curly and so I get the "mommy stop its too tangled"). **She has hair like the people from the other side, which is good hair, don't get me wrong...I AM NOT COMPLAINING. Ok. So child support on hold? Ugh...give me a break already. I just thought of that because I made mention of the OTHER SIDE and it popped in my mind. Ok SO I'm training right now, I'm in a class so I have to go. Technical stuff. See you later....Have a great day...Let's take the time out to Thank God for His time because without His time, WE would not be here. I'll chat with you later. Your girl KJ over and OUT! Be easy out there   ya   hear!**

Hey Hey Hey...its Kali J! on the check in and its raining like crazy outside today. I have on a spot TV sweat hood and a pair of babyphat sweats with old ass Reeboks. Reebok classics too...You which ones I'm talking about...the 54.11's... and I love them! Me and Alicia Keys...we're gonna bring those back. At any rate, I have them on and I LOVE them. Aren't they the most comfortable sneakers you've every worn? Damn straight they are. So its Saturday and I'm getting ready to get the night jumped off. Have to put myself together and that's pretty easy. I have to squeeze into the pants. I actually planned to wear these to Shaker Williams bday party at the Guitar Bar in Newark last month, but I fell asleep before my ride came. So I'm recycling the outfit...**SHUT UP..NO ONE SAW ME IN IT!** I didn't even get out of the house. So that's what I am wearing. I just wanted to check in right quick..have to call my man Haji (author of Black Moon)...check him out. He's really an unsigned "HYPE" - great writer. Ok. so I've been up since about 5 and I'm sure I won't get to bed until about five am. (taking a deep breath). . . Damn, I'm going to have some kind of sleep depravation come Monday...Oh well. So what's up with me? Just chillin', trying to make a dollar out of fifteen cents, still coming up short. **People just don't treat me like I treat them I tell ya family. Like I'm just sitting back waiting to see how things are going to develop over the next three weeks. that's it. just waiting to see. Well Let me run, this was suppose to be short and sweet. Have wonderful evening and please don't forget to pray!   Be   Easy   Babe!   KJ.**

10/10 - Its my party and I'll cry if I want to…cry if I want to…cry if I want to…You would cry too if it happened to you…Well I'm upset today. Got news that One of my friends was shot last night and brain dead, he's expected to pass away sometime today. He's in my book. My homey… TWO – FIVE…I can't believe it. So its back to my hometown of Mt. Vernon, NY for the funeral. This morning I read Deuteromy (sp?) chapter 22 I believe. Its talking about cleansing yourself every seven years. That every seven years you should forgive people and move on. Its bugged out how I find scriptures that speak directly to me at the moment in which I need them to talk to me. I just flip open The Bible and wherever it opens is where I start reading. I have to say a prayer for my friend …affectionately referred to as "FIVE TWO" in my book. (I flipped his name around to keep him in the 'cut') Damn, I'm going to miss him. We had good times TWO FIVE and I…I'm sure women across the globe are crying today. Such a damn shame. Such a shame. God Bless his children. What else is going on? Nothing. I will be at Nicole's Place today on Bloomfield Avenue in Bloomfield for a little champagne and cake. With my daughter and close friends. **I want to say Happy Birthday to all the October babies. I wish you Gods Speed and just everyone in general. "May God grant you everything you ask for during   your   quiet   time   with   Him."   Kj.**

"R.I.P. Two Five, sleep easy my friend... I'll miss you." This is so   hurtful.

10/11 - To bounce or not to bounce, that is the question. What's good family? just wanted to check in right quick. I'm doing some stuff and so I can't stay and chat. Just read the

Bible and try to be motivated about something in your life. Be happy for yourself and to everyone who has sent bday wishes my way...THANK YOU. Today I am going to clean my apt and finish packing and take it light. Oh...Boss Man is coming through today so that should be interesting...hmmmm, you know I will tell y'all what happened tomorrow. **Stay sweet! KJ. To my people in Money Earnin' Mt. Vernon, "Keep your head up!" Let's stay strong. R.I.P. Two Five...Damn life is crazy.**

10/12 - and its Hump Day y'all and payday for ME! which don't really mean shit cause I have so many things to do and unfortunately bills to pay...(taking a deep breath AND exhaling)...so its still raining in Jersey and I guess its kind of symbolic with respects to how things have been for just about everyone I know lately...But hey...At least WE're HERE to fight another fight... and dream another dream. So...Lets talk about how you can be successful at your place of employment. **there are THREE (3) things you can do that won't fail you with respects to evolving at your place of work...ONE = CARE, TWO=SHOW UP, and THREE=APPLY YOURSELF.** If we do these three simple things we will be noticed and the promotions and advances that had once escaped us will no longer be. We will begin to be not only be recognized but **COMMENDED AND SUBSEQUENTLY COMPENSATED** accordingly. let's stop blaming others for our lack of's...**Lets be Man/Woman enough to take our Boo's just as we stand to take our Applause. Ok well that's all I have to say for today. later...Kalico Jones**

10/14 - THE BIRTHDAY PART DUECE...So what's good y'all? Its me your girl on the check in and damn if it ain't still raining here in jersey. So I had another bday party at Nicole's place in Bloomfield on Wednesday and it was nice. Cake, presents, dinner and close family and friends. My daughter got me a fur pocket book and I have to tell you, its nice. I asked her where she got the money from to buy it and she was like, "they just gave it to me mommy." I would assume so with the amount of money we spend there. ALL

my gifts were HANDBAGS...What's up with that? Handbags and jewelry. that's nuts. At any rate, I had a wonderful time. Oh...and two bottles of champagne. of which we drank ...plus the another and then two bottles of wine. Can you say tipsy? to say the very least I think. So that was nice and then I brought my daughter into the office yesterday and she had a blast, very well behaved. and now today she will be visiting me once again. I have to take her bowling and so there it is...she's coming to bowl and then we will go to chuck e cheese and then toys r us and then home. I have a funeral in the morning and then I have to come all the way back to jersey and then go back to the Bronx - for **part TRES of the Bday celebration** at my brother Charlie's house...he goes all OUT for shit like this. Nice Cigars, Cognac, you name it...its how he does it when he does it like he do...if ya know what I mean. Me and boss man may have to put things on freeze, damn I just thought about it. I have to fix that right away. Oh...maybe not..I think my time out is going to be "late night" if you know what I mean. So my child support checks (affectionately referred to as "CSC's") have not been on time, but I'm told homeboy has made a substantial payment...YIPPEEEE!!! Ok and the Only reason why I am kicking that to you is because I have to keep it real. I tell you the bad, so its only right I tell you the good as well. So I'm thinking I have to reach out to Boss Man and let him know we have to coordinate times because that's Important and I'm spending time with someone during the day, a close friend and I'm not saying who because WE collectively decided that the "diary" is no place for this person. and people keep trying to figure out who is who and that's just too close for comfort...so no...I'm NOT giving up the name on that one. Oh...so I have the cover concept that is going to fuck da game up! yes, my daughter gave it to me yesterday and I am sending it off to my girl Candace to get the ball rolling on it. its nice. I'm thinking of using my little one on the cover of 4miles to freedom, I have to see how I feel about putting her face 'out there'. -...what else is going on? nothing. have to plan Thanksgiving...going south. have to see how that is going to fit in with all that's going on. Also, my cousin is having a baby...yes, she's a little young, but that's ok. she'll be fine I'm sure. her shower is Sunday in the Bronx as well Oh and I have to get my hair done and I have to do laundry and I must purchase something for my night with Boss Man. damn that's a lot of stuff. and did I tell you I need to try to find a car AND a place to live all over the weekend? damn right...so I'm going to do hair tonight and get all that done and out of the way. and purchase my little sum thin' sum thin for boss man for tomorrow - hopefully if I get back around in time...oh...no...there's a place across from me I can go to. got it...that's taken care of...I'm good. Ok so enough about me. What's up with YOU? how are things with you? How is your family? I hope fine. **You know when God steps in, people tend to step off!** So if you are living right and find that in your quest to better yourself, you lose "friends" along the way...don't get upset about it...just think to yourself that God did not make enough room in your life going forward for that person and GET over it! **We must understand that some people are not going to be in our lives forever...some are just around to get us to the next level in life and in order for us to get to the next level we have to LEARN from each of our experiences so we can evolve. . . its only right. its all part of my "live and let live" philosophy...as we can only live for ourselves and NO one, no matter how much they profess to LOVE your ass is going to "take the weight" for you on Judgment day. So be happy, love each other and don't forget to pray! later Kali J Moore. Be easy babe!**

10/17 - Just another manic Monday...what's good Family? Its your girl kj on the check in this fine Monday afternoon. I'm looking out of my office window and its a gorgeous day! So I never made it to my dear homey's funeral. had "transportation issues" and so that didn't go down for me. and my bday party part TRES at my brother Charlie's house was off the chain! the food was fantastic (thick ass steaks so juicy and tender I actually cut into it with a butter knife)...there was wine, there was salad, family, friends and of course...CAKE! my friend Mohamed showed up and one of my other friends was there as well. After the festivities, I came back to jersey, dropped off my little one and me and BOSS MAN had a night out. and I have to tell you this...IT WAS VERY NICE...I mean very nice...**I can't tell you where we were, but I can tell**

you this: I'm putting a "hint" on my site under the photo gallery section and if anyone can tell me where we were, I'm going to send you an autographed copy of all three of my books and a little sumthin' sumthin' I "took" from the place we were...ha ha ha. who says your girl don't look out? Ok. well I have to go. stay tuned for as the world turns starring me, YOUR HOST, kalico Jones. HAVE A NICE DAY Y'ALL. I WILL GIVE DETAILS TOMORROW. KJ

So its Wednesday already? Dayummmm. I'm feeling a little...well put it like this...I'm just feeling vulnerable. Since I've let my guard down with Boss Man I'm thinking its only a matter of time before I end up with hurt feelings. I guess that's the price I pay to play in the big kids park...At any rate, I'm in-like and I'm not going to apologize for it. I'm having a blast with Boss man and I've decided that I'm going to take it one day at a time. that's it, in a nutshell. (exhaling)...so last night we spent time together and my stomach jumps...can't believe it...it JUMPED. like a nervous, anxious, love sick something or another...and I have to tell you...I'm feeling him. Its not about money with us... or what he has or what I have its just about having a special friendship and that's fine by me...I like it this way because our times together MEANS a lot to both of us and so there it is. No Versace, no gucci, no prada, just me and him being together. Now if I could just do something about both of our phones ringing constantly...that would be great. So what else is going on? my little one missed the bus today...I was late. And to top that off, I missed an appointment this morning because of it. running late and behind...the story of my life...ha ha ha. and last night I spoke with my girl pudda for about three hours just about life and things that are going on with us, our families and our friends. it was a nice conversation. I love my daughter...(just something I was thinking this very second). **anyway...have a great day and try to mend a fence. If you have wronged someone...apologize so YOU can move on...even if they are not receptive. you can't hold on to things you've done way back when. On the last page of my book...when gucci came first ...I have a quote that goes a little something like this: "you should not suffer** the past, you should wear it like a lose garment take it off and let it drop." if Jesus loves you with all your faults and transgressions...why would you dare worry about what anyone ELSE thinks? EXACTLY...so dust yourself off and try again. I'm out...Don't forget to pray y'all...get on your knees   and   pray...   kali   j   moore.

Hey Hey Hey...its THURSDAY! and I'm stuffing my face (eating a LARGE turkey, avocado, cheddar, mayo, tomato, lettuce on French bread) and its like a foot long...and I'm eating the entire sandwich...GREEDY GIRL THAT I AM...So today began LATE. and I have no one to blame but myself. have to get my ass out of the bed and STOP having wine with dinner...So I found out from Boss Man that we were NOT at the place I thought we were. The shit I stole from the hotel had a different name on it...UGH...so the hints I was going to drop I can't and to top that off, he doesn't know how to send the two photos he took for me with his **INSPECTOR GADGET PHONE** to my email....GO FIGURE! LIKE he paid a grip (it was expensive) for a phone he can't maneuver (spell check). tonight I think we are going to spend time together, but don't quote me because I don't know. I do know that I am NOT going to put up with not being able to get "my time" and he knows it, so...let's see what happens. today is week two. (each day is equivalent to one week in my life). so...at any rate...we were on 1 & 9 and I can still do the contest **"guess where kalico was..."** if **you want.... here are two hints and if you guess the name of the place, I will send you copies of my books ...autographed of course! hint no. 1:** _______**Mary's Church (fill in blank) hint no. 2 Type of way to make eggs . Eggs** _____________ **(fill in blank)** now take both of those words (the missing words) put together will make the full name of the hotel. send your answer to kalicojones@yahoo.com this contest is on for everyone. But I will not send out more than 20 book pkgs. so the first twenty people with the right answer, hit me up. or you know what? You can post it to the site...go under **YOUR TIME 2 TALK and click on WHERE WAS KALICO contest and put your answers there**. Now if you can tell me what TOWN we were in...THEN I WILL SEND OUT A BONUS. ok so enough about that...lets get into what's going on with US today. I hope you are ok. Yesterday I went to see an apt. it was nice. but **A LOT SMALLER THAN WHAT I HAVE AND EVEN WHAT I AM ACCUSTOMED TO.** I am going back to see it again this evening, just to get that last look in before I make a final decision...then after that...I am going to think. and go from there. Boss Man told me it was a good look. the apt is close to all but away from where I am currently living, which is a good thing. ..I think. I'm trying to be on the down LOW in my new space...that's Important to me and my guests. So anyway, tonight me and my close friend – can't say who because people be reading this diary and they know who I am talking about and it just causes so much b.s. between us...so my friend will accompany me just as a second set of eyes on the apt. and after that...its off to the Halloween store, I think because my little one wants to be a "vampire lady" whatever that means. ha ha ha. ahh the beauty of youth...what can I say? **Today I want to talk about SHOWING UP. Showing up for life...don't be a slacker...in the words of Reverend Run, "Life gives to the givers and takes from the takers." lets be givers and by saying giver, I don't mean Give money, give to others, etc. even though that would be nice if you are in a position to do so...I mean GIVE UNTO THYSELF. Give yourself a chance...SHOW UP for life...Let's start getting prepared to live.** So many of us walk around and live our lives like we are just here, twiddling our thumbs until we die...no big deal... just skipping and whistling to DEATH ...LITERALLY. WE HAVE TO STOP THIS FAMILY...**We must in order to have the kind of life here on earth that God promises us in The Bible. In order to get our BLESSINGS and Gods promises fulfilled...we have to SHOW UP...what does showing up mean?** It means being on time, as promised and ready. **Translation: It means that we not only do what we say, but DO IT WHEN WE SAY WE ARE GOING TO and be willing to work! Doing what you say does not prevent you from being a liar...You can still do what you say and be a liar. If you don't do it WHEN you say you are going to do it...and if you don't do it AS Promised. Meaning you don't do it the proper way, in full, etc. So today lets begin to SHOW**

UP FOR LIFE. Lets give unto THYSELVES the gift of showing up on time as promised and ready / willing to work. Well that's my time for today. I will keep you in my prayers. Until tomorrow my friends...Kj

10/31 – To Trick or not to treat? That my dear friends is the question. Well today I am mommy the trick or treater. My little one is going to be supergirl! I like the costume. So today we will go around in Nutley and get some candy from the white folk. Ha ha ha. Nah, what I should say is that we are going to all those businesses where we spent our money. That's what we are doing. So right after work, I believe one of my "friends" is going to pick me up and take us around. Let's see how that develops because she gets an attitude sometimes when she believes she is the only person I can count on. Kind of like how men act when they realize you don't have a job, but got rent to pay… **"YOU SCRATCH MY BACK IF YOU WANT ME TO SCRATCH YOURS."** AND I'm not afraid to say Women are NO different in that respect. Don't believe me? Just go check out the lesbian scene, you'll see. And that's NOT me trying to play my lesbian sistas…shit…you know I "go there" when / if I am in the mood. Ha ha ha. Nah, not anymore, but yeah…I've played in that park and NO it ain't a secret. **Today I have learned that you have to handle your OWN business. When you don't and you have to go to people, you might as well pucker up, because if it's something they know you need, they tend to give you their ass to kiss. Its bugged out because any time anyone has asked me for a favor, whether its being given back or NOT…I NEVER ask them what they need it for. I never ask them "how did you get into this mess where you need me?" I never ask them shit. I just assume that if they are asking me, its because they need it and that's that. If I go to any of my friends, you can rest assure its because I NEED IT, because I would never put my ASS nor the ass of my little one is ANYONE'S POCKET.** And you know what I mean. **So that's the assignment for today: Get your ass out of someone's pocket!** You know the person who is holding that favor over your head or throws it in your face every time they get a chance. Put yourself in a position where you can give it back to them...if its something you cannot give back to them, then ... begin to distance yourself from that person. What are you hanging around for? They did the favor, you can't give it back, so MOVE on! **What good is going to someone if they are only going to throw it up in your face?** EXACTLY...you may as well sold your ass...at least then you keep you dignity...THAT'S RIGHT I SAID IT... and don't be talking about "kj how can you say that selling your ass is dignified?" Hear me clearly: "selling your ass meaning...you did it on your OWN, without enlisting the help of those who are going to talk about you...that's what I mean. And hell yeah...let me even think I have to go backward to take a step forward and ...it will be...ONCE, TWICE, SOLD....TO THE HIGHEST BIDDER up in this mother f@#@$@$!" AND DON'T GET IT twisted. Ok so now that I have set myself and all the women in the world back about fifty years. Let me put the disclaimer out there, **"I am not suggestion, saying, or directing anyone to sell their ass, prostitute, engage in sexual activities in exchange for money, things, etc."** and don't even think about writing my ass a letter behind this. (taking a deep breath)...you know I say the things most people wouldn't have the guts to admit they are THINKING! What else is going on with me? Nothing. Just getting ready to get outta here and do the mommy thing with my little one. I'm a little excited, I can't even front like I'm not. So lets check back tomorrow and see how I did. **And to all the parents reading this who will be out there tonight braving the elements like me holding the trick or treat bag when your kid says they don't want to carry it anymore... "GOOD LUCK TO YA!" HA HA AH. That's my time, I'm gone...or "ghost" since its Halloween. Kj.**

11/02 - What's up family? Its me your girl Kali J Moore checking in on ya. Tired of being yelled at over this shit with the courts by my boss at work. Ok. So as you know last week I was in court with the landlord 10/21. I can't stand Newark's court system. They just pile a bunch of folk in the room and holla and scream. The landlord finally showed, but the case was dismissed. The judge refused to listen to them on the grounds that they attempted to prejudice the courts by bringing up something that was going on in our other court case. Ugh, don't you just hate that. But luckily ...NO Thank GOD, my ass had the law on my side and thank God I was NOT dumb enough to listen to the advice of one of my friends. **Advice that was the equivalent to a train wreck.** The advice, although it was "not good" would have gotten me more time to get some things in order, but by no means was it legal. At any rate...I thought about it...and thought about it...and thought about it, and then I told my mother who said, "Kal I know you ain't even thinking about doing that! You know God don't like ugly, you can't do that!" and so I didn't. **and just when I thought I was going to give up...ALL my shit came through. ALL OF IT, meaning...LACKING IN NOTHING. Every last thing I needed came through, and to top that off...homeboy even sent a child support check!** Go figure. And they say "it never rains in southern California!" ha ha ha. But seriously and the case was dismissed on top of that. But here's where it gets twisted...The case is dismissed and what happened? These rain makers (they are Indian) I know, that's fucked up Kalico. . . But I can't stand them and as a "friend" pointed out...the "rain makers" as I so eloquently put it are US (kj's being ignorant)...these people are from some place else...ok. But back to what's going on...so they turn around and file papers with the courts to have the dismissal vacated and so I had to tell my boss that I would be out on the ninth – next Wednesday, to be in court AGAIN! He was NOT happy. I think the only reason I didn't get fired was because we have two people out on vacation. At any rate, he yelled and again...I couldn't do shit. I had to just sit there and take it because I need pay stubs. Ugh! My blood is boiling. So it's back to court yet again. This is bullshit! What else is going on? Nothing much! Still tired from Halloween. It was nice. My little one and our "friend" had a good time. I think our friend had a better time than the little one. It was nice. But I know it's going to end soon because she is the type of person who forgets what level our friendship is on and that's when the bug outs begin. So I'm just going to ride it out this time, hoping that it will not be the way it's always been. **Today's**

assignment: Tell someone you love them! And I'm not talking about an ex boyfriend or a boyfriend, I'm talking about your children or your mom and dad…someone in your family who you haven't told in a while or may think you are upset with them are just that things are not the same between you because they haven't been. Call them up and when the conversation is over…say, "I love you." I did that to my cousin La La and I have to tell you. When I got off the phone, I cried. It made me just think about growing up and how me being mad at her for dumb shit and just my OWN jealousy about some family matters that were really not her fault or the fault of any of the people who I consider to be my cousins…**I'm talking about FIRST COUSINS ONLY. And there ain't many of us: Me, Tweety Bird, La la, Carlos, Timmy, Joey, and Charlie that's it.** US. At any rate. I know she loves me too. Which reminds me, I have to call and check in. **So today…let's take direction from the Legend Stevie Wonder – call someone and tell them you love them. (singing)** *"I just called to say, I love you…I just called to say how much I care….yes I do…I just called, to say, I love you….and I mean it from the bottom of my heart." AND I LOVE YOU TOO. Have a great day, you deserve it. KJ*

11/05 - (singing) *"The way I feel about you…there just ain't not doubt it, I'm in love…"* I just jumped off Boss Man and so I'm feeling a little Tony the Tigress! **Can you say, "Incredible?" Oh baby!!! It's all good folks. He's just doing for me what I do for him and that's the truth. Although I don't allow myself to have the big "o" with him. I just don't. I gave it to him once, and that's it. I just don't want to have that kind of connection with anyone who is not my daughter's father or my husband…I'm sure you understand. So what's "it" all for you ask? It's for the thrill of the want. The passion that comes in lying in wait for someone to take hold of you and do the damn thing!** That's what its about. Nothing more than that. Haven't really had a "connection" since my daughters father and truth be told…I don't want one with anyone right now because I ain't even ready for it mentally, emotionally or otherwise…and I don't think it would be in the best interest of the other person to engage in that kind of next level interaction with me. I have too much shit going on. **You tell me what am I going to do with a person full time? EXACTLY. Nothing but make a big ass mess of things.** And so I try NOT to put myself in situations that could even be considered for next level intimacy/relations. There! I said it aloud for the FIRST TIME…and that's half the battle. So now you see the reason for most of the players in my life. It's been on hell of a year, huh? PYT, my dear EX the music industry man and now my person of the moment, Boss Man. Hmmm, I wonder…How the end would come for me and him. I think its just going to be a "fade away" because neither one of us have the guts to say goodbye. And again, he's damn near married. At least in my book anyway…'cause anything over five years is a commitment to me. **So why am I with him?** 'Cause I have nothing else better to do apparently, right? Damn shame. **You think a bitch still has low self-esteem?** I don't think so. You know I can't stand watching these talk shows and reading these books about bitches who mess with attached men having low self esteem, when that is NOT always true! **Why can't a bitch just be GRIMEY? Or a fucking DOG?** You know when men fuck with a bunch of women or "attached" women, you don't hear people talking about a nigga got low self esteem. EVEN the ones who fuck with other men during their marriage to WOMEN are not even looked upon as having self esteem issues, that shit is crazy. Double standard "peep"le, just a double fucking standard. **Well I'm not going to pretend I have low self esteem, just so you can justify whatever it is you may think about me, because my self esteem is JUST FINE! I will say I have serious intimacy issues because I may still be harboring feelings for the father of my child, but I WILL NOT say I have low self esteem and you can just go to hell for thinking that! So…There is no assignment for today. You can just analyze this (putting up my middle finger). That's just the way I feel today. Making me come to grips with my life, how DARE you! I'm going to take a nap now …I'm drained. Kali J Moore.**

11/09 – FIRED! Can you believe that? First off, the landlord is a jerk. He took me to court AGAIN today. So now that makes Four times in one month and today brings it up to five times in six weeks, can you say "fed up?" and rightfully so. I guess this is a good thing, because as I told you…the boss was on my last nerve. Just speaking to me and everyone else in a manner that is degrading. And you have to know that **if you allow a person to speak / treat you in a manner that is substandard or less than the manner in which you treat / speak to people or would like people to speak / treat you…THEY WILL ALWAYS SPEAK / TREAT YOU IN A MANNER THAT IS SUBSTANDARD OR LESS THAN YOU WOULD LIKE TO BE TREATED / SPOKEN TO.** And the beat goes on. So when EVERYONE around you begins to treat you fucked up…Don't blame them, blame yourself, because had you set the boundaries **FROM THE BEGINNING,** they would not feel comfortable in treating you in a way that makes you feel uncomfortable and that's my fault with my boss as work. I put on this "Kj is so soft spoken" front, even changed my voice during work hours at the advice of someone to sound "professional" when in fact there was NOTHING wrong with my speaking voice. A speaking voice does not make you sound professional…**WHAT COMES OUT OF YOUR MOUTH IS WHAT MAKES OR BREAKS YOU.** So I'm in this new world, with a different voice and the voice…well it made me sound like a weak ass bitch and so he treated me like one. At first the shit was subtle. Little things like, "do this" "in my office right now" in front of my peers and subordinates. And then it escalated to him not even being able to wait until I got in his office to speak to me. It was right in the middle of the office, in front of everyone. It was a disaster…and then…it began. OTHERS thought they could just speak / treat me any ol kind of way and in the midst of needing pay stubs for my apartment search…I COULD NOT QUIT. So it was just me showing up for work…doing the minimal of what was required, barely speaking to people and going home. So he just did me a fucking favor. And besides…I CAN COLLECT UNEMPLOYMENT FOR WHILE. So I have the apartment. I move in on the 15th and so that worked out right on time…AND JUST IN TIME. I guess

God really does know how much we can handle, because I was just about to give up. I mean I literally had stopped looking because I was just so tired of being told "no!" for one reason or another. So the smaller apartment it is. But its nicer and a better block and so that's what really counts. No I'm sorry. I have that incorrect. **What REALLY counts is a roof over my daughter's head.** So we could be in a room for all I care and our shit in storage, don't get it twisted! **So today's assignment / lesson is: "Don't allow people to treat you in a manner that makes you uncomfortable or feel less of a person. It's not worth it. Please stand your ground by demanding respect.** Now I'm NOT saying for you to jump up and yell and scream at the person who is treating you not so nice and I'm not saying to be overly sensitive to directives/comments/critiques from others. I'm saying…**if someone is disrespecting you…stand up for yourself. Take a minute to bring them to the side and just say… "I don't know if you realize this, but when you say/do (fill in blank), it makes me uncomfortable." And wait for their response. Nine times out of ten they are going to say that they didn't know they were being rude. And hopefully they will change their behavior. If not…then its up to you to change it for them…and that's by altering your attitude. Be assertive. Put some "authority" in your voice. That's my time, I'm outta here. Your girl kj.**

11/10 - and Thank Goodness it's over. I have to pick up my final check tomorrow. What's going on? Nothing, just packing. I have my new lease and I am looking forward to the change of scenery. I have to get the movers and the lifters. Ain't this some shit? Don't you know that some places only DRIVE your shit. It's your responsibility to get someone to move it in and out of the truck. Oh my goodness the entire world is lazy. I'm convinced. What else do you call it when movers DON'T MOVE? Ha ha ha. Its funny but it's a sign of the times ladies and gentlemen. Ok so today I want to talk about dating busted ass people. I say this because I got a letter from someone who is going to remain nameless. **She is going through the mills with her baby daddy. They have three children and she**

is in school part time and working. This young lady is dealing with a functional crack head baby daddy. He goes to work, but he is constantly high. She stopped letting him see his children and is thankful that the child support comes directly from his employer, or else she is sure she would not get it. He forgets the children's birthdays, refuses to help her buy winter coats and boots for the children and to top that off, had the nerve to call her on her birthday to ask if she would be interested in going to the "telly" with him (motel). She told me that she was "confused" and didn't know what to do. Now the only reason why I am bringing this to your attention is because we are ALL family in this arena <u>www.kalicojones.com</u> **and I feel it's my duty to try to bridge the gap that fucks us up as a whole.** *So here it is: First of all, YOU BETTER NOT GO WITH A CRACKHEAD ANYWHERE, ESPECIALLY A MOTEL, DO YOU WANT AIDS? Ok. I said it and I know, it's harsh, but the truth in the matter is, When I was out there (y'all knew I was going to go there), I did a lot of shit. Some shit I put in a book When Gucci Came First, most of it, <u>I did not</u>. <u>ALL of it I did high</u>. When you are high and getting high, you are NOT thinking about shit but gratification. That could be sex,* **or it could be anything you feel has <u>the potential</u> to make you feel good***. Most of the time with crack heads/ cokeheads, weed heads, etc. the gratification is a sexual one and so we forget about BEING SAFE. Come on, and keep it real. How many times have you "forgot" the condom and was NOT high or drunk? EXACTLY and so how in the hell do you think a crack head is going to remember while on a high...HE IS NOT. My dear friend. What you need to do is focus on your children and finishing up your degree. From what you've told me, you only have about six more months to go (may 2006) and so you need to thank goodness you are getting child support now, but put yourself in a position where you won't need it because more sooner than later...that will stop (I only see termination of employment down the pike for him). He can't remember the kid's birthdays is bullshit. He remembered yours when he called for ASS, so what does that tell you? He is only interested in whatever HE is interested in at the time in which he is interested in it. For three children you get enough money to buy winter coats and boots. (She told me how* *much she is getting). You get MORE than enough to handle your business. And so you need to be doing it. Don't be like me calling the kids father asking for shit you know good and well the kid don't need in hopes he will say something "nice" to you or want to see the kid. THAT DOES NOT WORK. You don't have to spend 100 on a coat. You spend about 40 bucks a piece and the same with the boots and that's for NAME BRAND (check out AJ Wright, TJ Maxx, Century 21, Daffy's, Burlington Coat Factory, etc.). You will have enough money left to do all the things you need to do for not only your children, but yourself and you better do them quick because just as I have too lost many a job during my "offensive" years…I'm sure he will as well. In the meantime, Keep your head up.* I know, that was hard, but this is tough love "peep"le and I have got to be honest with her. She is a sweet young lady and just as I have said many of times... **Don't listen to his family tell you, "girl, its going to get better. He just needs someone to stick by him." Fuck that. We don't have time for that. Who is going to take care of your 3, count 'em three kids while you stick by a crack head…NO ONE. The only reason why the family would tell you to "stick by him" is because they don't want his ass on their doorstep or sofa. Listen girlfriend…someone has to be the responsible party here and it looks like you win that role by default. Sorry, but it's the truth. And you ain't the first, second, third or last woman who is going to have to shoulder parenting all by herself. Today's lesson is: Learn something from what our sista girl is going through. If you are a single parent out here in the world…know that it's NOT the END of the world. We have to make for some kind of "mission failures" throughout life and being a single mom is NOT a failure. If the father of your child is fucking up…its HIS failure, not yours. Please keep that in mind because a lot of the time, we take HIS fuck ups and make them our own** and in doing so, WE put an extra burden on ourselves. **So with having said ALL that…Remember that <u>YOU</u> ARE ALL That. 'Cause it takes one hell of a woman to be a single parent , so take a bow, you deserve it! Ok well that's my time, I'm outta here. Your girl kali j moore over and out. Peace.**

11/14 - "Is the juice worth the squeeze?" Look at your bed partner and ask yourself that. You know why? Reading this book I realized that more times than not the "juice" was not worth the "squeeze" for me. Ha ha ha. I know, what a fine time to discover that kj, right? Yeah…but hey better late than never. So me and my friends were talking about the last guy we dated, oh excuse me for not keeping it real…Me and my friends were talking about the last guy we FUCKED And we collectively agreed that you are only as good as the last person you slept with. If he is busted, then you are busted. **Once, is a fuck up. Second time …you were confused. You were in need of clarification, so you did it again. The third time…MAKES YOU JUST AS BUSTED AS HIS ASS, SO DON'T COMPLAIN TO YOUR FRIENDS AND FAMILY ABOUT HIS WACK ASS SHOULD HE HIT YOU, CHEAT on you, STEAL FROM YOU, AND SO FORTH AND SO ON.** I say this because I've been down the "busted" road once or twice and so have most of the women I know and although you should not be ashamed of making a mistake…three and four times is by no means a mistake! YOU meant to be there, period and point blank. So in your quest to find true love and happiness…just know how some of US are judging YOU! Ha ha ha…I got some fucking nerve. Today's assignment: singing *(I just need time to see, where I wanna be. Say when you love some one, you just don't treat them bad…oh how I feel so sad…she's crying her heart to me, how could you let this be…I just need time to see, where I wanna be, where I wanna be)* **Today's assignment is: (drumroll please) "Nobody can be you, but you!" aka, Be yourself. If that means a little bit of make up is going to make you happy…then put it ON! if that means you gonna get a hair cut or some braids (then do it)…if all you really need is a little weave…GO FOR IT. We have to stop thinking that we are not US because we put on a little make up, or a set of nail tips … 'Cause those things are NOT what makes us, its our personalities that make us different and in some aspects, the same.** Just because you got a track or two in your head, does not mean you are not KEEPING IT REAL and don't let anyone tell you that. Screw them. **You do what is going to make you happy.** And if that means you want bigger boobs, shit…y'all know I deal with Cosmedica – Dr. Bellin and your girl has had work done and I'm going to get new ta-ta's and not because the ones I got now are lacking in anything…its just that I'm thinking about Lil' Kim'ing it 4real and I could give a damn less what anyone thinks. You know me by now I'm sure. Ha ha ha. **So be YOU and in the midst of being you…don't stop to think about what others think about YOU. 'cause trust me…they ain't thinking about what you think about them WHILE THEY'RE being who they are! I'm gone, KJ.**

11/21 - Sorry I haven't written in so long. What's up family, its Me the ONE and only coming to you on this fine day…Damn the weather is changing. Shit my ass is going to have to put on a bigger coat soon. So…I'm moved y'all its official and I'm enjoying my new place. I threw away so much furniture, but I had to, because the new place is substantially smaller – I don't have a dinning room and the living room is not even HALF the size I had before, but its all good. I ain't gonna front, its nice. So (taking a deep breath), I came this close (putting my pointy finger and my thumb as close as I can get them without letting them touch) to slapping the ever loving shit out of someone one because everyone who I thought was going to help me move…NO SHOW! I mean everyone. "Kj I'm going to help you" yeah right…that shit was right out the window when it came down to it. My friend Kevin was like, "I know you ain't got no friends now." And I'm like, "you damn right" and so I have cut off the remaining few, as I just could not allow myself to be a fake ass bitch. Of course I got the "Oh I didn't know you were talking about THAT day" and the "I tried to call you, but I didn't get an answer." All the bullshit folks, all the bullshit and for what? Its not like I give a damn! That's on them…It STILL got done, even though at one point I thought I was not going to pull it off. I even went to Boss Man to ask him for help, his response, "No" I asked why and he said, "I'm not the one moving, you are!" Can you say, "done with his ass?" Oh yeah, y'all know one thing about me if you know nothing else, If I come to you, its because I really need it. But hey…lets not say he didn't offer direction to the tune of about 5 hundred dollars for "friends of his" to move my shit. No thanks, I'll pass and I was out there with "E" moving my shit. Me, Eric, my former next-door neighbor and a downstairs neighbor. We moved it out and then me and "E" aka Eric, moved it in. Secret Crush left the office and drove the truck. I guess its all in a days work when you think of it and it just let me know that I have been making dummy moves all fucking year. Like how in the hell did I find myself with someone who would refuse to help me? And its not like he doesn't have money. He has NO money issues. This is purely about him just not giving a shit and that's all good. 'Cause in reality…I guess I don't give a shit either, because had I and I wouldn't be with him in the first place. **Anything I do with him is on my TERMS. I am available when I WANT to be available and he…well now he's history, (since he's with someone I guess that would make him herstory, right?)…no…I just checked with my girl Ruby who told me that since it's about him and me, he would be "mystory" At any rate, he's outta here so it doesn't matter. Time to "fade to black". Ok. So I've decided to live like I'm Michael Jackson…no one can get next to me aside from Hubby and a few phone buddies, but they better call me on my cell phone because my home phone is going to be private and unpublished. Today I have no assignment. Just learn from all my shit. I'm gone, KJ.**

12/01 - What's up Everyone? Sorry it took me so long to write, but as you know between the landlords taking me to court, being a single parent, trying to move, these books and just fake ass people in general, I have been really busy. As I told you, I have finally moved, but not before someone took it upon themselves to rob my old apartment. They didn't get away with much, just a fur jacket and a diamond ring that was worth more to me emotionally than anything else. There was no forced entry and so between the statement my neighbors gave the police and the investigation, I'm sure something will happen soon. What else? So I'm in my new place, without a phone might I add and it's a good thing. Hell I haven't even ordered cable, and for what? Me and the little one don't go past channel 13 and since the reception is crystal clear, it makes no sense for me to add yet another bill to my life right now. Especially since my cable was "free" in the other spot. My little one is doing well in her new school which is predominately BLACK (or African American) I never get why blacks are referred to as African American when we ain't stepped one foot in Africa and between us being all mixed up with other races, I just think its dumb. Why can't we just be American? ...at first I was like, "oh LAWD" this school is NOT going to work, but I have to be honest with you, (I guess I am a little prejudice), she has learned more here than the other school. They are reading already, but they don't offer a language and I can understand why. I mean what good is learning Spanish when you don't understand basic English? EXACTLY, it doesn't make any sense. So the language isn't offered until first grade and I'm ok with that. So ... She's a bit frustrated because they sing, "life every voice and sing" and she doesn't know that – coming from the "white" school, but have no fear, I taught it to her in a few takes so she can feel better when that time of the morning comes at school. What else is going on? Nothing much. Just finally getting a lot of stuff accomplished. It's amazing just how many things a person can accomplish when they have no phone. And my cell phone, the number has been changed and so it's difficult for anyone to get at me right now. (exhaling) Y'all know I just needed a BREAK. **So where's everyone?** Well, Absolutely NOTHING matured from my "relations" with **Boss Man**. Since before the move, I began to make myself unavailable...unseen. I just couldn't take his attitude any longer. I figured whatever woman could put up with that arrogance deserves him all to herself. I did let him come to my house the day before Thanksgiving, but that was just so he could see how I really live because when he and I got together my shit was packed and the apartment was in disarray. So he saw, and that was that. **Secret Crush** and I haven't been in contact since the move only because I just need to do some things for ME and my little one and she and I tend to do this thing where we get along for a few days and then she forgets we're not "together" and then it goes into this kind of a "why don't you like me" thing and I just can't deal with that anymore. She's a sweet person at times, but when you are sweet just to get something, then that makes you a PIG and I don't care if you are a MALE or FEMALE. **PYT** is out of the picture as well. I just got tired of bailing his ass out of jail. The last time I went to the precinct, I asked him on the ride home, "Is there anything you want to do with your life? Maybe I can help you." His response, "I want to be a famous rapper." (exhaling), that was the last time I saw him. His comment made it painfully obvious I was truly in the wrong lane. **VRJ** (vacation relations jump off) is still in North Carolina. He called me the other day and said, "Why did you call and hang up?" I replied, "Sorry wrong girl." He said, "My bad" and hung up. What in the hell does my bad mean? I have yet to understand that terminology. I didn't call him back. I'm sure we'll run into each other again one day. **My ex "boyfriend" who is in the music industry** and I don't speak often. I did make it my business to call him the other day and ask him for some money. His question to me, "Why should I give you shit?" Ahhh the beauty of "strong arming"… I can't tell you what I said, but I can tell you this…I met his secretary in the lobby of his label…she handed me a check. And my husband? Well he is on his way home, so all this "closure" is right on time. My radio show is going to air on powertalkfm.com (maybe) or I just may go back to artistfirst.com check back with me on that through the website www.kalicojones.biz. I am going to begin the second week of the year and then once per month for a little while, just until I get these last two books completed out and then I will go to every other week and then possibly once per week. I've decided that January 15th I will begin my search for possible part time employment. This will put me home with my little one long enough to get her situated in school, etc. Did I mention the apartment is NICE. Hardwood floors, nicer neighborhood and so I'm ok for a little while. Who is my man of the moment? NO ONE! I've decided to return to celibacy and that's NEVER a bad thing. It's best because hubby would have a damn fit if he knew about PYT and Boss Man after that whole thing with the kid from the music industry who turned out to be after "kalico jones." (exhaling) I'm telling you everyone around me has benefited some way or shape or form from knowing me. It's terrible the way I have allowed myself to be used, and most of the time, WILLINGLY. Just awful, but as I sit here and type this to you, this…the end of The Diary Volume One, I can make this promise, "I will not allow 2006 to catch me slipping." And speaking of slipping, don't you just love the new Lil Kim CD? I'm feeling number 5 on that joint, "Shut up Bitch!" It's the way I've been feeling lately. Just a lot of people yapping about me and my "issues" (taking a deep breath), I just don't understand what's so fascinating about my black ass…If you know holla at your girl…**So today's assignment is simple: Learn how to SHUT UP! You know the ONLY way a person can talk about you and spread your business is if you tell it yourself.** So lets learn how to keep some things close to us because again in the words of my grandmother Omega Lyerly Williamson who passed away about 6 years ago, "People always remember the bad, never the good." And that goes for your miseries as well. You know that shit that you have no control over that happens to you. People are so quick to keep your business on their lips. And so having been the victim of that OVER AND OVER AGAIN, I have promised myself that I would keep by business to myself. Anytime anyone asks me anything I'm going to say, "I'm sorry but I don't discuss my business." And I'm NOT fronting on that y'all. Because certain things we tell about ourselves are just so fucking unnecessary. Its like the people / person we tell are NOT going to do anything to help us and since we know this, why are we so free to give our business away? So having learned that lesson ….AGAIN…and yes, the HARD way…I have cut EVERYONE off. **EVERYONE is gone.** And you know what? Oh well and so what…'cause I don't give a fuck. **I'm determined to live in peace and I'm not going to DIE to get it either.** I'm just going to keep my business to my damn self and yes, that INCLUDES family. **So once again, the Assignment for the end of the Diary is: (drumroll please) "SHUT UP!"** and you know what I'm talking about folks, you know EXACTLY what I am talking about. Well that's my time. I'm outta here. This is the official end of the diary – and yes, it WILL be published. *(SINGING)* *"There's more to life than you know… Don't give up the fight, take one day at a time, you just got to have hope….so…don't be fool,   don't throw life away…don't be a fool, don't waste your life away…don't be a* *fool, don't throw your life away…don't be a fool, don't waste your life away…." LUV KJ*

A VERY SPECIAL THANKS TO:

Jesus! Thank you for holding me down as I discover "thyself." I've been told my "calling" maybe to do your will on another level, like ministering to women once I get myself together a little more…I don't know. The only thing I DO know, is that whatever reason I am here for, you can rest assure I will not fail the mission.

To my Family: Those who love and respect me and my daughter.

To my extended family: The readers of kalicojones.net / .biz, .com, etc, the members of <u>thekalicojonesproject@yahoogroups.com</u>, my myspace friends …MY audience…you guys know you ARE family. There are so many of you and I just want to say "thanks" for going through life with me. I love you and I appreciate all the letters of encouragement.

To Mike Moore: Thank you for being the one person who has never judged me. Thank you for being the one person who I never had to lie to. Thank you for being the one person who understands what it takes to be me. Thank you for your encouragement, thank you for sharing my dreams and allowing me not only room to make mistakes, but to grow as well. I love you and I'm glad what we have is Unbreakable.

To Robert Brown Jr: You are my rock. Thank you for being there for me and Ivana over the years. Your consistency could out last the energizer bunny! ☺ I love you very much. You define the words "Real" and "Man"

My thanks you's are over, as I have weeded so many people out of my life…There is no need to thank folks I don't speak to.

What's next? My daughter has published a book, **"The Dinosaur and Silva"** – www.thedinosaurandsilva.us
What a fantastic children's read. This book speaks directly to children; touching their emotions and intriguing their intellect. We've come to know dinosaurs as these gigantic scary creatures, but (a child herself) shows us a gentler side of the dinosaur. She effortlessly pulls the reader (child and adult alike) into this story from the very beginning. What a great book to introduce or re-introduce your child to the wonderful world of dinosaurs. The Dinosaur and Silva, with a great storyline and outstanding illustrations - tells the story of a little boy who finds a dinosaur and returns it to the museum. A short story with adventure, excitement and more! From newborn to grammar school, for story time or bedtime, this book is school friendly and can be used as a learning tool. Its something I'm sure you will enjoy reading to the child(ren) in your life.

What else? I am STILL attempting to launch my cosmetics line and my newspaper. I will keep you posted. For more information on me, and my publishing company WildChild Press, please log onto to www.kalicojones.net or send an email to: kalicojones@yahoo.com. Oh and you can catch me on myspace. Myspace.com/kalico_jones

"Whatever it is you are doing that is blocking your blessings…please stop it. God wants us to take advantage of all the things he has promised us in the Bible." – kj

And again, in the words of my father, the Pastor, "Jesus loves you and so do I…bye, bye, bye….bye."

"Dreams do come true."

Books by Kalico Jones:
1. When Gucci Came First
2. And To You Homeboy, I say "Thanks!"
   (follow up to WGCF)
3. Man Unnecessary
4. Kj Three Six Five (The Diary)

Books on the horizon:
5. The Shame of His Touch – WINTER 2007
6. 4 Miles to Freedom - FALL 2007

Books by WildChild Press Authors
1. The Dinosaur & Silva by: I.L.Williamson – AVAILABLE
NOW WHEREVER BOOKS ARE SOLD

Other books by Kalico Jones with excerpts:

WHEN GUCCI CAME FIRST

The book that started it all

And so your journey begins...

Last night, I was out with this guy "Q." He's a fellow PK (preacher's kid) at a bar in New Jersey. After having several drinks "Q" invited me back to his apartment. He said he had access to some good cocaine and since I hadn't seen him in a while I agreed to keep him company.

We walked two blocks from the bar to the apartment he shared with a friend who worked nights. Upon our arrival, "Q" told me that he had to go upstairs to get the "stuff" from a dealer who just happened to live in the building.

He returned 45 minutes later...

When "Q" re-entered the room. I immediately asked him how much my portion of the tab was. His response, "Nah Diamond, I got it." Now although my dear friend "Q" had offered to pay for our party favors, I didn't want him to think I owed him a "favor," so I gave him half the money he spent at his neighbor's house, $55.00.

I opened the little plastic baggie and scooped out some of an off-white, really close to yellow substance that was just passed off to me as cocaine and took a hit. Twice up each nostril. My nose froze immediately. I sucked my teeth and said, "There's too much cut on this shit...I can't sniff this crap, shit!" So pissed, having paid $55.00 for garbage, I grabbed a glass, filled it with Bacardi, dropped in two pieces of ice and decided to get drunk instead. But there was one problem, I started feeling high. I thought, "Damn, I hate being high off beat." I sat back on "Q's" bed, smoked a cigarette and waited for my high to come down.

30 minutes later...

My high was gone but my dear friend "Q" was just getting started. He was in the corner of his room (in front of the window, no less), rolling up a dollar bill like a straw. He snorted three lines of cocaine off the top of his dresser. I was flabbergasted and apparently that wasn't enough, because he then poured the little bit of cocaine left in the bag I had in a pipe and lit it!

Oh my goodness, he's a fucking CRACK HEAD! I gotta get the fuck out of here quick. I asked him to walk me back to the bar and he responded with, "Can I have a kiss?"

You should've seen the look on my face, utterly disgusted at this point (I just wasted $55.00 on bullshit, I can't get drunk and now he blows the little bit of high I had with this stupid ass question). "Sorry 'Q' but I don't do anything buzzed." He started laughing and took another hit of his dirty ass pipe. To this day, I have never seen a person suck up smoke the way he did. I know the pipe LOOKED dirty, but was it clogged too? Damn, he needs help. He blew the smoke towards my face and replied, "I respect that."

Yeah right...now you know his ass was lying.

"Can we please leave?" I said, as I felt it necessary to ask his ass a SECOND time, to walk me back to the bar. I put on my jacket and told him I was leaving. He said he needed to change his shirt (that took fifteen minutes). He then tried on several suit jackets (another ten minutes) and finally at 1:15am, we were on our way out the door. The bar was closed.

I walked home by myself in the freezing cold, clutching a torn piece of paper with his number on it.

I looked down at his number and thought, "I hope he doesn't expect to hear from me tomorrow." As a matter of fact, I hope he doesn't expect to hear from me ever again, fuckin' CRACK HEAD!

I know, I know, how can I call him a crack head, right?

Listen...I have a weird perception of people who do cocaine. I guess it's because I don't consider myself an addict, and that whole crack pipe, smoking coke thing seems so offensively "fiendish" to me (if that's a word). I feel like this: if you sniff it, that's okay, a rich mans high and as long as you can afford it, you DO NOT HAVE A PROBLEM. Now, if you SMOKE it, you're a fiend, period!

I guess my mindset on this is largely due to the fact that one of the TVs in my home was purchased from a pipe smoking fiend. It's a sick justification, I know, but as you will see, I've developed many sick justifications over the years.

When I'm not doing cocaine, I have a drink in my hand. I know it's substitution and you better not say shit to me about it, 'cause if you do, I'm gonna say, "At least I'm not getting high!" and I might tell you to go fuck yourself (depending on how many drinks I've had), so mind your fuckin' business!

AND TO YOU, HOMEBOY, I SAY "THANKS!"

The follow-up to When Gucci Came First

Yonkers 10701 – I found a place that would not only take a deposit, but would also allow me to move in a few days early. I called homeboy and asked him if he could move me and the baby's stuff out of storage. He did just that, but I don't think it was because he wanted to help. I just think it was because he wanted to know where we were going to be living. When I informed my mother of my need for money, she came right away, wrote a check directly to the landlord for the balance and me and my little one were set. Or so I thought. Until….

Homeboy found out I was "dating" Young Buchanan. Buchanan, he picked me up every morning, drove me to the sitter and then took me to work. He picked me up when work was over, drove me to the sitter and then took me home.

Pulling in the driveway of my new placc, and I notice homeboys Benz. I quickly got the baby out of the car, said goodbye to Buchanan and made my way in the house where I would find homeboy sitting on my bed watching television.
A startled me yelled, "What are you doing in my house?"

"I can come anywhere my daughter lives…what happened to your little boyfriend. He didn't want to come in?"

"That's not my boyfriend and what are you worried about it for? You're with everyone you can find…so don't start minding my business."

"My daughter is my business and I don't want her around another nigga. You got that?"

"Whatever…well can you stay for a minute, so I can take a bath?"

"Yeah"

And on that note, I got undressed and ran a nice, hot bath. Something I haven't been able to do with regularity since becoming a full time single parent. Its just showers and jump into my clothing, sometimes without even putting on lotion. Ahhh, it was so relaxing.

Relaxing UNTIL (damn can I get a break with the "untils")…Until homeboy came in the bathroom talking about how much he missed me and his daughter. He began to rub my back, started talking about how good I've been looking lately and that if I were to date anyone to please let it be someone who did not live in Mt. Vernon. Can you believe it. HE wanted to me to RESPECT HIS ass. Ha ha ha. I got out of the tub, "Where's the baby?"

"In her crib sleeping."

"Oh good. Now if you'll excuse me, I would like to put on some clothes."

"I've seen it all before." And before I could respond, he had his mouth on my breasts, his hands up my towel and I was feeling no shame. I let the towel drop and we made love right there on the floor of my bathroom. It was great and it was something I needed. . . PROOF that he still cared for me.

Yeah right, 'cause as soon as it was over, he was being paged by his "job."

Nigga please.

MAN UNECESSARY
(Why a lot of women feel as though they don't need a man in their life to be happy…a journey of hurt and adaptation)

Cynthia

Met her current boyfriend fifteen years ago in high school. They dated on and off through the years. She's a very successful business operations analyst, him: He's a single father and a bum.

You see Corey never took school seriously and Cynthia did. Always excelling in her studies, striving for more. Wanting a better life for herself and her family. You knew Cynthia was going to be successful. Everyone knew it. There was just something about her.

Corey on the other hand excelled in Class Clowning, Cutting and mooching off the brains of Cynthia. She did his homework assignments while he played football, she took his tests while he cut class, she did everything for him, and he was her FIRST.

While Cynthia was away excelling in college, Corey was back in the old neighborhood selling drugs, drinking and sleeping with the clients his business serviced. His daughter. The product of him getting sex from a crack head in exchange for drugs. When Cynthia found out, she was devastated, but forgiving nonetheless and there begins the end.

Cynthia takes in Corey's daughter. Cynthia purchases a home for them to live in. Cynthia purchases the three cars they have in the driveway. She enrolls Cori – his daughter in private school. And all the while no one even stopped to say "thanks." No one, not even Corey. And why on God's earth would he? He was used to Cynthia bailing him out and this time, although taking in a child was big, it was no different.

But Cynthia felt it was her duty to help Corey because they had so much history. And through all his class clowning, playboy antics and sex with crack heads she never once stopped to notice the signs.

Corey displayed signs of a looser way back when they were teens, but Cynthia was so blinded by the moments of her first time she just couldn't find her way to the truth.

"She's my daughter!"… "She's my daughter!" Corey would yell during arguments with Cynthia, and two days and an apology letter later, Cynthia would forgive Corey's behavior and take him back, not saying a word or expecting him to explain his reasons for treating her so badly.

Until Tuesday. Tuesday would be the day Corey was scheduled to work late. Cynthia never expected him home before ten. She gets a call from a friend of Corey's who would like Cynthia to drive to a hotel where she would find Corey in bed with another woman.

She has since sold the house, sold the cars and moved. She still takes care of his daughter.

Corey has since tried to come back to her. On several occasions proposing marriage, but Cynthia is done with him. She has moved on.

Man, truly Unnecessary

Lesson here: There are usually signs to a looser, and if you look hard enough, you will find them. Notice the looser traits.

Judy

Never dated outside her race. Never once dating a white man. She's black, she's pro black and everything she says and does is black. No getting around Judy, an African American woman with a lot of self pride.

Until the day a black man robbed her as she stopped to try to help him.

Minding her own business driving down I-95 heading home after a long day at work. It's three o'clock in the morning and Judy is tired. She noticed a car on the side of the highway and slowed down. It was a man in a suit waving his hands, he was in need.

Judy pulled over.

"Are you okay?" Judy asked through her <u>rolled</u> <u>down</u> window.

"No, my car just died on me, I don't have my cell phone, and do you have a phone I can borrow to call someone?"

"Sure"

And Judy goes into her purse, takes out her cell phone and hands it to the man through the window. He walks away shouting into the phone to someone …maybe a mechanic. "You fucked up my car, you should come get me…I'm at exit 16 off I-95 South."

And the man walks back over to return Judy's cell phone. Judy takes the phone and looks down while putting the phone back into her purse. When she looks up again, there is a gun to her left temple.

"Get out of the car bitch!"

"What?"

"Get out of the car bitch…I don't want to hurt you!"

His hand is shaking, Judy is afraid, She gets out of her car slowly.

"Good girl, now give me your fuckin' purse!"
Judy gives him her purse. He jumps in her car and drives off.

She is in the middle of nowhere. At what is now three fifteen in the morning. With no means of communication. As the day breaks someone stops to her cries for help.

A white man.

He calls the police, and waits with her until they show. She is very grateful.

They never caught the guy.

And the car he was standing next to…not even his. That same car had been on the side of that road for weeks, Judy just never noticed.

She has since moved because her license, keys and the rest of her identification was in her purse.

She has changed her taste in men to exclude Black men.

BLACK Man Unnecessary!